Emily Austin

Everyone in This Room Will Someday Be Dead

atlantic·*fiction*

First published in hardback in the United States of America in 2021 by
Atria Books, an imprint of Simon & Schuster, Inc.

First published in hardback in Great Britain in 2021 by Atlantic Books,
an imprint of Atlantic Books Ltd.

This paperback edition published in Great Britain in 2022 by Atlantic Books.

1 2 3 4 5 6 7 8 9

A CIP catalogue record for this book is available from the British Library.

Paperback ISBN: 978 1 83895 375 1
E-book ISBN: 978 1 83895 374 4

Printed in Great Britain by Clays Ltd, Elcograf S.p.A.

Atlantic Books
An imprint of Atlantic Books Ltd
Ormond House
26–27 Boswell Street
London
WC1N 3JZ

www.atlantic-books.co.uk

For Christina and Matthew

part one

Advent

There must have been an explosion. I hear ringing interspersed with a woman's muffled screams. Everything is black. I blink repeatedly.

Black. Black. Black.

I blink once more and see sunlight. The towering silhouette of a streetlight forms in front of me. The light is green, but I am not moving. I glance behind me. A beige van is expelling smoke from its bent hood. There is shattered glass across the concrete road—

I remember now. I was about to sip my coffee. I heard a car horn, looked into my rearview mirror, and watched as that minivan plowed into the trunk of my car. My airbag exploded, and I involuntarily punched myself in the face.

I am now covered in both the scorching guts of my erupted thermos, as well as a concerning gray dust that was emitted when my airbag detonated. I turn my hazard lights on and glance again at my mirror. The screaming woman has emerged from her van. She is rushing toward me.

I am overwhelmed by the smell of my deceased coffee as it resurrects itself in the form of stains on my car's upholstery and burn scars on my chest. Sunlight beams directly into my eyes, and I still hear ringing. I close my eyes and focus on the blackness behind my eyelids.

The woman raps her knuckles on my window, but I keep my

eyes sealed shut. I tend to cry when I am overstimulated. Keeping my eyes closed might stop me from succumbing to that humbling tendency.

"She's not opening her eyes!" The woman's muffled voice shrieks through my window.

"Is she dead?"

I keep my eyes closed but wave an arm to demonstrate that I am alive.

"Why are your eyes shut?" she asks. "I thought I'd killed you!"

Does this woman think that all dead people shut their eyes?

"Can you hear me?" She knocks on the window again.

Rather than fill her in regarding how I am closing my eyes to avoid crying in public or exposing her to the dark realities of wide-eyed death, I decide the easiest thing to do now is open my eyes.

White light floods my vision.

I hear the woman say, "Oh, honey," pacifyingly as tears begin to throw themselves off the cliff of my nose.

"I'm fine," I lie.

I discovered the corpse of my pet rabbit when I was ten years old. I was planning to split my apple with her. Instead of sharing a moment and some fruit with my pet, I came face-to-face with her lifeless remains. Eyes wide open. Dead.

"Are you okay? You're bleeding, you know."

I lean my face closer to the rearview mirror and stare into my reflection. My nose is bleeding. My moment with the mirror also reveals that I have bloodshot eyes and a pale, watery complexion; however, it is possible that these afflictions beset me before the accident. I haven't been looking in mirrors that much lately.

"And your arm . . ." She gestures toward my arm.

I look down to discover that one of my arms is sitting abnormally in my lap. The impact of the airbag has either broken or dislocated it.

Despite both my car and my arm being broken, I am driving myself to the emergency room. I resolved not to involve an ambulance because I do not like to be a spectacle. I would rather be run over by another van than be surrounded by paramedics touching me inside such a conspicuous vehicle.

My foot is pressing down on my gas pedal so delicately that I am barely moving. I am crawling down the road with the airbag hanging out of my steering wheel like it has been disemboweled.

A large white truck is tailgating me. Its driver keeps honking its horn.

I grip the steering wheel, cognizant of the fact that if another car rear-ends me right now, there will be nothing left to cushion the blow.

I glare at the truck as it passes me like it is a predator hunting me. I clench my steering wheel while I stew intensely with the reality that I am a living, breathing thing that is one day going to die. Reckless drivers can snuff me out. I am trapped inside this fragile body. I could be run off the road. I could be crushed by a van. I could choke on a grape. I could be allergic to bees; I am so impermanent that a measly bug could hop from a daisy to my arm, sting me, and I could be erased. Black. Nothing.

I stare at the creases in my knuckles and begin consciously breathing.

I am an animal; an organism made up of bones and blood.

I study the trees as I crawl past them. I do this to occupy my mind with thoughts that are not related to my own fragile mortality.

That is a pine tree.

A maple.

Another pine.

Spruce.

My death, and the death of everyone I love, is inevitable.

Pine again.

I head toward the receptionist's desk and position myself in the center of his view. I wait patiently for him to look up from his paperwork to greet me. I read the posters plastered on the wall behind his desk, to appear occupied, and to distract myself from the fact that every passing moment brings me closer to my ultimate destination. (Death.)

One poster is titled: THE HUMAN PAPILLOMAVIRUS! The odd use of an exclamation mark is what drew my eye. The model hired to pose for the poster is grinning so aggressively that I can see every single one of her enormous teeth. I am staring into her beaming eyes, wondering how I too can achieve happiness. Does living a life unburdened by the fear of catching HPV result in that level of euphoria? If so, shoot me up.

"What's the problem today?" the nurse finally asks me.

I want to tell him that my problem might be that I have yet to receive my HPV vaccine; however, I have already been mentally reciting what to say, and so I announce: "I was just in a small car accident."

"What?" He glances up at me, surprised. "Were you really?"

"Yes."

"Oh, dear. Are you okay?"

That is a strange question, I think. My presence as a prospective patient in this emergency room implies that I am not okay.

Despite thinking the question is strange, I tell him, "Yes, I'm fine." I add, "Well, I think that I may have broken my arm, but I am okay in general. How are you?"

He stands up to look at my arm. He then looks me dead in the eyes and squints. "You are a lot calmer than you usually are when you come in here."

Failing to fashion a more articulate response, I stammer, "Th-thank you."

Compelled now to direct the conversation away from my usual lack of composure, I decide now is the moment to share: "And I would like to be immunized for HPV, please."

While waiting for my number to be called, I occupy myself by amateurishly diagnosing everyone in the waiting room with the condition that I imagine they are suffering from.

That man has the flu.

That lady has cancer.

That kid is faking it.

After completing my assessment of everyone in the room, I hear a familiar voice shout, "Hey there!"

I can see through my peripheral vision that a nurse is waving at me.

I pretend not to see her. I act very focused on the floor tiles.

Not intuitive enough to recognize that I do not want to be addressed, she re-shouts, "Hello!"

I grit my back molars and look up at her.

"Nice to see you!" she hollers.

I smile weakly. "Nice to see you too, Ethel."

She smiles back at me while a different nurse, whose name is Larry, walks toward her. Larry also looks over at me. He waves. "Back again, are we?"

I nod.

"Do you work here, or something?" the patient sitting next to me pries.

"No," I reply—just as Frank, one of the hospital janitors, points at me and shouts, "Hey, girl!"

I am being interviewed before I can see the doctor.

"Are you on any medication?"

"No," I reply. "Well, I have been taking a lot of vitamin D recently."

Last week when I came to the ER they told me that nothing was wrong with me, and that I should consider taking a vitamin D supplement.

"Just vitamin D? No other medication?"

"No."

"Does your family have a history of heart problems?"

"No."

"Is there any chance that you could be pregnant?"

"No."

The nurse purses her lips as she writes down my responses. I interpret her pursed lips as an indication that she is judging me. I responded that I take no medication, which means no birth control, and I responded that there is no chance that I could be pregnant—consequently suggesting that I am likely celibate. I am not. I am just gay, and thus blessedly exempt from the hazard of pregnancy.

"No chance at all?" she repeats.

"No," I say, watching her lips purse again.

"This might hurt a little," the doctor warns me.

"That's okay." I nod.

She moves my arm quickly. It makes a disconcerting popping sound.

The nurse in the room raises her eyebrows at me, impressed.

She says, "Wow, you didn't even flinch. You sure are brave."

"Thank you." I nod.

I did not flinch because it did not hurt. I am not going to admit that, however, because I would prefer to impress this nurse with my bravery. I would also prefer pretending that I am brave because I suspect that it should have hurt, and the fact that it didn't is likely a symptom of some much larger medical problem.

The nurse is staring at me.

"Are you okay?" she asks.

"What?" I look at her.

"Are you all right?" she asks me again.

"Oh." I nod. "Yes, I'm fine."

I broke my arm once before. I was in the fourth grade. I made a dicey acrobatic move on the monkey bars and sunk into the gravel below the jungle gym like a shot bird. I lay there, staring up into the faces of my rapt classmates as they crowded around me.

I have always hated being the center of attention. Despite my arm being broken, and despite what I would classify as stunning pain, I assured everyone that I was fine until they disbanded.

I was not fine. I had fractured two bones in my arm.

"I need you to check for redness around the cast every day," the doctor instructs.

"Okay." I nod.

"And if your arm ever feels warm, or if you develop a fever, come back to the ER, okay?"

"All right." I nod again.

She flips through some papers on her clipboard. "I see that you've been coming into this hospital a lot recently. You've been complaining about chest pains and breathing problems. Is that an ongoing issue?"

"Yes," I reply. "My chest feels tight a lot."

"It sounds like you're having panic attacks," she tells me. She then looks down at her clipboard and says, "I can send a referral to a psychiatrist."

They always send referrals to psychiatrists. I never hear back.

"In the meantime, have you considered taking a vitamin D supplement?"

* * *

"Are you able to pick these up on Wednesday?" the pharmacist asks me after I hand her my painkiller prescription.

"Wednesday?" I repeat.

"Yes." She nods. "Would that work for you?"

"That's three days away," I comment.

She frowns. "No it isn't. It's tomorrow."

"O-oh," I falter. "Right. Sorry, I've been sleeping a lot lately. It's affected my perception of time."

She frowns at me again.

I clench my toes in my shoes. I don't know why I shared that.

"I've been feeling sick," I lie quickly. "I'm battling this nasty cold, and I've been sleeping too much—"

I realize as I fabricate this lie that this woman is a health care professional, and therefore she might somehow be able to sense when people are faking illnesses.

"I feel much better now, though," I say to negate the lie.

She replies, in a tone that exposes absolutely no sincerity, "I am so glad to hear that."

"Hello?" I struggle to answer my cell phone.

It is sunny out. My cell phone's screen brightness is too dim to read the caller ID.

"Are you ignoring me?" the caller confronts me.

I recognize that the caller is Eleanor. She is the girl I'm seeing.

Rather than answer no like I had planned, my tongue trips over itself and I produce no audible noise.

"Hello? Are you there?"

"Yes, I'm sorry," I spit out.

"Why didn't you text me back? You know, I can see when you've read my texts. It's not very nice to ignore me—"

"I'm sorry," I repeat. "Could we please talk about this later? I just got into a small car accident and—"

"What? Are you okay?"

"I don't know," I confess. "I'm trying to figure out the bus."

My car is being towed to my apartment.

"Do you know how to get to my house from the gas station on Alma Street?" I squint up at the yellow bus stop sign above my head. "Do you think I take the ninety-four or the ninety-seven?"

"You don't know if you're okay?"

"Well, no, to be completely honest, I don't. I've been feeling unusually tired lately. No matter how much I sleep, I still wake up feeling exhausted. I think that I might have some sort of imbalance—"

"No," Eleanor interrupts me. "I meant from the car accident."

"Oh. Yes, I'm fine. I'm more concerned about having a vitamin deficiency, honestly. I think I need more calcium or something. I feel really weak and foggy-headed. Do you drink much milk?"

A brittle, elderly man is offering me his seat on the bus.

"I can't accept it," I tell him.

"Sit, sit," he insists.

I shake my head. "No, thank you, that's kind of you—but I'm fine."

"You're injured," he flags, nodding at my new cast. "Please, these seats are reserved for people like you. I insist that you sit."

I glance at the decal above the seat depicting a pregnant woman and an elderly man with a cane. I am neither; I am a twenty-seven-year-old woman who couldn't possibly be pregnant. I would consider myself to be the lowest priority passenger on this vehicle. I have a minor injury on a component of my body that does not influence how difficult it is for me to ride a bus.

Instead of explaining this, I reluctantly accept the seat. I tell the old man "Thank you" four times.

"Thank you."

"Thank you."

"Really, thank you."

"Thanks so much."

Whenever the driver brakes, the old man stumbles. I am nervous that he is going to fall completely. I imagine him losing his footing and propelling across the bus. I think about how old people have porous, fragile bones. I think about how old people can die from falling. I start to picture myself attending this man's funeral.

I am wearing all black.

I am telling his loved ones that he died because of me.

"This is all my fault," I explain.

I got off the bus two stops early so the old man would take his seat back. The bus doors opened in front of a coffee shop. Instead of walking directly home, I walked into the shop.

After I ordered a large cup of milk, the coffee shop employee asked me to "please take a seat." I thought that was a peculiar request, because I didn't order a drink that takes time to assemble.

Rather than question her, I just sat down.

I spend a few moments wondering why she asked me to sit. I then begin wondering why it matters to me why she asked me to sit. Why do I need to know what her rationale is? Why can't I just trust that the people around me have their own justification for their requests and their behavior? Why can't I be like a dog and sit when I'm asked to, without wondering why?

I glance at the small crowd of people surrounding me. Maybe we are like dogs. Everyone here is waiting for their drinks like trained animals. I look down at my hands, and then at the hands of the people around me. These are our paws. We are creatures.

My leg is shaking restlessly.

I open the news app on my phone to distract myself. I begin rolling my thumb over the stories.

There was a school shooting last Wednesday.

Multiple celebrities have been caught sexually assaulting other celebrities.

The glaciers are thawing.

Sea turtles are going extinct.

I decide to veer off the popular news page. I click an article titled: WEIRD WAYS PEOPLE DIE.

Lottie Michelle Belk, fifty-five, was fatally stabbed by a beach umbrella blown by a strong wind.

Hildegard Whiting, seventy-seven, died of suffocation from carbon dioxide vapors produced by four dry ice coolers in a Dippin' Dots delivery car.

"What happened to your arm?" A little girl tugs on the sleeve of my coat.

"I was in a small car accident," I explain as I look away from an article about a man and a lava lamp. The man could not get the lamp to work, so he put it on his stove and turned the heat on low. The liquid in the lamp started to move and bubble before it overheated and exploded. The lamp popped and the colorful wax, clear fluid, and shattered glass flew through the room. A piece of the glass flew into the man's chest, pierced his heart, and killed him. All the comments beneath the article ask what possessed this man to conduct such a harebrained experiment, but I once microwaved a lightbulb when I was a teenager, out of blind curiosity. I understand how the train of human thought can derail. It is tragic both that this man has died and that his stupid impromptu attempt at entertaining himself misfired in a way that will now define him.

I wonder if my death will be what defines me.

"Can I sign your cast?" the kid tugging at my coat asks.

I look at her dirt-encrusted fingernails, and then at her pink, slobbery face.

I answer, "Sure," even though I would prefer it if she didn't touch me.

I sit, a martyr for this child's happiness, while she draws with a red permanent marker all over my new cast. She keeps accidentally drawing on my skin and on my clothes.

When she finishes, I ask her what it is she drew, and she tells me it's a dog. I look down and examine what appears to be a drawing of a penis with eyes, and sigh.

The coffee shop employee shouts my name, so I stand up.

She hands me some sort of smoothie, and I accept it without flagging that she must have misheard me when I ordered.

I guess I probably mumbled.

I think that I am allergic to whatever was in that smoothie. My tongue feels like it's two times larger than it is supposed to be.

"For fucks sake," I groan out loud while rubbing my eyes with the edge of my new cast.

Someone touches my shoulder.

I turn and gape into the face of an elderly woman framed by a habit. I gasp because I didn't turn expecting to come face-to-face with a nun.

I am not religious, but still would not have chosen to say "for fucks sake" in front of an old, devotedly religious woman had I known she was within earshot.

She beams at me. "Are you okay, dear?"

"I'm fibe," I answer. My tongue has expanded so much that I now have a speech impediment.

"You sounded frustrated by something," she comments.

"Oh no, I'm fibe," I repeat, smiling insincerely.

She smiles back at me. "Can I offer you a church newsletter?"

She hands me a folded piece of yellowed paper.

I have started to collect dirty dishes in my bedroom. My smoothie cup from earlier today is sitting on top of a small stack of cups, plates, and bowls. Piling the dishes feels sort of like building a block castle. Every dish I add is risky. At some point the castle is going to collapse.

Thinking about washing the dishes feels a lot like thinking of going for a jog.

I will do it tomorrow.

I bought the last three editions of *Guinness World Records* before I was fired from my job at the bookstore. I bought them thinking I could return them after I read them. It was my lazy alternative to the library. Now I can't return them without confronting my old employer, who thinks I am untrustworthy and irresponsible. I'm worried if I did try to return these books, he would just accuse me of stealing them.

I was a bad employee. I find it hard to wake up, so I was rarely on time. I often missed entire shifts. I don't think I added much value when I was present, either. I don't have the right personality for customer service. A customer once asked me if I was really an employee of the store, or if I was just three possums in a trench coat. I was so confused by the remark, the customer had to explain it to me. She said that possums are notoriously skittish. I said, "But what about the trench coat, though? I'm not wearing a trench coat. And aren't possums kind of small? Wouldn't I be like five or six possums in a trench coat, if I had a trench coat?"

She complained to my boss about me. He made me sit in the back room and listen to him preach about the five pillars of good customer service. I was so distracted by how impassioned he was by the topic, I couldn't retain anything he said.

I crack open the most recent edition of *Guinness World Records*. I flip through its glossy pages. I read that the oldest human to ever live was 122 years old. She was a woman named Jeanne. She died in France.

I touch my greasy hair, turn the page, and wonder if there is a record for the longest a person has gone without showering.

* * *

My heart is pounding at a faster pace than a rabbit's when being accosted by a fox. I am standing in front of my bathroom sink, telling myself repeatedly that I am fine.

I am fine.

I feel like someone is sitting on my chest, but that is fine.

I tear open my bottle of vitamin D, pop two tablets in my mouth, and chew.

"This should cure me," I say out loud, knowingly deluded.

I haven't inhaled properly for at least five minutes. There is no oxygen reaching my brain.

I should go to the hospital, but every time I go to the hospital, they say it is just anxiety.

Is this just anxiety? Is it worth risking that this is a real heart attack? What if that car accident exacerbated a legitimate heart attack?

I reach for my phone and dial a number that I have memorized.

A man's voice says, "Hello, you have reached Telehealth. If you are currently experiencing a medical emergency, please hang up and call nine-one-one. How can I help you?"

"Hi," I say, breathless. "I'm having an attack."

"Please go to the emergency room."

"I've been there too much," I explain, panting. "The nurses know my name. That isn't normal, is it? I can't go back."

"You've already gone and seen a doctor?"

"How can I tell if it's a heart attack or a panic attack?" I clutch my chest.

"If you change positions, does the severity of the chest pain change?"

"Let me check."

I lie down on the cool bathroom tile, clutching my knees to my chest.

I pause to listen to the rapid thud of my heart.

Thud.

Thud.

Thud.

"Sort of," I say.

"It's likely a panic attack, then," the man explains. "Do you have issues with anxiety?"

"Apparently," I say, the pain in my chest easing slightly.

"Do you have anyone you can talk to about that?" the man asks me after a quiet moment passes.

"I have you," I say.

He laughs.

"How is the old bookstore treating you these days, sweetie?" my mom asks me while slopping a heap of mashed potatoes onto my ceramic plate.

"I got fired," I admit while shoveling a forkful of the potatoes into my open mouth.

I once read that human beings can live solely on potatoes. A potato contains all the essential amino acids humans need to build proteins, repair cells, and fight diseases.

"You got fired?" my dad chokes out. "What? Why would they fire you?"

You would have to eat about twenty-five potatoes a day to get the recommended amount of protein, however, and you would have calcium deficiencies.

"Hello? Why did you get fired?"

Eating just potatoes wouldn't be exactly healthy, but you would live longer than solely eating foods like bread or apples.

"Are you deaf?" My dad waves his hand in front of my face.

"What?"

"Why did you get fired?" he asks, his face slightly red.

"I don't know," I say, despite knowing that they fired me because I didn't show up for five consecutive shifts.

"Did you get caught stealing books or something?" my brother, Eli, jokes.

"Have you been handing out your résumé?" my mom interjects before I can respond to Eli's allegation.

"Yes," I lie.

We all stew quietly for a moment in my unemployment.

My mom sighs. "Should we open a bottle of wine?"

"No," I say quickly.

"What?" My dad looks at me. "Why not?"

"Because," I insist, "I'm on medication." I hold up my broken arm.

"You're on medication?" my dad says. "I thought you said the car accident and your injury were both minor? Are you badly hurt?"

"I'm fine."

"And yet none of the rest of us can have a drink?" he scoffs.

"That's right," I maintain.

"There won't be any more issues." My dad shook hands with my principal. "Her mother and I will handle it. Thank you, Dave."

When I was fifteen, my parents were called to my school because I was being suspended for two days.

My class had gone on a field trip earlier that day. When we were leaving, my friend Ingrid and I took the seats at the back of the bus. A group of girls confronted us there. They insisted we give them our seats. I started to stand up, to comply, but Ingrid refused. She held my wrist and said, "We're not going anywhere."

The girls who wanted our seats started calling us lesbians.

Ingrid was not a lesbian. She was often accused of being one, however, because she was my friend, and there are some misconceptions about how it spreads.

Everyone on the bus was looking at us. People were laughing. A guy named Brandon started shouting, "Dykes!"

"Stop calling them lesbians!" Mrs. Camp, the teacher supervising the field trip, finally intervened. "What an awful thing to say!"

The girls had to sit down in the seats in front of us. Ingrid felt so enraged that she took her lighter to the ends of their hair. The girls weren't hurt, but their dead ends got a little fried, and the bus stunk.

Mrs. Camp made Ingrid and me go to the principal's office. The other girls weren't sent. I saw Mrs. Camp consoling them as Ingrid and I walked to the office. She patted their backs and said, "I know that was scary."

My dad lectured me while he and my mom drove me home. He said, "When you grow up, you're going to realize you could have worse problems than stupid girls bullying you on the school bus. You need to keep your nose clean."

"It wasn't even me who—"

"I don't care. The people you hang out with are a reflection of you. You shouldn't hang around this Ingrid girl if she's lighting people's hair on fire—"

"Those girls were—"

"I don't care! You should've kept your head down."

My mom was silent.

Different-sounding sirens are intermingling outside my apartment. Together they are creating a vibrating, hostile music that I am unable to sleep through. I open my eyes. I stare at the ceiling above me.

I fell asleep on the beach one summer, and Eli buried me up to my neck in the sand. I woke up completely immobilized. I couldn't get up without him digging me out. I feel like that now. I feel chained to my bed.

I kick my legs until my blankets unchain me. I muster all the strength stored in the caverns of my body to stand up.

There is a bright orange light framed in my window. I approach the light and peer outside. The house across the street is on fire. There are fire trucks, ambulances, and police cars circled on the front lawn. I stand at my window and stare down at the glowing house. Flames have engulfed the upstairs. They are burning through the roof. I hope no one is inside.

My eyes dart, looking into the windows. I am trying to spot silhouettes of people. The windows upstairs are glowing. There are no shadows, just bright yellow light. I can't make out if anyone is in there. The windows downstairs are expelling black billows of smoke. I can't see through it.

I pat my chest with my fist to steady the thump of my worried heart.

The firefighters are blasting water into the flames, but the fire is still raging. I think the roof is caving in.

The sirens are so loud that I can't hear anything but them. I hope no one is screaming for help. I feel panic twinge in my chest. I watch the water blast from the hose and tell myself the fire is going down, even though I can't tell if it is.

People outside are shouting. What are they saying? I can't make them out. I open my window. The late November air is warm from the fire. The smoky, acrid smell of the burning house seeps through my screen. I try to hear what the people are shouting.

"Where's the cat?"

"Is the cat out?"

I press my forehead up to the cool glass and scan the darkness, searching for the missing cat.

My search for the cat is obstructed by the people who are crowding around the house. An audience is forming. They are standing in their pajamas, watching the commotion. I notice that some of them are holding take-out coffee cups. A man has his kid on his shoulders.

A yellow eye contained in the decomposing carcass of a seagull watched me sunbathe the same day my brother buried me. It was in the middle of August. I was nine years old. My parents had taken me and Eli to Port Stanley, and they had unknowingly laid our beach towels a stone's throw from a hot dead bird.

As the day progressed, I noticed living seagulls would visit the dead seagull's body. I imagined that they were doing so to pay their respects. I thought I was witnessing the poignant wake of a seagull.

My dad noticed the carcass after a while and said, "I think those disgusting sea rats are trying to figure out how that other gull died."

"Shame about what happened across the street, eh?" the woman who lives in the apartment next to mine comments as I lock my door behind me.

I look at her. She is dressed in a pink bathrobe, and her hair is wrapped in a towel.

"Yeah," I reply, wondering why this woman is lingering in the hall.

"Scary living in an apartment building," the woman continues, now eyeing me up and down. "You never know if your neighbors clean their lint traps or leave their candles unattended. Of course, you have a fire extinguisher in there, don't you?"

"Of course," I lie. "What kind of irresponsible asshat doesn't have a fire extinguisher?"

I devoted the past four hours of my life to locating a store that sells fire extinguishers. After visiting three stores, and speaking to five salespeople, I was finally able to charge a sixty-dollar, top-of-the-line fire extinguisher to my now-almost-maxed-out credit card.

I am now quashing my compulsions to grunt, swear, and pause for breaks while I smuggle my shiny new fire extinguisher into my apartment. I am doing so with one working arm. My prying neighbor, who I am afraid will spot me with this and realize that I lied to her, is oblivious to the lengths that I have gone to to safeguard her life.

I feel the apparatus slip slightly from my sweaty grip. I start to picture myself dropping it. I think of it rolling down the stairs and crashing through the floor. I think of the noise it'll make. I picture it crashing through someone's ceiling, plummeting through the air, and clunking against the skull of some poor, unsuspecting victim. I imagine my neighbor emerging from her apartment in her pink bathrobe to confront me and the murder scene.

I drop my keys twice while I fumble to unlock my front door. Once I finally get inside, I kick the door shut behind me, and toss the fifty-pound apparatus onto my unmade bed. It immediately bounces from the springy mattress into the air and crashes clamorously onto the floor.

My heart twinges.

I rush over to inspect the damage. I see that it landed directly on the remote for my TV, which I carelessly flung to the ground last night.

I examine the damaged remote. It is cracked down the middle. Five of its buttons are pressed into the plastic and are now unclickable. I tell myself, *It's okay. I can just change the channel from the TV from now on*, and chuck it back on the ground. Its batteries fly out like gutted innards.

I watch the batteries roll across the floor, and then I scan the room. What else am I supposed to do to ensure that I am not responsible for killing the people who live in this building?

I check my lint trap.

I throw the two candles that I own out.

I unplug my stove.

I pull the cabinet below my oven open. I look down into the drawer at heaps of mail and paper. It dawns on me as I scan the mass of combustible material that I am a hazard.

My apartment has limited storage. I have been keeping all my paperwork here. I never cook, so the danger isn't imminently threatening, but still.

I kneel in front of the cabinet and start shoveling through the mass of unopened mail, newspapers, and letters.

I shift through a lot of overdue bills before spotting an advertisement.

It says: ARE YOU FEELING LOW?

Yes.

DO YOU NEED SOMEONE TO TALK TO?

Apparently.

COME TO 1919 PEACH TREE CRESCENT FOR FREE MENTAL HEALTH SUPPORT.

The words LOST CAT confront me from a sad, wrinkled poster plastered to the telephone pole outside my apartment. Mittens, seven years old, last seen napping in his favorite windowsill, has been missing since his house caught on fire. He is friendly and responds to his name. His family is offering a reward for his safe return home. He is gray with white front feet—hence the name "Mittens."

"Mittens?" I call into the dark bushes as I walk by them.

"Here, kitty kitty."

I peer over a fence into a backyard. There is frost on the grass.

"Mittens?" I call out into an open garage.

"Mittens? Are you in there?" I hush into the darkness beneath somebody's front porch.

"Come out if you're in there, Mittens."

1919 Peach Tree is the site of an enormous gothic church. I am standing on the lawn in front of this intimidating building, allowing myself to soak in the realization that I was duped by an evangelizing advertisement. This is not the location of free therapy; this is where people are converted to whatever religion this church hawks.

I stare down at the paper and recognize as I do that it is the paper given to me by that nun.

"Beautiful building, isn't it?" a man's voice says from behind me.

Startled by his unexpected presence, I trip over nothing.

He chuckles, extends his hand toward me, and says, "Hi, I'm Jeff."

I stable myself and reply, "Hi, Jeff."

"It's nice to meet you, dear. Are you here about the job?"

I open my mouth to reply. I stop myself before the word no escapes. I notice Jeff's white collar. He's a priest.

I stammer, "Y-Yes."

"Wonderful!" He claps his hands together.

"We lost our previous receptionist to the Lord just last month," Jeff tells me as I sit down in his office.

Losing someone to the Lord makes it sound like God steals people.

"Oh, I'm sorry," I say, while trying to veil how uncomfortable I feel being in the presence of so many Jesus figurines. The figurine nearest me depicts Jesus looking sorrowfully up toward the sky. I look away from his mournful eyes and glance around the room. This office reminds me of my bedroom when I was nine and obsessed with sea turtles, except Jeff is obsessed with crucifixes. I had a turtle bed set, turtle posters, and turtle stuffed animals. Jeff has a mixed-media gallery wall behind his desk with a wooden cross, a gold cross, a ceramic cross, and framed photos of crosses. There is a cross-shaped candy dish in front of me that contains dusty Werther's Originals, and a dirty coffee mug with a renaissance painting on it of Jesus holding—you guessed it—a cross.

"Thank you, dear," he says.

I start to picture a world where Jesus had been killed using a different murder device. I picture little ceramic guillotine figurines. I imagine miniature nooses hung above children's beds. Electric chair necklaces and earrings.

"I know Grace has been committed into the hands of God," he adds.

I stare forward, unsure of how to respond. Should I ask for a Werther's?

He looks down at his hand, at a ring on his finger.

"This was Grace's ring," he tells me. "I wear it to remember her."

I don't know what to say. I eye the ring. I wonder why she left it to him.

"Now." He clears his throat. "Everyone who has been applying for Grace's old job has been—oh, how shall I put it?" he hums. "Well, let's just say the applicants have all been eligible for a discount at Denny's, if you catch my drift?"

I force a laugh to demonstrate my good humor.

"They all ride the bus for free on Wednesdays, if you know what I mean?"

I force a laugh again.

"I know I am not one to talk." He smiles. "I am seventy-two myself, can you believe it? Do I look it?"

I open my mouth.

"Oh, now don't answer that!" he says, chuckling again. "But seriously, I would love someone young in here. Do you know how to use the internet?"

"Do I know how to use the internet?" I repeat.

He nods. "Yes, I am looking for someone familiar with the internet. Are you acquainted?"

"Well, yes—" I begin to reply.

"Wonderful!" He claps his hands together. "Wonderful, wonderful, wonderful! And how is your hearing?"

I stumble to say, "It's regular, as far as I know. I think I heard everything you've said—"

"Well, little lady." He grins. "I think you might just be our gal! You're Catholic, of course?"

"Yes," I say, even though I am an atheist lesbian.

He slaps a hand on his desk. "You're perfect!"

Two Jehovah's Witnesses came to my door when I was seven. They asked me if I was baptized. I answered no, and they told me that was because my parents were atheists. I remember their voices deepened when they said the word "atheists" as if it were an obscenity. Being seven years old, I was inclined to take notice of swear words—so I committed the word to my memory. I spent the next three years calling people atheists, having no clue what it meant, thinking I was a cutting trash-talker.

My teacher gave me an F on a spelling test, and I muttered, "What a freaking atheist."

Gemma Igmund started a rumor that I was gay, and I confronted her. "Shut your God damn atheist mouth, Gemma."

My mom made me go to bed early, and I screeched from the top of the stairs that I was living in a family of cold-blooded atheists.

I exit the church like I am escaping a crime scene. I peer over my shoulder as I scuttle down the street, worried the priest is following me.

The advertisement that lured me to the church is still clutched in my fist. I uncrumple it once I have darted far enough away from the church that I am confident I am not being watched. I examine the ad for any indication that the free therapy it promotes is being offered by a Catholic church. I turn the paper over, confirming that there isn't so much as a decorative crucifix on it.

My eyes are open. I am lying awake in my bed. It's the middle of the night. I can't fall asleep. I am thinking intensely about churches and religion. I am especially ruminating on the concept of hell.

I blink. I start to think intensely about fire, and about what it might feel like to burn to death. I picture blazing, effulgent flames. I picture sweltering, blistering skin.

Every time I try to roast a marshmallow, they always catch on fire. The white chewy sugar and gelatin bubbles golden before it engulfs in flames, and it doesn't burn or turn black until the flames have encased it for a while.

I start to imagine what might go through a cat's mind in a house fire. I picture hot flames latching on to strands of cat fur. I think about scorching cat skin and singed cat bones.

Cats sleep all day. They like to lie on pillows in warm patches of sunlight. They are timid animals; they are easily spooked. They hide under beds and in corners of closets when they are scared.

I sit up. My heart is beating irregularly.

Am I having heart palpitations?

I put my hand to my chest.

I feel the speed of my heartbeat increase rapidly.

I feel like my ribs are a birdcage and my heart is a bird on fire.

The doors to the emergency room open automatically when I stand in front of them, confirming that I exist physically. This is a comforting affirmation.

I head toward the receptionist's desk. The nurse sees me coming. I watch her deflate as she exhales.

She is exasperated by me. She thinks that I am a hypochondriac. She thinks I am wasting her time.

"What's the problem today?" she inquires coolly.

"I think it's my heart," I explain.

"Mittens?" I call out from the sidewalk.

I kneel to view under a car. The cement is cold.

"Mittens?"

"Are you down there?"

"Can you hear me?"

My mom is organizing our family photos. There are hundreds of photos of my family spread out on the kitchen table. They are being placed into piles by year.

My old report cards are also stacked on the table. They must have been stored in the same box. I flip through them. I see that I earned high marks before the sixth grade, when things took a dip. My report cards from earlier years have comments like "Gilda is a quick learner," and "Gilda is a pleasure to teach." They describe me as "curious" and "inquisitive." After the sixth grade, the comments change. They say, "Gilda is socially withdrawn," "Gilda has difficulty concentrating," and describe me as "low energy." I notice a particularly stark comparison when I see that my third-grade teacher recommended I be placed in a gifted program, whereas my seventh-grade teacher recommended I be put in a class for slow learners.

"How are we supposed to eat dinner here?" my dad snarks, looking down at the piles of pictures and papers.

"Oh, just look at you two!" My mom ignores my dad, holding up a picture of Eli and me at the beach. Eli is wearing goggles and I have bright orange water wings on.

"You look insane," Eli snorts at me.

My mom frowns. "She does not, Eli. Come on."

"Everyone in our family is perfectly sane," my dad says.

I take the photo from my mom to examine it up close. I look at my fleshy child face, and at how wide Eli is smiling.

Sometimes I wonder if I have really been the same person my whole life. I stare at the picture, and think: Is that really me? I have this bizarre feeling like I was a different person at every other stage of my life. I feel so removed from myself then. Sometimes I feel like I was a different person a month ago. A day. Five minutes. Now.

"Why would you paint that, Eli?" my dad said.

The high school was doing an art show. Eli's art was on display in the front hall.

He painted a self-portrait of himself dead. It was a startling oil painting. It was incredibly realistic. From a distance, I thought it was a photo. He painted pale, waxy skin. His eyes were open, but lifeless. His arms were crossed on his chest. You could tell he was dead.

"It's a really good painting—" I started to say. It was very detailed; you could see all the pores in his skin.

"It's horrible," my dad interrupted me.

My mom cut in. "It's a horrible, good painting. You're so talented, Eli. We just wish you had painted something less morbid—"

"All of your teachers are seeing this," my dad remarked, exasperated. "They're going to think you have a screw loose. You are embarrassing us. I'm disappointed in you."

"When I was your age, I was paying a mortgage, working forty hours a week, and raising you and your brother," my mom tells me while handing me a large mug of orange pekoe.

I wrap my fingers around the mug, realizing as I do that it is too hot to touch. I rush to put the mug down on the counter. I shake my hand after putting it down in a vain attempt to fling the burning sensation off.

"How are you going to support yourself if you can't keep a simple job at a bookstore? I really hope that you don't plan to just marry some rich man, sweetie. I can't bear to think—"

"I'm gay," I remind her.

"Exactly!" she retorts. "It would be especially dishonest."

"Is it worse to be dishonest or to be unemployed?"

"What?" She contorts her face. "What kind of question is that?"

"Would you rather I be honest, or that I be employed?" I ask again.

She shakes her head. "What I would prefer is that you sort that kind of thing out for yourself. You are a grown-up."

There is room on my credit card for twenty dollars. I am about to purchase a sandwich, reducing that number by five.

Today marks one month since I was fired. The only food left in my fridge is rotten.

"Is this everything?" the cashier asks me, nodding at the sandwich I have placed on the glass counter between us.

I nod and begin to enter my PIN into the debit machine. I consider while doing so that my rent is eleven hundred dollars and that it is due in two weeks. I think about my car, utilities, credit card, gas, internet, grocery, and phone bill. I think about how I was ticketed last month for parking five minutes too long on a deserted residential street. I think about the cost to repair my car. I think about my depleting shampoo bottles and deodorant. I think about the cost of fruit, vitamin D, and about how I need to buy ibuprofen.

"Thank you," I say to the cashier as I leave the store poorer.

I wish that I hadn't lost my job at the bookstore. I knew that if I did not go to work I would be fired, but I still didn't go. I don't know what's wrong with me. I've been exhausted. I don't have the motivation to wake up in the morning, let alone the drive to go to a bookstore and interact with people.

What's an easy way for me to make some money? Should I take up sex work? I doubt there's much of a market for lesbian sex workers, and I am a bad actress—so straight sex work is out of the question. I suspect that it would not be hard for my male clients to discern through my gagging and crying that I was not enjoying our business transaction. That said, I'm sure some guys would be into that. Maybe that's my niche market—gross men who like to revolt sad gay women.

Alternatively, I could just go along with working at the church. Like the sex work option, I would have to play a role, but I think I might prefer to deceive the Catholic church than to have sex with sordid men.

An infomercial for butt pads is blaring on my TV. I fell asleep with the TV on because my remote is broken, and I was too tired to stand up to turn it off. Instead of standing up, I added the cup I'd been drinking out of to the dirty-dish tower in my room, and fell asleep.

The volume of the infomercial is louder than the program that played prior. The host of the infomercial is screaming, "Call now and you'll get a second butt pad for free." Women on the TV are modeling jeans before and after wearing the product. One woman is telling the audience tearfully that these things changed her life.

I look at my phone. There's a text from my brother. It says, **fjmekr.**

I frown at the text for a second before replying, **Is everything okay?**

He replies: **j4riiiiiiir.**

Where are you? I text.

Eli's eyes are glazed over in a way that reminds me of our dead bunny's eyes. I keep looking into his face, searching for his usual eyes.

It's after midnight. We are sitting in a booth in a bar with a tin ceiling. The table is sticky and the room smells like soured beer. There are white Christmas lights strung around the bar, and a red neon sign on the wall that says: BOTTOMS UP.

Eli is chugging his beer like it's water.

I stare at the tracks his fingerprints make in the condensation on his glass. I notice his fingernails look like they have chipped nail polish on them.

"Have you ever considered what thoughts go through cats' minds?" I ask.

He sips his drink.

"Do you think they think about death, or anything like that?" I ask.

"I doubt it." He sips his drink again.

I look at his depleting glass and at his foggy eyes.

"I think maybe you've had enough—" I start.

"Do you ever wish that you were someone else?" he interrupts me, sipping his drink again.

I nod. "Yeah."

We sit quietly for a moment.

"Do you think I should accept a job at a Catholic church?" I ask him.

He laughs. "What the fuck?"

He leaves the table to go to the bathroom. When he's out of view I drink what's left in his glass and then chug what's left in the pitcher.

I am balancing on the curb like it's a tightrope. I keep losing my balance and falling off.

"Hey, Eleanor, guess what?" I hear myself slurring.

There are no cars on the road and it's dark out. I am walking in the shadows between the streetlights.

"I got a new job. Don't ask me where." I hiccup. "You don't want to know."

I dip a toe into the church like I am testing the water in a hot bathtub. It has been two days since I had my accidental job interview here. I stand at the entrance, waiting to see if my body boils before fully submerging myself in the building. God shows no signs of planning to smite me as I completely enter the church, ready to begin my first day as an undercover atheist.

I am wearing the only dress that I own.

I wander through the building until I locate Jeff's office. I knock when I find his door.

"Come in!"

He looks up at me as I enter. He has large, thick glasses sitting low on his nose. He is wearing a red knit sweater vest. He says, "Oh dear it's you."

I am not sure if he was using the word "dear" as a term of endearment, like "sweetie" or "honey," or if he was saying, "Oh dear" as in, "Oh no."

I smile uncomfortably and remain silent until I can better gauge the tone of our interaction.

He stands up. "I failed to ask you some pretty critical questions when we met earlier, didn't I?"

I stare at him, concerned now that he's unearthed something about me.

"Like for example . . ." he continues, now looking at me over the rim of his glasses. "What is your name?"

"What's my name?" I repeat.

He smiles. "Yes, forgive me, but I didn't ask! What is your name, dear?"

I exhale, relieved that my cover has not been blown.

"Gilda."

part two

Twelvetide

"**This is where** we keep the computer." Jeff introduces me to an enormous desktop computer. He just finished giving me a tour of the church, to orient me on my first day. He has his hands on his hips, and he is frowning apprehensively at the primordial, beige machine.

"Do you know how to turn it on?" he asks timidly.

I press the prominent Start button. The computer makes a noise like a revving lawn mower.

"Wow!" Jeff's face lights up with the monitor. "I can't believe you got it going already!"

I smile nervously, pleased to discover that this man is easily impressed.

I am sitting at my desk, flipping through a pile of church bulletins. Jeff handed me a stack to read. He said he wanted me to familiarize myself with the church's news and events.

I feel like I am wearing a costume. I keep forgetting I am wearing a dress, and I have not been crossing my legs. I feel like I have the words "atheist" and "gay" stamped on my forehead.

Something is fluttering in my chest, and my hands feel clammy. What am I doing here? I should leave.

The fluttering feeling intensifies. I close my eyes.

Black.

I need to distract myself.

I open my eyes and stare at the nameplate on my desk.

Grace Moppet.

My leg is shaking. The fluttering feeling starts to subside.

Grace Moppet.

Grace Moppet.

Grace Moppet.

Sometimes, when I stare at something long enough, I become so focused on it that it mollifies all my other senses. Grace's name is written in gold. Corners of the letters are rusting. The *r* looks like it was written in a different font than the other letters—

"Gilda?" Jeff's voice interrupts my train of thought.

I look up at him.

"Are you able to email?" he asks.

I pause for a moment before replying, "Yes."

He claps. "That's wonderful! I haven't been able to access the church's email since we lost Grace. Could you check it for me, please?"

Grace was either an absentminded person, or generously forward-thinking. She left behind a Post-it Note with the church's email address and password written on it. The password to StRigoberts@ StRigoberts.com is "Password."

I log in and learn that the church has 203 unread emails.

The first email is from someone named Viola Blackwell. It's a forward containing pictures of dogs dressed in pumpkin costumes. Viola has included a personalized message within the forward, which reads:

ADORABLE. THE THIRD LOOKS LIKE MY PEACHES.

I assume Peaches is the name of her dog.

I move on to the second email, which reads:

Grace

I haven't heard from you in ages! How are you? What's new?

Love,
Rosemary

I reread the email twice before a frog forms in my throat, and my eyes start to fog up. Rosemary must not know that her friend Grace is dead.

My hands start to feel clammy again.

A picture of what I imagine Rosemary looks like starts to take shape in my mind's eye. I imagine that she is petite and frail-looking. Her hair is short, white, and permed. I imagine that she uses a cane, or maybe a walker—or maybe, God help me, a wheelchair.

Am I going to have to break it to sweet, decrepit old Rosemary that her friend Grace is dead?

I glance at the email again.

I haven't heard from you in ages!

That is because she is dead.

How are you?

Dead.

What's new?

Nothing is new with Grace, or ever will be again.

I start to type *Grace is dead*, but then click Backspace, Backspace, Backspace. That wording is insensitive; it's too blunt.

Grace is no longer with us.

No, that's too vague. She might think that Grace was just fired, or that she quit.

Grace has given up the ghost.

She is beyond the veil.

She's freed her horses.

Grace has passed away.

I do not know how to phrase this properly. I have never had to tell someone that their friend died before. I didn't expect to be responsible for this. I—

A crushing heaviness weighs down on me suddenly, with no warning. It's as if an invisible giant just plopped down on my chest. I gasp, but I can't inhale. My heart is pounding. I feel an overwhelming sense of dread.

Dread.

Dread.

Dread.

I stand up, panicked.

How do I get rid of this feeling?

I don't think that I will ever get rid of this feeling.

I feel like a cat in a house fire, cornered in a room with no windows.

Dread.

Dread.

Dread.

I feel like I am so far underwater that the surface is sixty stories above me.

Dread.

Dread.

Dread.

I can't scream. I can't open my mouth. Am I dying?

AM I DYING?

I pant. My throat makes a deep, audible gasping noise as a small amount of air travels inside my lungs.

I gasp again, slugging in small gulps of oxygen.

It's passing.

I put my hand to my chest and focus on breathing.

I'm okay.

I'm okay.

I'm "okay" in the loose sense of the word, meaning mostly: I can breathe. I am probably, however, not truly okay. Something is obviously wrong with me. I feel like I just escaped a bear attack. Why does my body react like it is being chased down by predators when it's not? Am I physically in-tuned to some sort of impending doom that I can't perceive otherwise? Am I sensing something, or am I just out of whack? Why do I feel this terrible physical dread? Do I have cancer? Am I—

Stop.

I need to focus on something other than this. I glance around the room. I look at my computer monitor. I zero in on my draft reply to Rosemary.

Grace has passed away.

Why am I dealing with this? This isn't my problem. I can't help that Grace is dead, or that everyone failed to share that with whoever Rosemary is. I have nothing to do with this. I am an impostor at a church; I'm not a grief counselor. I don't owe Grace or Rosemary anything. I don't really owe anyone anything. I am an animal, brought into existence without my consent, left scrounging to get by. I have my own problems. I have a full plate: I have to pay my bills; I have to pass as a Catholic; I have to clean my lint trap; I have to focus on breathing.

I hover my cursor over the Delete button, and then click. Erased.

My leg is shaking. I need to distract myself more.

I open the desk and fish through the drawers, pulling out pens, erasers, and other things to look at. I pause when I open a drawer containing one unfinished crossword puzzle, half a pack of gum, and a romance novel. I stare tragically into the drawer, at the empty spaces in the crossword puzzle, and at the scrap of paper bookmarking the center of the novel.

"Gilda?"

I look up. My vision is blurred by the tears that have built up in my eyes.

Jeff tilts his head. "Is everything okay, dear?"

I blink, tipping the tears out of my eyes, down my cheeks.

"Allergies," I lie.

"Allergies?" he repeats, his eyes glancing at the frost on the window.

"I'm allergic to dust," I lie, wiping my face.

"Oh." He nods, accepting that explanation. "It is kind of dusty in this old place, isn't it?"

"Hello?" I answer the phone on my desk.

It's noon. I have made it through half of my first day. This is further than I thought I would get.

"What time is mass this Sunday?" an old lady with an unstable voice asks me.

I have no idea.

"Let me ask Father Jeff," I tell the woman. "Could you please hold?"

"Okay," she says.

I knock on Jeff's office door.

"Hi, sorry to bother you, but what time is church?"

He looks up from his book and answers, "Mass is at seven a.m. every weekday, eight p.m. on Saturday evenings, and at nine and eleven on Sunday mornings, dear."

"It's every day?" I clarify.

He nods. "Yes."

I walk back to my desk, pick up the phone, and repeat, "It's at seven a.m. every weekday, eight p.m. on Saturday evenings, and at nine and eleven on Sunday mornings."

"Okay," the woman replies before she hangs up.

"Hello?" I answer the phone at my desk again.

"What time is mass this Sunday?" a familiar voice asks me.

"Is this who just called?" I question.

"What?" says the woman. "No."

"It's at seven a.m. every weekday, eight p.m. on Saturday evenings, and at nine and eleven on Sunday mornings," I say cautiously, concerned now that I am being prank-called.

"Okay," she says before she hangs up again.

* * *

"What time is mass this Sun—"

"All right," I interrupt her. "Why do you keep calling me and asking me the same thing? Am I being initiated?"

"Oh dear, have I already called? I'm sorry."

It dawns on me that this woman is forgetful. My face heats up as guilt for confronting her about her senility washes over me. "No, no, I'm sorry," I say. "Mass is at seven a.m. every weekday, eight p.m. on Saturday evenings, and at nine and eleven on Sunday mornings."

"Okay," she replies faintly.

More than 75 percent of the emails this church receives are forwards from Viola. I spent my morning reading and deleting all of her politically conservative chain letters and motivational stories oddly juxtaposed with pictures of cartoon characters.

Following that harrowing task, Jeff asked me to put flyers on all the pews. After completing that to-do, he asked that I man the telephone, and continue to monitor our emails.

There have been no calls or emails for the past two hours. I have therefore spent my afternoon sitting, staring forward, and covertly reading the news on my phone. There's been an earthquake in Japan. Hundreds dead.

I keep combing my fingers through my hair. Shaking my leg. Fidgeting.

"Are you okay, dear?" Jeff asks me as he passes by my desk.

"Yes," I reply too quickly, feigning a smile.

That is the fourth time that he has asked me if I am okay. I must not look like I am okay.

I stare forward, into the black computer screen in front of me— at my reflected face.

I think my neutral expression is too deadpan. I need to be more cognizant of the way that my face relaxes. I can't allow my face to rest; I have to consciously flex it into a semi-smile to placate Jeff.

Smile.

Keep smiling.

Does this look unnatural?

Smile.

I probably look like a manic lunatic.

Am I a manic lunatic?

"Is it difficult for you to type with that cast?" Jeff asks me, gesturing to my broken arm.

I look down at my cast. I stare at the penis that kid drew on me.

I cover the drawing with my hand. "No. Well, it makes me a bit slower, I guess, but I can manage."

"How did that happen?"

"I was in a small car accident."

"Dreadful," he tuts. "Car accidents can be very frightening. I'm glad that you're okay."

"I'm okay." I nod, solidifying that assumption.

I'm fine.

Impostor syndrome is a psychological pattern in which individuals doubt themselves and have a persistent internalized fear of being exposed as a fraud. Last year my friend Ingrid told me I had it. I had just told her that I didn't feel like I belonged at my previous bookstore job. I told her that I didn't really get *1984* and that I hate poetry—so I wasn't sure if working at a bookstore was right for me. She told me, "You have a classic case of impostor syndrome."

I told her that I'm not sure that's a real syndrome. I said I wonder if everyone's an impostor. What if beneath every lawyer's suit and every stay-at-home-parent's apron, everyone is just a baby who doesn't know what they're doing? I wonder if anyone really identifies as the adult they've morphed into.

I remember being sixteen and feeling eleven. I remember thinking, how could I be a teenager? I remember finishing high school and thinking, am I grown now? Is this what it feels like? I feel the same as I did before.

I think I am an impostor. Twenty-seven years ago I was a baby. Before that I was a clump of cells. Before that I didn't exist. How could I be a bookstore clerk, or a Catholic, or a woman, or a person at all? I'm a life force contained in the deformed body of a baby. Of course I'm a fraud. The fact that I'm able to carry myself through life without being crushed beneath the psychological weight of being alive proves that I'm a con artist. Aren't we all con artists?

I close my eyes.

I'm lying to a priest and to this church about who I am, but that's okay. I'm working here and pretending to be someone I am not because that is what I would have to do anywhere.

I inhale.

I have to make money to pay my rent, and buy food to sustain my existence, because that is the purpose of my life.

I exhale.

I have to push the sadness I feel about Grace and Rosemary and forgetful old women deep into the grottoes of my stomach, next to my thoughts about cats in house fires, because this is what it means to exist. This is how people stay alive.

"What are you so unhappy about?"

It is eight a.m. and I am sitting at my desk in the church.

"What?" I look up. A portly man is looming over me. He is wearing a plaid short-sleeve button-down. He has tucked the button-down into cargo pants. He has sunglasses perched on his forehead like a headband.

"You look miserable," the man clarifies.

Fuck.

"I'm not miserable," I lie, frantic. "I was just concentrating."

"Concentrating on what?"

I hold up the book that I'm reading.

He squints. "The Bible?"

I nod. At my previous job, I spent my downtime reading. I had been getting into graphic novels and thrillers. Here, my reading options are a little slimmer. I had to pick between the Bible, a book of hymns, and something called a catechism.

"Are you the new secretary?"

I nod again.

"Well, you sure are better-looking than our last one!" He cackles.

I reply, "Thank you," quietly, despite feeling affronted by that comment.

Why is this old man thinking about my appearance at all? Did he think that I would feel flattered by him exposing that he's spent part of our two-second interaction assessing my appearance, while insulting a dead woman's looks?

I watch him roar at his own comment. At his face reddening. His eyes squinting. At him slapping his knee. I wonder what it's like to be him. To vocalize the stupid thoughts he has without considering how others will interpret them. He just fumbles happily through his day, saying whatever he is compelled to—while I am over here laboring to produce appeasing facial expressions.

Smile.

Keep smiling.

Am I frowning?

"I see you and Barney are getting acquainted!" Jeff sings as he passes by my desk. "Barney's our accountant," he explains.

Barney winks at me. "Nice to meet you, honey."

"Nice to meet you too," I lie.

A new email notification pops up in the corner of the computer screen. I double-click it, happy to finally have something to do, and read:

Grace,

I found a recipe for maple cookies that are to die for. I've attached it to this email for you. I know how much you love a new recipe. I think I've finally found one worthy of sharing with you. I wish I could send you a batch of the cookies instead of just the recipe. Living far away from each other has so many downsides, doesn't it?

Please let me know if you like them. I hope to hear from you soon. I miss you.

Your friend,
Rosemary

"Are you okay?" Jeff asks me. Hot tears are streaming down my face.

"I'm fine," I lie as I blast past him toward the bathroom.

I am standing inside the church's cramped, one-person bathroom. I have my hands on both sides of the sink. I am staring into the oxidized mirror, trying to psych myself up to return to my desk.

Pull it together.

Why am I so upset? Why do I care that Grace will never eat a cookie again, or that Rosemary doesn't know that? I don't even know these people. Why does it matter to me that this woman was not informed that her friend is dead? Why do I care? There are sadder things happening on this planet right now than old women dying after living long lives—

Oh, but that makes it worse. Of course there are sadder things. This is a drop in the bucket. The world is full of so much sadness that it eclipses the sadness of this. That doesn't actually make this any less sad, it just means that there is so much potent sadness on earth that this becomes trivial. Everything becomes trivial. Nothing matters. Cats are being burned alive in house fires. Old women are dying and their friends don't know, but they'll die soon, too; they'll leave half-read books in their desks for younger people to find, who will die one day too, and the cycle will repeat, and repeat, and repeat until the sun swallows the earth, there's some sort of nuclear catastrophe, or—

Stop.

I stare into my own red eyes in the mirror.

You need to think about something else.

I focus on my reflection.

I look like a clown in this outfit. I pull at the collar. I tried to dress professionally. It must be obvious to Jeff that I am uncomfortable in this. I look ridiculous.

I exchange a pitying look with my reflection to communicate with myself that I feel sorry for me.

"Look at us," I whisper to myself. "What are we doing here?"

My face looks strange. Is it the mirror? It is a sort of warped, vintage mirror. Maybe it's distorting my face. My eyes look enormous, and my mouth looks so small. Was my mouth always that small in comparison to my other features? Is that really my face? Am I looking at a painting? Who is that?

"You need to think about something else," my mom told me.

I was crying at the end of my parents' bed. It was the middle of the night. I was ten years old.

"Think about something else," my mom said again.

I had a dream they died. It was a vivid dream. I woke up thinking it was true. I rushed to their bedroom to see if they were alive. It was too dark to see. I had to turn their lights on.

My dad shrieked, "What the hell!"

"Are you okay?" My mom sat up, panicked. "What's wrong?"

"I dreamed you died," I said. I was hyperventilating.

*   *   *

I stole a roll of crackers from the church. I don't know when to expect my first paycheck, and the only food to my name is a block of cheese. I hesitated as I pocketed the crackers. According to the book I was reading today, stealing is one of the top ten worst things a person can do. I decided to carry on with the theft, however, because hell does not exist, and if it does, I'm already slated to go.

My neighbor bombards me as I try to enter my apartment. "Did you see that story on the news about that couple running a drug ring out of their apartment?"

I pause to look at her before turning my key. She's wearing slippers. Her pink pajama pants are covered in images of small martini glasses.

"Terrible what people do from their homes," she adds, eyeing the cast on my arm. "It puts everyone around them in danger." She looks me up and down.

It turns out the crackers I stole are the body of Christ. After eating more than half the bag, I googled the cracker brand and learned that I paired marble Cracker Barrel cheese with God's transubstantiated body. I had originally googled the crackers so I could leave them a review. I planned to write: *BORING. Whoever created these is unimaginative. These crackers are tasteless and bland.*

"Eli is drunk," a man's voice tells me.

I was asleep before answering the phone. My vision is blurry.

"Wha—?" I mumble. A whistling noise is coming through the cracks around my window. A winter wind is fighting to get inside my bedroom.

"Your brother," the man repeats. "He's fucked up."

"Where is he?"

I find Eli sitting on a bench downtown eating a hamburger bun. He is not wearing a coat, and it's started to snow.

"Where did you get that?" I ask, nodding at the bun.

"I found it," he replies.

I take Eli home, to our parents' house, in a cab.

He tells the cabdriver that he loves him.

He says, "You're the best cabdriver that I've ever had."

I ask Eli to drink a glass of water.

He refuses.

"You'll regret not drinking water," I explain, nudging the glass I have poured for him into his wobbly grasp.

He tells me that I am annoying and bats my hand away. Water slops onto my legs and on the carpet.

Eli is crying and throwing up in the bathroom.

He keeps shouting that he's ugly.

"You're not ugly," I assure him as he hurls into the sink.

Eli lives with my parents. He dropped out of college two years ago and moved back home. He was going to school for visual art. He was in his last year when he dropped out. He hasn't been able to keep a job since moving back. My dad's friend had him working in his wood shop last year, but Eli quit. He said he hated it.

He retches into the toilet.

This bathroom is next to their bedroom. Despite how loud Eli is being, neither of them have stirred.

I know they can hear us. They are pretending to sleep. They are not capable of sleeping through this kind of disturbance. When I lived here, I couldn't so much as sit up in my bed before one of them materialized.

"Going somewhere?" my dad's voice would echo through the dark hallway every time I even thought of sneaking out.

"Your sister is weird," I heard Max Hardstark tell Eli through the vent in my bedroom. It was after school. I was in high school, and Eli was in middle school, but we took the same bus. I had walked immediately upstairs after getting home to avoid having to converse with Max.

"She's gay and she wears weird pants," Max said with a mouthful of snacks provided by my parents' pantry.

I had no idea my pants were weird. I was used to criticism regarding my lesbianism, but the pants comment struck me like a golf ball to the head in a boat.

Just as I had removed my pants and begun inspecting the rest of the pants folded in my dresser drawers, assessing whether they too were weird, I heard Eli shout: "Are you fucking kidding me, Max? Look at your fucking pants! You wish my sister weren't gay!"

"When did you come out?" Eleanor asked me. We were on our second date.

I never know how to answer that question because I don't feel like I am out. I feel like I am in a constant state of coming out, and like I always will be. I have to come out every time I meet someone.

We were at a restaurant. Earlier the waitress asked us if we were sisters. Neither of us came out to her; we just said no. Technically, therefore, I was not out at that Applebee's.

I assume that when someone asks me when I came out, they mean when did I first tell someone I'm gay, so I replied, "I was eleven."

I told Eli. We were in my bedroom. We were doing a quiz from a magazine. The quiz was supposed to tell us the name of the person we would marry. I got the name Kevin. I remember hoping I would get a gender neutral name, like Robin or Jordyn. I told myself that if I did, I would take that as a sign to tell Eli I'm gay. I remember looking at the magazine and thinking, *I would rather die today than marry a Kevin*. With that in mind, I announced, "I think I'm gay." I had barely finished my sentence before Eli said, "You're definitely gay. Do the quiz again as a boy so you get your real name."

"Is that the age when you realized you were gay?" Eleanor asked.

"No," I said. "I've always known I was gay, I think. Whenever I played with dolls, I'd make up romantic storylines about two girl Barbies. Before I even knew the word 'gay,' I knew I was gay."

"How are your parents with it?" she asked.

"They're okay," I said. "I haven't been disowned or anything."

She laughed. "That's a low bar."

"How are yours?" I asked.

"Similar," she replied.

I felt out of my body on that date. I had not dated someone, or socialized much, in over a year. I felt uncomfortable. I kept biting my fingernails and the insides of my cheeks.

"When did you come out?" I asked her.

"When I was twenty-two," she said. "I came out to my boyfriend first."

"How did he take it?"

"Not well," she said. "He thought I was just trying to find the easiest way to break up with him. He accused me of cheating on him. He said I'd have a new boyfriend within a month. He just invalidated me, and basically insisted I'm not gay."

When the waitress came over with our food, I thought: *Why did Eleanor date a person like that to begin with?*

"This looks good," Eleanor said, nodding at her cajun salmon.

"How long were you dating your boyfriend?" I asked.

She had taken a bite of her food. She covered her mouth and said, "Three years."

"Three years?" I repeated. "Why would you date someone so awful for three years?"

She laughed. "He wasn't all bad. He was just insecure, and had some toxic masculinity problems. Outside of that, he was very funny and smart." She sipped her drink. "Have you ever dated someone you regret dating now?"

I thought about it.

"I'm probably the person people regret dating," I said.

She snorted. "I'm sure that's not true. I can already tell you're a catch."

I am sitting amid a small crowd of senior citizens who have assembled in the church pews. Barney is sitting next to me. I am picking at my plaster cast.

My knees hurt. I eye the people around me to see if anyone else looks tortured by this relentless kneeling.

"Do your knees hurt?" I ask Barney.

"Of course my knees hurt," he answers, hushing. "But I think the pain pales in comparison to crucifixion, don't you?"

"I wonder," I mutter, rubbing my agonized knees.

"These people come here every day, you know. We're the church's regulars," he whispers to me through the corner of his mouth. "I guess you're one of us now," he adds, nudging my leg.

I have never attended mass at a Catholic church before. I am a wolf in sheep's clothing, or a sheep in wolf's clothing, depending on the perspective.

My palms are sweating. This church is ornamented in many life-sized statues of angels, and I can feel all their stony eyes on me.

Organ music starts to play. Jeff begins walking down the aisle like a bride.

He bows when he reaches the altar at the front of the room. I glance at Barney and at the people surrounding me for cues regarding what we should be doing right now.

Jeff makes the sign of the cross, and then says loudly: "In the name of the Father, and of the Son, and of the Holy Spirit."

To my horror, the crowd surrounding me replies in unison: "Amen."

Startled by this, I put a hand to my chest.

We have lines?

Jeff shouts, "The Lord be with you!"

Once again, I am startled by the crowd surrounding me replying together, "And with your spirit!"

I feel my heart racing. Is the whole thing going to be like this?

"Brothers and sisters," Jeff continues, "let us acknowledge our sins, and prepare ourselves to celebrate the sacred mysteries." He pauses.

I say, "Amen," but no one else does. Fuck.

We stand quietly. I feel sweat trickle down my brow.

Suddenly the crowd begins to recite, off the cuff, "I confess to almighty God, and to you, my brothers and sisters, that I have greatly sinned, in my thoughts and in my words, in what I have done and in what I have failed to do, through my fault, through my fault, through my most grievous fault; therefore I ask the blessed Mary ever-virgin, and all the Angels and Saints, and you, my brothers and sisters, to pray for me to the Lord our God."

I stand mute. Stunned.

The jig is up. It is astounding how well this crowd has the script memorized. Barney is bound to notice that I don't.

I feel the blood rush out of my face, and my body turn cold.

I need to get out of here.

How do I get out of here?

I should pretend that I feel sick.

I turn to Barney and announce: "I'm about to hurl."

He dives out of my way, and I bolt to the ladies' room.

After spending an hour and a half sitting on a toilet, I finally muster the courage to exit the bathroom. As I step out, an organ pipes abruptly. I clutch my heart, alarmed by the startlingly brash, unexpected noise.

"Jesus Christ," I mutter, while trying to steady the thud of my heart. Thud.

I wouldn't mind knowing whose big idea it was to install organs in God's so-called houses when they were clearly manufactured by the devil himself. Organ music reminds me more of Halloween and demons than it does of heaven and cherubs. This is the instrument played in every Dracula movie, I'm sure of it. Are they meant to scare us? Are we supposed to be frightened?

I glance around at the church. I look up at the towering pillars, and at the tall, arched roof. I notice that the stained glass windows turn all the sunlight red. Maybe this place is meant to scare me. I do feel very small in this enormous, echoing space. Not to mention, there is an alarming statue of a crucified man at the front of the room. I appreciate that it's emblematic, but the fact is it's gruesome imagery.

The organ plays loudly again.

As I walk around the church, I imagine that I am a vampire, and that the unnerving organ music is narrating all of my eerie movements.

I am a creature of the night, here to drink blood.

I sleep in a coffin.

Sunlight burns me.

"Gilda?"

Thud.

Startled, I turn to look at Jeff.

"Don't forget to genuflect in front of the tabernacle." He winks.

I smile. "Of course."

What the hell does that mean?

Eleanor keeps texting me. I don't feel comfortable responding at work because I'm worried Jeff and the Catholics will be able to sense I am doing something gay.

Hello?

Gilda?

Why aren't you replying?

There is a new email from Rosemary ticking like a bomb in the church's inbox. I am eyeing the subject line like I would glowing animal eyes in a forest. If I move slowly enough, maybe the email will walk away and I won't have to confront it.

The subject line says: *I need your prayers.*

I wonder why she needs Grace's prayers.

Oh my God, is she sick?

Despite not believing that prayers reach anyone, it still depresses me to picture a person asking for prayers from someone who is too dead to pray.

I open the email.

Dear Grace,

It is with a very heavy heart that I share with you that my dear Jim has passed away. We are all doing our best to be brave about it. It was a stroke. Quite unexpected, but the kids are doing okay. Cindy's pretty upset, but you know my Cindy.

So strange to be a widow after fifty-two years. I'm finding it hard to sleep alone. I wish it had happened after Christmas.

Add us to your prayers if you could, Grace. I hope you've been doing better than me. I would love to hear from you . . .

Your friend,
Rosemary

My face is hot, and I am heaving. I am, once again, crying on the toilet in the church's bathroom. All I can think about is poor, sad Rosemary and poor, dead Jim.

"Pull it together!" my life force instructs my body from the ceiling above me.

I can barely inhale.

"You don't even know Rosemary and Jim!"

"I know! I don't know what's wrong with me!" I explain to my spirit, hysterical.

Barney strides up to my desk with a hand covering his mouth and nose.

"Is it catching?" he asks, his voice muffled beneath his grimy paw.

"What?" I furrow my brow.

"Your bug," his muffled voice explains. "Your sickness. Do you think I could catch it?"

"Oh." I remember. "No, I think it was probably just something I ate. I had some iffy-looking bread earlier," I lie. "It was probably that."

"You're not pregnant or anything, are you?"

"What?" I furrow my brow again.

"It would be quite the scandal for the church's new secretary to be with child out of wedlock." He snorts.

I look at his chortling eyes and recognize as he wheezes that he's teasing me inappropriately. He thinks suggesting I might be pregnant is funny.

If I were pregnant, it would be immaculate conception.

I watch him cackle while I think about the actual scandal that could be unearthed about the church's new secretary.

"Were you mugged?" my neighbor asks me from her doorframe.

I am covered in dirt because I spent the last forty minutes chasing an animal who I believed was Mittens. I crawled on my knees through muddy snow. I tore the sleeve of my coat on a thorny vine. I was half an inch away from grabbing the ass of a raccoon before I realized. The raccoon turned to look at me, exposing a black mask and pointy nose—as well as an expression that communicated he was deeply confused by my pursuit of him.

"I was gardening," I lie to my neighbor, because the truth is too much of a mouthful.

"Gardening?" she repeats, narrowing her eyes at me.

It is one a.m. I was researching what to say in mass when I was sidetracked by an article that claims priests used to kill themselves to be with God.

A notification obstructs the article on my phone.

It's Eleanor. She's texted me, asking, You up?

I text back Yes, and return to my article.

I guess this is why Catholics teach that suicide is a sin. They were running out of priests.

Another notification obstructs the article. What are you up to? Eleanor asks.

I write back: Researching the order of mass.

I guess heaven sounded so good to the holy men that they thought, hey, what are we waiting for?

She texts again, You're what?

*   *   *

The local morning news is playing on my TV. I fell asleep with the TV on again because my remote is still broken. I keep falling in and out of sleep, witnessing small tidbits of the news in between my own dreams.

A local nurse has confessed to murdering five senior citizens.

I am dreaming that I am very tall.

All of her victims were her patients, but none of their deaths were attributed to her.

I can see the tops of trees.

She was over-injecting them with drugs. If she hadn't confessed, she would have never been caught.

Birds keep getting caught in my hair.

"This woman is insane," reports a man on the sidewalk.

I stretch my arms into the sky so far, my fingertips reach the end of earth's atmosphere and touch the cold black space.

A baby is being baptized today. Her mother is holding her at the front of the church. I am sitting in a back pew, watching.

I spent all of yesterday decorating the church for Christmas. It is the end of November. I had to carry fake Christmas trees, garlands, and candles up from a storage room in the basement. Every string of lights I labored to untangle would not turn on. I had to test each bulb.

I observe the lights in the room. I wonder if anyone attending this baptism senses the effort I put into elevating the ambience of this space.

The baby has been stuffed into a puffy white dress. She keeps crying, and her mother keeps cooing, "It's okay, it's okay, it's okay."

It must be difficult to be a baby. Everything must be so confusing.

"It's okay, it's okay, it's okay."

That baby has no idea why her parents put her in that uncomfortable outfit. She doesn't anticipate that an old man in a robe is going to dunk her head underwater today.

I stare at her pink face as she screams. I relate to her. She's uncomfortable and confused, just like I am. Why am I here? Why are you doing this to me? Why are we wearing these ridiculous clothes?

I bet that baby would be absolutely baffled to hear why she's enduring this. Imagine someone forced you to wear a miniature wedding gown, dunked you underwater in front of an audience of your loved ones, and then explained that their rationale for doing so was so that when you die your spirit would fly to the clouds. If I were this baby, my first words would be "fuck off."

The baptism is over. The baby's soul has been saved. Now if she dies, God forbid, she will no longer have to suffer eternal hellfire, unlike some of us. Thank God she is no longer fated like me, because I am holding her, and I am afraid that I might drop and kill her.

We were about to migrate to the basement of the church for a reception when I was stopped by the mother of the baby. She touched my arm and asked if I could please hold the baby while she fished for something in her enormous diaper bag.

I should have said no, but it felt impolite to refuse to hold someone's baby.

My arm is in a cast and this baby is hysterical. I am battling an intrusive thought right now involving this baby's soft spot and the marble floor beneath us.

Stop imagining that.

I am not sure if I am holding her wrong, if she just wants her mom, or if she is having a psychotic break. She is throwing her skull backward into my jaw and screeching.

Screech.

Screech.

Screech.

"You're a natural," the baby's mother compliments me.

"Are you being sarcastic?" I ask, but she doesn't hear me.

"Do you have kids?" she asks me over the baby's bloodcurdling cries.

"No," I reply, trying to off-load the distressed baby back to its mother.

I am troubled by the primal instinct I did not know I possess, which responds to distressed babies with a feeling of extreme physical anxiety and alertness. It's as if each cry is a line of coke. Every time the baby screeches I feel my pupils dilate.

"You want them though, right?" she asks, finally taking the baby away from me. She starts jiggling her up and down.

"N—Yes."

She grins as the baby pukes on her shoulder. Baby vomit rolls down her back.

"Are you married? Seeing anyone?"

I shake my head.

"Just haven't met the right guy yet, or—?"

"Yeah, exactly," I declare, afraid it's obvious that I'm lying.

"I should introduce you to my brother-in-law," she suggests. "He's really cute, honestly. He's Italian. He runs his own business. That's why he's not here, actually. He's with a really important client. He's so in demand. He cooks! You would love him. Are you on Facebook?"

I pause. I am on Facebook. I don't use it much, but I'm pretty sure my presence there is palpably gay. I distinctly remember liking *The L Word* and *Ellen DeGeneres*. I have definitely left positive reviews for multiple lesbian dive bars. All of that is theoretically explainawayable; however, I have also unambiguously identified myself as being "interested in women" in my About Me, and my current profile picture, if I remember correctly, is of me holding hands with my ex-girlfriend. I may be misremembering the exact phrasing, but I'm pretty sure I captioned that photo "Me and my girlfriend (we're gay)."

"I'm not," I lie, my hands sweating.

"Oh darn, okay—well, why don't you just give me your phone number, then?" she suggests, handing me her phone.

* * *

There is a nun standing next to me. She and I are both standing near a table covered in a nice spread of coffee, fruit, squares, and other assorted refreshments. There is a poinsettia on the table, and a large sheet cake frosted in pink icing that says: GOD BLESS LUCY ON HER BAPTISM.

I am not sure what I should be doing right now. I keep putting my hands in my pockets, and then taking them out again.

Should I be standing here?

Am I allowed to eat this cake?

I feel like I should be having small talk with the nun. I glance at her.

"I read once that baby diapers never decompose," I say.

That is the first topic that surfaced in the murky puddle of my mind where I concoct conversation starters.

She turns to look at me. "Is that true? Boy, that's bad news. Babies produce a lot of diapers."

I nod. "Yeah, it means that landfills are just teeming with the unrecyclable diapers of babies who have since grown up and died."

"Wow," she replies, hushed. "That is disquieting, isn't it?"

I nod. "Garbage is more lasting than people."

There is a palpable silence.

I reach toward the coffee on the table. I pick up one of the white Styrofoam cups.

"I wonder if this cup will be on the earth longer than I will," I consider out loud, while I struggle to pour myself some burnt-smelling coffee.

The nun looks down at her own coffee cup. "Well, I just turned eighty-six," she says, "so I am quite sure that mine will outlast me! I bet even those biodegradable ones will outlast me!" She snorts.

I feign a laugh.

I am googling how long it will take the garbage in my trash can to decompose. I have emptied the contents of my garbage can out on my kitchen floor, and I am investigating each piece of trash.

Tin cans last for fifty years.

Batteries last for one hundred years.

Plastic bottles last for 450 years.

Do you have any pets? Eleanor asked me.

We matched on a dating app. We had been messaging for about an hour. She told me she worked at a tech start-up, and I told her I worked at a bookstore. She said she liked my photo, and I told her I liked her picture at a zoo. She was standing next to a baby giraffe in it.

No, I replied.

I can't get a pet because one day it would die, and I doubt I'd recover.

Do you? I asked.

No, she replied. I wish. I've never had a pet.

I wasn't sure how to respond to that, so I didn't.

After a while, she messaged me again.

Have you ever had a pet?

Yes.

What was your first pet's name?

Flop.

What kind of animal was Flop? she asked.

A bunny, I wrote.

Cute. So did you grow up around here?

Yes, did you?

Yeah. What was the name of the street you grew up on? she asked.

Maple Road. You?

Fairview Ave.

All of the conversations I was having with my "matches" were similarly dull. I'm not well versed in small talk, and every conversation felt the same. We would tell each other what our jobs were, compliment each other's photos, and ask each other insipid questions until someone finally stopped replying. I was lying on my kitchen floor, mindlessly swiping through profiles, having the same conversation over and over.

What's your mom's maiden name? Eleanor messaged me.

I started to reply but stopped. I scrolled up in our messages and reviewed the questions she'd asked me. I thought, *Wait—is this person trying to steal my identity?* She'd asked me all the questions required to access my email or my bank account.

The more I thought about it, the more I convinced myself she was a scam artist.

I gave her a fake name. I said, **Kenny.**

She kept messaging me. Even though I thought she was trying to access my bank account, I kept replying. I figured I don't have money to steal anyways, and was excited to be liberated from the pressure of establishing any romantic rapport. I no longer cared if I said something stupid or weird. If she was a stranger motivated to scam me— who better to burden with my conversation?

I asked her, **What do you think the point of life is?**

She said, **I'm still trying to figure that out.**

I said, **Do you ever think about space? Black holes?**

She replied, **Yes, all the time.**

She sent me videos about dark matter. She told me about a book she read. *A Brief History of Time.* She talked about time travel, and aliens. She said she'd tried LSD once and that it made her feel more in tune with her life and nature. She said she observed plants as if she had never seen them before. Everything seemed more alive.

She told me about a drug called DMT. She said most people who do DMT see the same thing. They see creatures they call Machine Elves. When you do DMT, the elves greet you, saying, "How wonderful that you're here! You come so rarely! We're so delighted to see you!"

I thought that was interesting. We talked about whether Machine Elves were real creatures who we can't sense unless we're on DMT, or whether DMT does something to the human brain that creates the same hallucination.

She suggested we try DMT together, and I said, **No way.** She asked why not, and I said because I know in my bones that if I did DMT, or LSD, or any other hallucinogenic drug, it would be the last thing I ever did because I have chronic panic attacks and would likely kill myself.

She asked me if I was in therapy. I told her I'd gotten referrals to psychiatrists, but I never hear back. She said, **Yeah, it takes a long time.** She told me she'd gone to therapy because she has abandonment issues. She said her dad left her family when she was ten, and her mom was neglectful. She has self-esteem issues because of it. She's afraid of being alone.

I asked her if therapy helped her, and she said it had, but not completely.

She asked if I thought there was a reason why I'm anxious, and I said, "I think it might be hereditary."

I told her my dad had a mental breakdown when I was a kid after my uncle died. He rarely left the house for months. He had extreme mood swings. He kept accusing my mom of wanting to leave him, and he stopped showering. I remember our neighbor asking me, "How is your dad doing?" I answered truthfully, "Not great." I think the neighbor sent him a card, or something, because my parents found out what I said. They both screamed at me. I remember sitting at the bottom of the stairs while my mom lectured me about privacy, and my dad shrieked "I'm fine!" at the top of his lungs into my face.

I told Eleanor that I think I have mental health issues on my mom's side, too. I said one Thanksgiving, after topping off a bottle of pinot grigio, my mom's sister Dorothy told me she thought my grandpa was bipolar. He had rage issues, she said. She told me every picture hung in their house growing up was positioned oddly to cover the holes he'd punched in the plaster. I figure my mom minimized my dad's outbursts because her dad acted like that too.

Why do you think your dad didn't acknowledge he was having problems? Eleanor asked.

I don't know, I replied. I think he saw it as a weakness. I think maybe his parents taught him not to talk about that kind of thing. He cares about appearances.

I asked her about her relationship with her parents. She said she rarely speaks to her dad. He usually forgets her birthday. He never calls her. She has to call him. Her mom is better, she said. She's apologized for being absent, and they have a better relationship now.

We kept messaging each other for a couple days. I stopped thinking she was a scam artist.

So, why are you on this app? she asked me.

I downloaded the app while lying on my floor, thinking about how I hadn't dated anyone in over a year, and about how I'd distanced myself from the few friends I'd ever had. I was trying to pinpoint why I felt especially depressed lately, and thought maybe it was because I wasn't connected enough to anyone. In a blinding moment of energy, I tapped on my cell phone screen until this app was downloaded. I had to take a selfie.

I'm just trying to connect with someone, I replied. What about you?

Same, she said.

"Do you know how long it takes a glass bottle to decompose?" I question Eleanor over the phone.

"Gilda, it's two in the morning."

"Oh. I'm sorry—" I express. I didn't realize what time it was.

"That's okay." She yawns. "I just had a dream about you, actually. You were in a cookie-eating contest. You were eating Samoas."

"Interesting," I reply. "Samoas, though? I prefer Thin Mints. Was I winning?"

"Yes." She laughs.

"Okay good."

She's quiet.

"I'm sorry for waking you up," I tell her.

"That's okay. I don't mind."

"Goodnight."

"Goodnight."

I am studying the ceiling above my bed, wondering how old my apartment building is. It's a two-story walk-up. It used to be a shoe store with apartments for the shop owner upstairs. I look at the molding bordering the room and wonder who else has lived here. I think about what their lives might have been like. I wonder what they thought about when they looked up at this ceiling. I wonder how long this building will exist, and about who will replace me in this spot in the future.

I wonder if anyone has ever died looking at this ceiling.

I wonder if I will die looking at this ceiling.

"One day I am going to die," my internal dialogue asserts. That reality reverberates in my skull like a shriek in a cave. I am going to experience whatever it feels like for my life force to finish. Face it. Whatever animates my body will stop. Black. Nothing. That isn't just some alarming scary-movie fear; it's true. People will have to deal with my corpse.

I break through the hospital doors like I am a bird escaping a subway station after being trapped inside for weeks.

I need help.

"Are you okay?"

I am not.

"Is it your heart?"

It might be.

"Can you speak?"

Am I not speaking?

When I was a kid I used to lean back in my chair at school. I remember feeling like I had leaned too far and was about to fall fully backward. That's how I feel right now—except I am not in a chair and the sensation is lasting. When I was a kid, I always caught myself. I was always able to stop myself from falling completely.

"Am I falling completely now?"

"No. Calm down."

"I can't."

"Calm down."

"I would love to!" I am screaming at the receptionist.

She's behind glass and has picked up the red phone mounted on the wall beside her.

"You need to calm down!" she tells me again.

I think I just flipped a table over.

"Are you okay?" the man sitting in the room with me asks.

I look at him. He is holding a bloody cloth up over his eye.

I nod.

"You keep hitting yourself in the chest," he remarks.

I didn't realize I was doing that. My heartbeat feels irregular.

I look at him. He has blood all over the chest of his T-shirt.

"Are you okay?" I ask him.

"Me?" he replies. "I've been better."

"What happened?"

"I got in a fight," he explains. "What about you? What happened to you?"

I pause.

"I'm dying."

He makes a face. "You're dying?"

I nod.

He exhales. "Yikes. How long do you have?"

I answer gravely. "I have no idea."

*　　*　　*

Sometimes I fixate on how disgusting humans are. I think about how we do things like litter and invent nuclear bombs. I think about racism, war, rape, child abuse, and climate change. I think about how gross people are. I think about public bathrooms, armpits, and about all of our dirty hands. I think about how infection and diseases are spread. I think about how every human has a butt, and about how disgusting that is.

Other times I fixate on how endearing people are. We sleep on soft surfaces; we like to be cozy. When I see cats cuddled up on pillows, I find it sweet; we are like that too. We like to eat cookies and smell flowers. We wear mittens and hats. We visit our families even when we're old. We like to pet dogs. We laugh; we make involuntary sounds when we find things funny. Laughing is adorable, if you really think about it.

We have hospitals. We invented buildings meant to help repair people. Doctors and nurses study for years to work here. They come here every day just to patch other people up. If we discovered some other animal who created infrastructure in the anticipation that their little animal peers might get hurt, we would all be absolutely moved and amazed.

I am observing a nurse as if she is a deer in a meadow; a portion of wildlife in scrubs with latex gloves and sensible sneakers on her hooves. I watch her prepare a gurney as if I'm watching a bird build a nest.

"Are you sure you're okay?" the man next to me asks me again.

I wipe tears off my jaw.

"Yes, thank you, I'm fine."

"You're just thinking too much," Frank, the hospital janitor, tells me while mopping the tile floor beside me.

Frank and I have spoken before, on my previous visits. About a month ago, I threw up on the floor and he mopped it up. I apologized profusely and explained I felt anxious, and was having chest pains. He said it was okay, he understood. Now when he sees me, he greets me like we're old friends.

He asked me what brought me in today and I said, "I feel anxious again."

There is no one in the waiting room but him and me. I am the last patient waiting.

"You might not feel so anxious if you just occupied yourself a little more." He rinses out the mop in his soapy bucket. "You're probably just too in your head," he says. "I bet that's your problem."

"Okay." I nod. Maybe that's true. "How do I occupy myself?"

"I find I feel less anxious when I spend my time trying to make the people around me happier," he shares. "Maybe you should try that."

Snow is plummeting down from the clouds and coating everything. All the garbage and dog shit on the road is being tucked under a glittery white blanket. My coat, hat, and hair are covered in snow. I am like the garbage and dog shit; I am being tucked under the snow blanket as well.

I glance around at the sad sacks shivering at the bus stop with me.

"I love your coat," I compliment the stranger standing next to me. I had been mustering the courage to say it for the last ten minutes.

She turns. "Are you talking to me?"

I nod, humiliated. "Yes. I was just saying that I love your coat."

"Thanks . . ." she says cautiously, clutching her coat tighter to her body as if she's preparing for me to try to steal it from her.

The man driving this bus keeps slamming on the brakes.

I gave my seat up to a wobbly pregnant woman. Despite losing my balance and smashing my face on the back of another passenger's skull, I still make a point of saying "Thank you very much" to the bus driver before escaping his bus.

"You're welcome." He nods.

"I really appreciate the ride," I reiterate.

"Please hurry up and get off my bus," he replies.

Barney is struggling to carry a pile of cardboard boxes into the church.

"Can I help you?" I ask, running up beside him.

"Yes," he grunts, handing me every box in his arms.

Barney has BO, and the smell has transferred onto the boxes. It is as if I am carrying two boxes of putrefied garbage and ham.

He doesn't open the door for me as I struggle to carry the boxes, one-armed. He lumbers ahead of me, happy to be freed of his chore. I shove a foot in the closing door before it shuts completely, and heave my way into the building like a disabled pack mule.

"How did these get so knotted?" I ask Sister Jude as we untangle a box full of rosaries.

"Someone must have put them away carelessly," she sighs.

I think it was me.

I almost break the rosary in my hands as I undo a particularly tight knot.

"Be careful!" she says, taking the rosary out of my hands in the same way she'd confiscate a knife from a toddler.

"Breaking a rosary is bad luck. It means someone's mad at you," she explains.

I have a feeling that if I broke a rosary, that person would be her.

My phone is ringing.

I pick it up and say, "Hello," as cheerfully as I can manage.

"Hi there!" The voice matches my enthusiasm. "Am I speaking with Gilda?"

"You sure are," I reply, still trying to present as cheery.

"Hi, Gilda, this is Giuseppe. My sister-in-law gave me your number—"

Oh no.

"I was wondering if I could take you to dinner?"

Fuck.

"Do you like sushi?"

"Y-Yes."

"Perfect!" he replies. "When are you free?"

How am I supposed to make Giuseppe feel happy if I reject him? How am I supposed to uphold this façade as a Catholic heterosexual if I refuse to go to sushi with an Italian bachelor?

"Hello?" Giuseppe says.

"Hi," I choke out.

He laughs. "What day works for you?"

I pause.

"Can I get back to you?" I ask, the cheeriness in my voice waning.

"Sure!" he replies. "I'll text you so we can arrange a day that works. Sound good?"

"Okay," I say.

"Awesome! Talk to you soon, then. I'm really looking forward to meeting you!"

"Are you?" I ask, to verify that I have managed to make this stranger happy.

He laughs. "For sure!"

I made coffee for Jeff and myself. I am carrying both cups from the church kitchen to our offices. This is difficult to do with my broken arm; I have one cup pressed to my chest with my cast. Coffee keeps splattering out of the cups and scalding me. I am smiling despite it. I am presenting as happy because people prefer that. I am less likely to brighten people's day by wincing and scowling while being burned.

I knock on Jeff's door. "I brought you a coffee."

I hand the cup to him.

My hands are bright red.

"Well, aren't you sweet?" He beams, accepting my offering. "Thank you, dear."

"No problem," I reply, smiling too.

I log into the church computer. I open the most recent email from Rosemary and pause.

I stare at the email for a moment before typing:

Rosemary,

I'm sorry for taking so long to reply. I've been ill, but I'm doing a lot better now.

I am so sorry to hear about Jim. I don't know what to say to make you feel better, but I want you to know that I wish I did. I hope you're able to feel even an infinitesimal bit of happiness today despite all of this.

Love,
Grace

Just as I click Send, something is activated in my chest and my heart explodes. I stand up, accidentally knocking my coffee off my desk. Coffee splatters on the carpet and on the boxes I carried into the building for Barney this morning.

I can't breathe.

I can't breathe.

I can't breathe.

My skin hurts. If sensitivity were a color, the saturation of my skin would be an intense red.

I feel intensely red.

*   *   *

Someone is knocking on the bathroom door.

I am drenched in my own cold sweat.

"Are you okay in there?" Sister Jude asks me.

"I'm fine," I lie, but I'm not.

I don't think Frank's medical advice was right. I don't think focusing on other people's happiness will do anything to cure my anxiety. I tried to spend my morning making the people around me happier and I've been rewarded with a bruised skull, scalded hands, an unwanted date with a guy, and a panic attack.

I stare at my mouth in the mirror.

Smile, I tell myself.

Smile.

I read once that fake smiling can trick your brain into believing you're happy, which can then spur actual feelings of happiness.

I gape at my smiling reflection. I stare into my own lifeless eyes as I grin manically at myself like a deranged chimp.

I am opening the boxes I spilled coffee on, to inspect whether I destroyed what's inside. I rip the tape off one box, hoping to discover insides that can be easily cleaned off. I am disappointed to unearth piles and piles of sodden paper. I pull out one of the wet sheets.

The paper says, in large red lettering: SAVE YOUR CHILDREN FROM HOMOSEXUALITY.

"What the fuck?" I say out loud.

"What happened to the flyers!" Barney wails from behind me.

"I have no idea!" I lie.

Hey Gilda! This is Giuseppe. Are you free for sushi on Friday? an unknown number texts me.

I start to type no but erase it.

I'm sorry, I write instead. I have plans.

No problem! How about next Friday? Or next Saturday?

I rapidly search my mind for a believable excuse I could use to reject both of those proposed dates. Maybe I should pretend I am the sole-support of my aging grandma, and that I can't spare a single evening away.

No, that won't work. What if he asks to meet her?

Maybe I should say I've got a terrible illness, and my evenings are full with doctors appointments and blood tests.

No, that won't work either. He could tell Jeff. It's difficult enough pretending to be a straight Catholic; I can't pull off being a straight, sick Catholic. It's too much.

I type and erase, type and erase, until finally I write, **Saturday would be great.**

On Friday, I will just text him that I've caught the flu.

Fantastic! he replies.

"How did you cut your hand?" the nurse sewing stitches into my knuckles asks.

I fell asleep with the heat set too high. I gasped myself awake, my lungs full of hot air. I thought my house was on fire. I felt foggy-headed and confused. I started shouting, "Where's the cat? I don't want the cat to die!" before I remembered that I don't own a cat. By the time I had processed that, I had also registered that there were no flames or smoke.

I turned the heat down. I then walked to the bathroom, mistook my own reflection for an intruder, and punched my mirror.

"Who are you!" I shouted, quickly making a fist and attempting to defend myself.

My cracked reflection and I both laughed when we realized the mistake I made.

"How did you cut your hand?" the nurse repeats.

"Oh," I mouth. "I was fishing for something out of the garbage and didn't realize there was glass in there."

The truth is too much of a mouthful.

I am struggling to hold my hand still. I am involuntarily shaking.

She stops what she's doing and asks, "Are you feeling anxious?"

"A little, yeah," I reply.

"I have some anxiety issues too." She smiles. "Have you ever tried mindfulness?"

"No. What's that?"

"It's paying attention in a particular way," she explains. "On purpose, in the present moment. It might help you. Do you want to try it?"

"Sure," I answer, though being deeply present in this moment of getting stitches sounds unappealing. "How do I do it?"

"Think about your senses. Ask yourself: What do I see? What do I hear? What do I smell? What do I taste? What do I feel? Why don't you look around the room right now and tell me, what do you see?"

I glance around the room.

"Hospital stuff," I reply.

"Like what?" she probes.

I look at the wall. "A poster about the flu shot."

"What else?"

"A black chair."

"What else?"

"You."

"What do you smell?"

"Nothing. Bleach, I guess."

"What do you hear?"

"The fan in the ceiling. People talking outside the room."

"Can you taste anything?"

"My gum."

"Do you feel anything?"

"My knuckles hurt, I guess." I look down at my hands; one is in a cast and the other is bloodied with stitches. "My arm hurts," I say, holding up my cast for the nurse.

I see stars in the dark sky through my bedroom window. I see light snow falling. I see my curtains swaying. I see the shadowy silhouettes of my furniture. I see the plates piled next to my bed, and around my room. I smell my dirty hair and the burrito I ate in my bed. I hear cars in the road beneath my apartment, driving through slush. I hear the fridge hum. I hear air entering my nostrils and leaving. I feel my blankets on my skin. I feel the ache in my broken arm and my knuckles.

I think deeply about the ache in my arm and my knuckles.

I sit up. Where are my painkillers?

I start rifling through the pockets of my clothing. I look behind my bathroom mirror, on my kitchen counter, and under my bed.

The aching feeling pulses.

I empty the contents of my vacuum cleaner, despite the fact that I have not vacuumed in at least six months.

I know I didn't accidentally throw the painkillers out because I just spent the last two days meticulously examining all of my trash.

I toss all the clothes in my drawers onto my unmade bed. I search through my empty dresser. I open my backpack. I search through every pocket.

I lie down on the floor of my bedroom, breathing heavily, now fixating on the pulsating pain radiating from my arm and my knuckles.

I stare up at my ceiling and then down at myself.

Wait. Am I looking down at myself?

How could I be looking down at myself?

That is my face. Those are my eyes; that is my body, wearing my shirt, my pants, and my socks.

"Think about the aching feeling," I tell myself, trying to remain in tune with my body.

I don't feel anything. It is as if I'm a corpse.

"Think about the aching feeling," I suggest again to myself, as I feel my life force gravitate into the sky.

"Think about the aching feeling!" I repeat, as I feel myself soar over the city, over the country, over the planet, over the solar system, over the galaxy, into the deep, expansive, empty blackness.

I stare down at the speck of the cosmos that my body occupies.

I am a mite; I am smaller than a dot.

"One day, you are going to die," Jeff's booming voice echoes through the church. "Everyone in this room will someday be dead."

I am chewing on my fingernails. I wish he had chosen a different topic.

"Look around," he instructs. People stir in their pews. "Some of us won't be here next year."

A baby starts crying.

"It's important to remember every day that passes brings us closer to the day that we die."

He drones on, saying words like "eternal life," "the paschal mystery," and "sacrifice." I glance at the people surrounding me, hoping to exchange a look with someone who is as unsettled by this homily as I am. I look at their bright eyes, watching Jeff at the pulpit, untroubled, absorbing his words, nodding.

I have successfully camouflaged myself as a Catholic for almost two weeks. There have been a few close calls. Yesterday, for example, I shrieked, "Jesus Christ!" after stubbing my toe on a kneeler, right in front of the Catholic Women's League. I snorted and said, "As if," when Barney made a comment about how lucky my future husband will be. All in all, though, I have been accepted as what I present myself to be.

I am a mild-mannered Catholic girl.

I read the Bible.

I plan, one day, to have a godly husband.

I will go to heaven when I die.

"Gilda?" Jeff interrupts my thoughts.

I look up at him.

"Are you going to answer that?" he asks, nodding at the ringing phone on my desk.

"Oh," I splutter. "Yes, of course."

He smiles weakly.

"Hello?" I put the phone to my ear, expecting to hear the senile woman who keeps calling to ask what time mass is. Jeff has left the room, so I toy with the idea of telling the woman that the Catholic church has been canceled, and that she should enjoy the rest of her Sundays without worrying about mass.

"Hello, this is Deputy Parks from investigative services with the city police," a woman with a deep voice replies. "I am calling in regards to Grace Moppet. I understand that she was an employee there?"

"Y-Yes," I answer. "Well, I was told she was. I'm actually her replacement. I didn't know her."

"Is there anyone around who knew her?"

I have the phone muted and held up to my ear. I am eavesdropping on Jeff while he talks to the police.

"Grace went to the hospital a number of times last winter," the police officer tells him. "Our records show she had pneumonia, suffered a fall, and that she also had a large number of tests done. Did she seem well at work? Healthy?"

"She took a few sick days," Jeff answers. "She had a good disposition, though. She seemed quite happy and content. She seemed healthy."

"She had an MRI done in January," the officer says. "It looks like she had the beginnings of dementia. Did she talk to you about that? Did she show any symptoms of that?"

"Oh dear." Jeff's voice softens. "She didn't mention that to me, no. She was forgetful, but it must not have advanced much while she was still with us. She seemed fine. Can I ask why you're looking at Grace's medical records?"

The officer clears her throat. "I'm not sure if you've been reading the news, sir, but a local nurse named Laurie Damon recently confessed to intentionally over-injecting elderly patients with drugs to end their lives. Our office has been tasked with investigating all of her patients to assess whether they might have been victims. Unfortunately, the reason I'm calling is because our records show that Grace was one of Laurie Damon's patients."

Jeff is quiet.

"I see," he says after a quiet moment. "That is difficult news to hear."

"I'm sorry," the officer says in a softer voice. "She may not have been a victim. We're just investigating every possible case to ensure that the proper justice is served."

Jeff clears his throat. "God bless you for that."

I google "Laurie Damon" and read every news article listed.

She went to the police and confessed to killing her patients.

She has been a nurse for over twenty years.

Her living patients are flabbergasted by the situation.

"I must be a terrible judge of character," Mae Ross reports. "I thought Laurie was a good person."

I am running my fingers along the fabric of my seat cushion. I am hyper attuned to how my fingertips feel moving over the plaited threads. I am stewing with the fact that I am sitting in a chair occupied recently by a woman who is now dead, and who was maybe murdered.

I wonder how often I occupy spaces that were recently inhabited by dead people.

I wonder who will occupy the spaces I've inhabited, after I'm dead.

If I get buried, my coffin will be my last space. No one will ever occupy that space but me. That's a comfort—to have a spot reserved only for me forever.

I guess bugs might bunk with me.

Rodents.

I start to think about worms.

Maggots.

Stop.

I slam open the Bible in front of me, shaking my head like an Etch A Sketch. Pictures of eye sockets and grubs crumble like a broken puzzle in my mind's eye. I fight to stop the image from reassembling by humming, and by telling myself to read something distracting.

I pick a page arbitrarily, like I am selecting tarot cards. I tell myself that whatever page I land on has been provided to me by some higher cosmic power.

I stare down at my preordained passage and absorb a story about a woman named Jezebel who is thrown out a window, trampled by horses, and eaten by dogs.

A new email notification pops up on the computer. It's from Rosemary.

> Grace,
>
> I can't tell you how excited I was to finally see your name in my inbox!
>
> You've been ill? I'm sorry to hear that. What's been wrong?

We've been doing all right over here, all things considered. The service for Jim was lovely and my kids are being a huge help to me. I am very lucky.

I also know my Jim would want me to be okay, so I've been focusing on my art, and on my cat. I am trying to be a better "pet mother," so I have put Lou on a strict diet. She's lost a full pound since I've done so, but she keeps trying to sneak into the cupboards. I found her inside the garbage can a few days ago. She'd eaten, honest to God, half a banana peel.

Get well soon, Grace.

Love,
Rose

My heart sinks deeply into my body. I begin to type, "Grace might have been murdered . . ." when Jeff enters the room. He sees me typing and smiles.

"You are one busy bee, aren't you?"

I nod. That's me, all right.

"Don't let me interrupt," he says as he enters his own office.

I sit motionless for a full minute, thinking about how sad Jeff sounded when the police spoke to him about Grace. I think about how terrible it would feel to learn your friend is not only dead but was maybe murdered. I imagine this grieving widow seeing an email from Grace in her inbox and feeling excited. I imagine her opening the email, eager to hear from her pal, reading that she's dead, and then having a heart attack.

I erase what I was writing and type:

Rose,

I am glad to hear that you have been doing okay. I am also thrilled to hear that Lou is slimming down and getting healthy.

There is a cat missing in my neighborhood. If Lou were lost, where do you think she would go?

Love,
Grace

Are we still good for sushi on Saturday? Giuseppe texts me.
Fuck. I forgot about that.
I'm sorry, I've double-booked myself, I lie. Can I take a rain check?
Of course! How about next weekend?
Sure, I write.

I arrive at work the next morning to find yet another email from Rosemary waiting for me.

Grace,

I think Lou would go right under the back porch and stay there until someone found her. She is quite timid, my Lou.

It's getting pretty cold out. I hope that missing cat is found soon and doesn't freeze out there. I can't believe it's December already, can you? I find time goes by so quickly . . .

Are you all ready for Christmas?

Love,
Rosemary

I am using the flashlight on my phone to look under my neighbors' porches.
I am shouting, "Mittens? . . . Mittens?"

My hands are cold, my feet hurt, and I am beginning to accept the dark reality that Mittens is gone. Dead. I continue shouting "Mittens," to assert to anyone who sees me in their backyard that I am not a burglar. I make clicking noises with my tongue, and say, "Mittens? . . . Mittens? . . . Mittens?" Over and over, fruitlessly.

At nighttime in the winter I always look for lit-up windows with open curtains. I like seeing a snapshot inside other people's houses. I look at what show the TV is playing. I look at the furniture. Even when I see the TV is playing an uninteresting show and the house is filled with outdated, ugly furniture, I always wish I were inside.

The house across the street has a Christmas tree. The lights on the tree are all white. There's a cat sitting on the windowsill. There's a woman playing her piano.

I tighten my scarf across my face and continue to stare into the window. I think about how comfortable it looks inside, and about how cozy the little cat looks.

My mind wanders back to Mittens. I think about his grieving family. I picture the sad image of those people on Christmas without their beloved pet. I picture an empty cat bed beside a Christmas tree next to a depressing, untouched ball of yarn.

My mind wanders further to Rosemary, and to the image of an old woman without her husband on Christmas. I think about how she spent almost her entire life with him. I picture his empty chair at their dinner table. I picture Rosemary struggling to carve the turkey because her husband used to do that. I think about the days before Christmas; I imagine that she comforts herself in her grieving by imagining how much she'll enjoy Christmas—but then when it comes, she realizes she doesn't feel any better. She might even feel worse.

*   *   *

I open the church's email, hit Reply, and write:

> Dear Rose,
>
> I feel the same way about time. At the end of every day I think, Didn't I just wake up? Every new year I think, Didn't last year just start?
>
> Rose, I want you to know I'm thinking of you this Christmas. I can only imagine how difficult it is for you this time of year after losing Jim. Please tell me if there is anything I can do to help you get through this time.
>
> Give Lou my best.
>
> Merry Christmas.
>
> Your friend,
> Grace

"This is my date, Gilda." Eleanor introduces me to a set of her co-workers. We are at her office holiday party. I am holding a drink.

We are in a party room at a restaurant. Mariah Carey's "All I Want for Christmas Is You" is playing softly. There are red linens on the tables and white candles lit around the room.

"Great to meet you, Gilda." One of her coworkers shakes my casted-hand too aggressively. Some of my drink slops over the rim of my glass onto my hand.

I had been deliberately nursing my drink because holding it has given me something to do with my hands. I don't like to be in social situations without something to do with my hands.

"How did you two meet?" the man who spilled my drink asks us.

"A dating app," Eleanor answers.

"How long have you been seeing each other?" the other man pries.

"Just like two months, right, Gilda?" Eleanor turns to me.

I have no idea how long we've been seeing each other.

"We just love Eleanor," the man who spilled my drink tells me while I struggle to contribute.

"So, what do you do for work, Gilda?"

I sip a ration of my drink to give myself a moment to formulate a response.

"I'm an administrative assistant," I reply.

"Oh, do you enjoy that?" the man snoops.

I sip my drink again.

"Do you want to go find our seats now?" Eleanor asks me.

I look into her eyes and nod, unsure of whether she's asking me out of a true desire to find our seats, or if she is in tune enough to my feelings to know I wanted a way out of the conversation.

"Excuse us." Eleanor smiles at her coworkers.

I think she knows.

Our table is in a corner. My seat faces away from the wall, giving me a view of the whole room. I am looking around at the crowd of people, listening to the sounds of clinking plates and voices chattering.

I am inside of an ecosystem that I don't belong in. These people spend a significant amount of their lives together. They attend meetings, go for coffee, eat lunch. They are a community with relationships and shared objectives. It's strange that I am in this room. I feel like a foreign object inside of a body, waiting to be rejected.

"How is your arm feeling?" Eleanor asks.

"My arm?" I repeat back, confused.

She snorts. "You have a broken arm. Did you forget?"

"Oh." I look down at my cast. I breathe air out my nose, "I did, yeah. Sometimes it hurts, sometimes I don't even notice it."

"I assume now is one of the times you don't notice it?"

I blow air out my nose again. "Yeah."

"Do you think that your new job will have a holiday party?" she asks.

I have been vague with Eleanor about my new job. I told her I work in an office as a secretary, which is technically true.

"I doubt it," I answer.

I decide not to mention that even if it did, I definitely couldn't bring her as my date.

"What's the company called?" she asks.

"The company?"

"Where you're working," she follows. "Your new job. Where is it?"

I have a plate of pastry puffs in front of me. I pop two in my mouth rather than reply.

"You love those, eh?" She smiles.

I nod.

"Thank you for coming to this." She nudges my leg from under the table. "I know you don't really like these kinds of things."

I look up. She and I look into each other's faces for a beat before she laughs.

"You must really like me to come here," she goads.

She wants me to tell her I like her.

"I do really like you," I tell her.

"What do you want your life to be like when you're old?" Eleanor asked me.

We had just started seeing each other. It was the first night I slept over at her house. We were lying on her bed with the lights off.

"It's hard for me to picture being old," I said.

When I was younger, I used to imagine different lives for myself. I thought about becoming a veterinarian, or working for an animal shelter. I thought about going to college, traveling, or moving far away. Other times, I thought I might buy a van, refurbish it, and drive it around North America. I liked to daydream about what I might do, where I might go, and what might happen to me. I don't do that anymore. I can't see myself older.

"What do you want?" I asked her.

"I want to live in a cottage," she said. "I want a perennial garden and fruit trees. I want to learn how to make bread, and how to do pottery. And I want a cat."

A hazy picture of her garden formed in my mind's eye. I saw fuzzy images of hollyhock and lavender. I pictured an orange cat sleeping under a fruit tree.

"That sounds nice," I said. "What would you name the cat?"

"Whatever you want," she joked.

"Apparently, one of the neighbors is agoraphobic," my dad gossips.

My mom is spooning small hills of canned peas onto all of our plates.

"I guess Joe from next door tried to shovel her driveway for her, and can you guess what she did?"

Before any of us can venture a guess, he tells us. "She screamed at him from her window to get off her property."

"Good Lord," my mom tuts.

"Can you believe that?" my dad says after spooning peas into his mouth. "Apparently, this woman doesn't leave her house." He chews. "She doesn't want anyone near her."

He looks at me. "Can you imagine not leaving your house for days, Gil?"

I stare at him.

"Isn't that insane?" he asks.

I look at Eli. He's pouring himself red wine. He has had three glasses in the last half hour.

"Anyways, she's a crackpot," my dad sighs. "We've got nutjobs in the neighborhood, I'm afraid, folks."

*   *   *

Eli runs a blue Sharpie over my cast. The felt tip squeaks against the plaster. He has one eye closed and one eye open. He's covering up the penis dog drawing with a forest. He's drawn little evergreens and mountains. Right now he's drawing a river; the water reflects the sky and the tree line.

I can't draw. Last year I was roped into playing Pictionary with my friend Ingrid and her coworkers. I had to draw "the elephant in the room." Everyone guessed my drawing, of what I believed looked like an elephant in a room, was of a toad.

"Is it a toad in a box?" Ingrid had asked loudly.

"It didn't look anything like a toad," I tell Eli while I detail the story.

He's using a Wite-Out pen to draw ripples in the river.

"Can you draw animals in the forest?" I ask him.

He draws birds in the sky, a duck in the water, and a deer lying under a tree.

"I tried to paint a picture of Flop once," I tell him.

"Our rabbit?"

I nod.

"How'd it turn out?"

"Terrible."

A muscular woman with a low ponytail, wearing a dark monocromatic outfit, is standing across from Jeff. From the back, she looks like a girl I dated named Ruth. Ruth and I dated for six months or so when I was twenty-one. She broke up with me. She said I had no ambition and that I was strange.

"Ruth?" I approach the woman, afraid Ruth has resurfaced to blow my cover.

Ruth hated me.

The woman turns around and I am relieved to discover that she is not Ruth. She is a police officer who looks a little like Ruth.

"Gilda, this is Officer Parks," Jeff says.

She reaches her hand out to shake mine. I hold out my casted arm.

"Nice to meet you," she says while hesitantly shaking the fingers that emerge from my cast. "I hope this doesn't hurt your arm."

"It doesn't," I reply, though it does a little. "It's nice to meet you too. Sorry, I thought you were someone I know."

"Oh, who?" she asks.

I swallow. I can't answer that.

"Uh," I sputter. "Just someone named Ruth. She was just a friend."

Why did I say *just* a friend?

"She was *a* friend, I should say," I correct myself.

I swallow again. That correction made it worse.

"What happened to your arm?" She mercifully changes the topic.

"I was in a small car accident."

"Oh, I'm sorry to hear that."

"Thank you."

"I was just telling Father Jeff that I'm investigating a case involving Grace Moppet." She redirects the conversation again. "Is it all right if I look around?" she asks Jeff.

"Of course." Jeff nods. "Let us know if you need anything."

She smiles. "Thank you."

Are we still good for sushi tomorrow? Giuseppe texts me.

Fuck.

I am dreaming of sashimi, he adds with two sushi emojis.

No, I write back. I'm sorry. I add. I'm not feeling well.

I add two barfing emojis to match the way he communicates.

Oh no! he replies with a sad face. Do you want me to bring you soup?

I type no again but erase it. That's very nice of you, I write instead. But no, thank you. I'm too sick to eat.

Should I put more barfing emojis?

Aw, he replies. That's okay. We can reschedule. He adds a smiley face.

I reply, while frowning, with a matching smiley face.

The church finally paid me. I went to a café to celebrate with a coffee; however, I discovered that all the money I took out and put in my wallet is missing. I am starting to doubt my atheism because this might be proof that God exists and hates me.

I am holding the coffee in one hand, and my empty wallet awkwardly in my casted hand. A cashier is waiting for me to pay for the coffee.

"It's two dollars and twenty-five cents," she tells me.

The heat from the coffee is absorbing into my hand and traveling up through my body. My face is sweating.

I often hold my money in my hand before even entering a store. I do that because I am excessively anxious about holding up lines while people wait for me to fish through my wallet. Today I felt bold enough to enter this coffee shop without going through that usual neurotic routine, but I have been vindicated.

"I don't have any money," I confess in a whisper as that awful realization washes over me.

Her bubbly smile fades into a nervous frown. "Oh, well, I'm not allowed to give it to you for free—"

I splutter, "I wouldn't have asked you to."

She takes the coffee back. "I'll just pour it out."

"I got married right after I turned twenty-five," Barney announces proudly. He is sitting on the edge of my desk.

The amount of space his body occupies in such close proximity to me is making me feel uneasy. I keep inching my chair back.

He is telling me about his marriage because he and I just witnessed a young couple enter Jeff's office. They are meeting with Jeff for couples' therapy before their wedding. This is apparently something the church mandates. Catholic couples must discuss marriage with their priest before their wedding, despite the fact that priests are barred from marriage and are supposed to have little to no experience in romantic relationships.

I wonder what they talk about.

"I met my wife in church," Barney continues prattling.

I have not been replying to anything he has said, but he hasn't noticed. He is capable of talking purely to himself. I am contributing nothing to the conversation.

Officer Parks knocks on the doorframe. She is with another police officer.

"Good morning," Barney greets them. "Father Jeff is just in a meeting. Do you want me to interrupt for you?"

"No, that's all right," Officer Parks says. "We can wait."

They sit down on the chairs outside his office.

"Anyways," Barney turns back to me. "Our wedding was beautiful. It was really just gorgeous. We got married in April, so we were worried about rain, but it turned out to be a really nice day. It was just lovely."

I wish he weren't sitting on my desk.

"She was wearing a lace dress, and I wore a full tux."

I glance at the police officers. They are speaking quietly to each other.

"Her sister was her maid of honor. Darla. Cute girl."

I wonder what they're talking about.

"She came from a great family, my wife."

I eye the officers' uniforms. They have badges on their shoulders. They are wearing ties. Why would their uniform include a tie?

"Really great people. Irish."

The shoes they're wearing look impractical. They look like men's formal shoes. Can they run in those?

"My father-in-law, boy, that man was a treasure. Let me tell you."

Officer Parks looks up at me. I look away quickly.

"And her mother! She had us over for dinner every Sunday night. Can you imagine?"

I hate it when people catch me looking at them.

"She was a great cook. She made beef tenderloin and cabbage rolls. She was a great lady, really. She made spaghetti. Beef Wellington."

I am staring at my hands while Barney rambles. His voice ebbs in and out of my awareness while I think about how wrinkles form. I wonder how many times skin has to fold for a wrinkle to form. I flex my fist. I look at the lines in my palms.

"How old are you?" Barney asks me.

I don't register the question. I am transfixed by my hands.

"Gilda? Earth to Gilda?"

I look up. "What did you ask me?"

"How old are you?"

"I'm twenty-two," I reply. "No—wait," I correct myself. "I'm twenty-seven."

He snorts. "The clock's ticking."

Every dish I own is now on the floor of my bedroom. I find the prospect of collecting these dishes, let alone washing them, exceptionally daunting. Envisioning myself picking up even one cup knocks the wind out of me. I'd reached for a cup earlier, and it felt as if I'd run a marathon. I almost immediately fell asleep.

There is ice in my boots, my socks are soaked, and my toes are freezing. I am walking to work. The streets are lined in mounds of dirty snow and garbage. My throat burns from the cold air, and my lips are cracking. I look ahead of myself and note the snow is almost the same color as the sky. It's as if the whole world is off-white and grayish.

The utility poles have red ribbon wrapped around them. Under every other streetlight hangs a limp, sun-bleached wreath. The city must reuse these decorations every year. The ribbon is wrinkled and torn in places. The wreaths are all falling apart.

Someone is dead. There is a coffin at the head of the church with white peonies draped over it. There is a green wreath to the right of the coffin, framing a photo of a pretty teenaged girl with long black hair. A herd of people are sitting staring forward at the coffin. The room is silent except for intermittent sniffs.

There are advent candles at the altar. Three of the candles are purple and one is pink. Jeff began lighting them last week. Every week he will light another. Last week he lit a purple one, this week he will light a second purple one, next week he will light the pink one, and on the last week—he will light the final purple candle. I would have expected the pink candle to be lit last, since there is only one; however, for a reason I don't understand, it is lit third.

The first candle, according to Jeff, symbolizes hope. The second candle represents faith. The third, pink candle, symbolizes joy, and the fourth candle symbolizes peace.

I look around the room and note that it does not feel hopeful, faithful, joyful, or peaceful in here at all. It feels bleak. Miserable.

"Eternal rest grant unto her, O Lord," Jeff proclaims. "Let perpetual light shine upon her."

The girl in the coffin was killed in a car accident. There was ice on the road, and she didn't have snow tires. She drove into a tree.

My chest is deflating and inflating as I breathe.

I think I might be inhaling and exhaling too deeply.

I am staring at the motionless coffin, thinking about how the girl inside it has a motionless chest.

She has all the same organs and body parts as me.

She has lungs.

A heart.

A brain.

I look at the people dotted across the pews. I look at all of their mouths. I stare at the mouths of the people in the front. The woman who I think is her mom is stone-faced. Her mouth is still. She looks shell-shocked. The man who I think is her dad has his face in his hands. I can't see his mouth. I can see tears emerging from beneath his palms, rolling down his neck, and wetting the collar of his shirt. I keep watching until finally he reveals his mouth, and I witness his grief-stricken frown.

Tears form in my eyes.

I look away from them to other people in the pews. I wonder how everyone else here knew her.

I scan the faces of the people sitting in the back of the church. I wonder who they are. Old neighbors, maybe. Strangers who work with her dad.

Jeff is rushing by my desk with his face in his hands. He does not know I am sitting here. I snuck in as the funeral ended, to escape the crowd. He doesn't see me because my computer is so massive that it obstructs me from his view.

He is struggling to unlock the door to his office because his hands are shaking.

He has tears rolling down his cheeks.

I am sitting as still as a rabbit in high beams, hoping he doesn't notice me.

He finally opens the door and shuffles inside.

I hear the *click* of him locking the door behind him.

*   *   *

I am staring down at my hands, trying to distract myself from the mental image of Jeff crying in the room next to me. I am looking at the painting Eli drew on my cast. I am gazing at the ducks in the water.

Jeff is an old man. His hands shake when he tries to hold objects. His voice is wheezy, and his posture has sort of curled into itself. He wears his pants too high.

My eyes fog up. I can't stand thinking about an old man crying.

Jeff must attend a lot of funerals. It's strange this one has affected him so much.

I can hear Jeff sniffing through his door.

Should I be comforting him? What if I slip up? What if I say something like, *Don't worry, Jeff, life is meaningless; it's strange and inexplicable that we exist to begin with. We are all basically dead already in the grand scheme of things, and our feelings of sadness are pointless—they are just how our meat sacks react to the chemicals in our bodies.*

I hear him sniff again.

Fuck.

I knock on the door.

I hear rustling noises and Jeff's voice cracks, "Just a second!"

I hear him blow his nose before opening the door sporting a phony smile.

"Hello, dear," he says. "Come in."

I look into his bloodshot eyes. His irises are gray. His eyebrows have sunk over them, and there are bags, wrinkles, and age spots encasing them. "What can I do for you, Gilda?" he asks. He runs his hands through the thin wisps of white hair that he has remaining on his almost bald head.

"Are you okay?" I ask.

He presses his wrinkled lips together and smiles. I notice light reflect in his teary eyes.

"I am all right, thank you, dear. I have just been feeling a bit blue."

I don't know how to respond.

"Because of the funeral?" I ask.

He nods. "Yes, because of the funeral." He clears his throat. He touches the ring on his finger. "I've also been thinking a lot about my friend Grace. The service today was the first since her funeral. It made it difficult for me to avoid thinking about her life and her death."

"Did you find out if that nurse killed her?" I ask.

I realize after the question escapes my mouth that maybe I should have worded it more gently.

"Did Barney tell you about that?" Jeff asks.

I open my mouth, then close it and nod.

"I haven't heard," he says. "But that is weighing on me, yes. That's a large part of why I'm not feeling my best, to be honest. I'm very troubled by it." He investigates my face and smiles. "You're astute, aren't you, Gilda? You're good at sensing what's wrong with others. That's a real skill, you know. I'm lucky to have someone around me who is so discerning and thoughtful."

I don't know how to respond.

I feel the beginnings of an uncomfortable silence bud.

"I was thinking," I blurt, to stop the silence from growing. "Maybe I could build the church a website?"

"A website?" he repeats.

"Yeah," I say, staring at his sad mouth for approval.

He beams. "You want to make the church a website?"

I built a single static HTML web page with a photo of the church, its address, and one sentence that reads: "Join us for mass any day of the week," and you'd think I'd just fed five thousand people with two fish and five loaves of bread. Barney and Jeff are losing their minds, showing everyone who comes into the church our new website. Officer Parks came by again today and Jeff told her, "Gilda's a computer whiz! She did this with one hand!"

Barney added, "Would you believe this only took her a day?"

My ego, now inflated from all the esteem the elderly parishioners have been bestowing upon me for building a web page, begs now that I take this a step further. In an effort to contribute to the modernization of this church, and to quell the guilt I feel for double-crossing Jeff, I have taken the initiative to also create a Twitter page for the church. So far, I have only accidentally "liked" two inappropriate tweets from the church's Twitter account, forgetting I was not logged into my own personal Twitter account. Both inappropriate tweets involved pictures of women's butts.

"You're such a great help," Jeff tells me, placing a cup of coffee in front of me.

"Thank you," I say, worried he'll see the computer screen.

It's my friend Ingrid's birthday. I am standing outside of her apartment with a bottle of wine and a stuffed yellow duck.

Ingrid and I were childhood friends. Every year on our birthdays we always get each other a stuffed animal. I'm not sure if she'll remember that tradition or not.

She opens the door. She's wearing bright red lipstick.

"Gilda!" She hugs me.

She smells like alcohol.

"Come in!" She beckons me inside.

There's a small crowd of people sitting on the ground around her coffee table.

I don't know anyone here.

"Hi," I address the room.

Everyone looks up at me.

"What's that?" A guy with a curled mustache nods at the duck in my hand.

"It's a duck," I reply.

When Ingrid turned eight, I bought her a stuffed panda. She named the panda "Gil" after me. That year, she bought me a stuffed sea turtle. I named it "Ing" after her. We played that Gil and Ing were best friends, like we were. We played that they were adopted sisters, and that they fought bad guys together. For some reason, the bad guys were a stuffed SpongeBob SquarePants doll, and a tie-dye Beanie Baby we named Dr. Rude.

Ingrid was born the year before me. She failed second grade and was bullied for it. I was bullied too, for reasons I find more difficult to pinpoint. I had bad social skills, I guess. We found each other when I was seven on the outskirts of the playground, trying to avoid everyone else. From then on, we sat next to each other in class. We had a similar sense of humor, a similar taste in music and TV shows, and we were trauma-bonded from the bullying. We arranged our schedules in high school to match. She was my partner for every assignment that needed a partner from age seven to eighteen.

When Ingrid turned seventeen she had a sleepover. She invited me and two other girls named Kylie and Fatima. I did not know Kylie or Fatima well.

I gifted Ingrid a stuffed polar bear that year. She squealed when she opened the gift bag, thrilled.

Kylie and Fatima laughed at my gift. Kylie whispered something into Fatima's ear. I couldn't hear what she said, but I'm pretty sure it was something disparaging.

Ingrid's bedroom window was open and we were crowded around it, smoking clove cigarettes and blowing the smoke outside.

"Do you have a boyfriend?" Kylie asked me.

I had recently taken to wearing a rainbow bracelet, despite preferring not to wear bright colors, just to avoid having to establish my sexual orientation with the people I interacted with.

I held my wrist up to her, to showcase the rainbow and to communicate I was gay.

She said, "Oh my God, you shouldn't be at a sleepover with girls."

Before I could process the slight, Ingrid stood up for me. She assured Kylie that I wasn't a sexual predator, and told her to shut up.

"Still, isn't that like a boy sleeping here?" Kylie said.

In a moment of bravery, I said, "Kylie, I don't find you attractive, so don't worry about it."

That comment must have triggered some insecurity in her because she changed her attitude. She spent the rest of the night talking to me, being interested in me. When the other girls were asleep, she tried to make out with me. I didn't want to.

She later started a rumor that I was stalking her. One of our teachers called my house to tell my parents I wasn't allowed to talk to Kylie at school anymore. I never spoke to her to begin with. My dad told me to stop wearing my bracelet, and to keep to myself. Ingrid stopped being friends with Kylie because of it, but a lot of people believed I was a creep.

My phone vibrates.

I look down at a text from Giuseppe. It says **Hey Gilda! This is a little last minute, but are you free tonight?**

I look at the time. It's nine p.m. Do last minute nine p.m. dates mean the same thing to heterosexual Catholics as they do to us lesbian athiests? I hope not because 1) this man knows me as the receptionist at a Catholic church, and this might be an insult to the character I'm playing and 2) I would rather be shot dead.

If I keep telling him I'm busy, he's going to suspect something is up.

I look around Ingrid's apartment. I take a picture of Ingrid from across the room.

I send him the picture, proud to have proof that I am busy, and write, I can't, sorry. I'm at my friend's birthday party.

No worries. Tell her I said happy birthday! he replies. Let's do next Saturday then?

I'm sorry, I work, I reply.

I could pick you up at the church after? he writes.

I try to think of an excuse.

I type, Okay, awesome.

Next Saturday, I will pretend to break my leg or something.

"I can't believe I'm twenty-eight," Ingrid laments on her balcony. "I feel like we were just fifteen, don't you?"

I nod. *Clock's ticking*.

"I swear, if I woke up tomorrow in my parents' house, in my old twin bed, and were told that everything that happened between then and now was all just a dream, and that I had to go to school, I'd believe it," she says. "I'd totally believe it."

"Me too," I reply.

If I woke up tomorrow and was told my entire life was a simulation, I'd believe it.

"Do you think the rest of our lives will go by this quickly?" she asks.

Ingrid is drunk. She's dancing in the kitchen with the stuffed duck I gave her.

Her friends keep talking about people who I don't know. It's difficult for me to contribute to the conversation. I'm drinking too much to fill the time.

"Molly's anorexic," a girl with blunt bangs announces to the room.

"Tommy's got the stupidest tattoo."

"Did you see Isla's profile picture? I almost unfollowed her."

I considered not coming tonight. I didn't feel like leaving my house. I barely know Ingrid anymore, and I don't like being around people who I don't know.

I sip my drink.

I watch Ingrid spin around the kitchen with her duck.

I sip my drink again only to discover that my cup is empty.

Ingrid and I are not close friends anymore. She isn't the same person. She's a grown-up. I don't know her; I know the teenaged version of her. I'm at this party because I feel indebted as a friend to the shadow of the kid that she used to be. It's strange I'm here at all. I wonder how long it takes the cells in our bodies to replace themselves. I wonder if I'm literally no longer the same person I was when Ingrid and I were friends.

Drinking is bizarre. I'm poisoning myself.

"Would anyone like a glass of my wine?" I offer loudly, deciding I want to off-load the rest of my bottle.

The girl with blunt bangs holds her cup out to me.

"Thanks." She smiles as I pour wine in her glass. "I'm sorry we're talking about people you don't know."

"That's okay."

She holds her phone out to me, showcasing a photo of a girl with bushy brown hair and blue eyes. "This is the girl we're talking about. She's strange-looking, isn't she?"

I squint at the photo.

"What do you think? Do you think she's strange-looking?"

"Uh," I examine the photo.

"Be honest."

"Okay, uh."

"Just tell me what you really think."

I don't know what to say.

She nods, encouraging me to say something.

Say something.

"I think our appearance is meaningless," I sputter. "We're all just skeletons covered in skin."

The girl stares at me.

I feel outside of my body.

She snorts. "No, seriously, what do you think?"

I am at a bar with Ingrid and her friends. I wish I weren't. I am trying to escape the environment I am in by absorbing myself in my phone. The cell reception in the bar is poor, and so I have resorted to rereading my recent text conversations. I have realized that Eleanor texted me eight times today and each time I forgot to reply. The bar is too loud, and people keep brushing their arms against me. I feel drunk and uncomfortable.

I weave through a crowd of people and hold my phone above my head.

Hi, I text Eleanor.

It doesn't send.

Hi, I text again.

Failed to send.

Hi.

Hi.

Hi.

The message turns blue. A little note beneath it says: Read 1:23 A.M.

A bubble tells me she's typing.

You ignored me all day, she writes.

Someone's drink sloshes out of their cup down my back. A man is jumping beside me, rubbing his arms against mine. A primal impulse to scream engulfs me. Maybe if I behave insanely, I can scare off the people surrounding me. Maybe if I scream as loudly as I can, I will be given the personal space I need to breathe in air that others haven't already exhaled.

I am almost drunk enough to give in to screaming, but the training imposed on me to present as fine even in situations where my insides are wailing, restrains me. I remain cool.

I'm at a bar, I text Eleanor, deciding not to address her comment. I wish I hadn't ignored her, so maybe if I pretend I didn't, it will be as if I didn't.

She doesn't reply.

I wish I weren't, I type.

She doesn't reply.

Will you come get me?

Eleanor is driving me home. She helped me buckle my seat belt because I am having dexterity issues.

"You drank too much," she comments.

My brain feels too small for my skull. I feel like it's sloshing around in my head.

"Did your friend have a nice birthday?" she asks while she adjusts the heat.

"She feels fifteen," I tell her.

"What?"

"Never mind."

"Did you have a nice time?" she asks.

I hiccup. "No."

I watch heaps of snow plowed to the curbs blur past the window as we soar down the street. I am thinking about how warm I am inside this car, and about how cold it is outside.

I start to think about homeless people in the winter. I think about sleeping in the snow. I think about being thirsty and having no clean drinking water. I start to feel guilty for having an indoor bed and water. I unroll my window. Cold air blasts my face.

"Why did you open that?" Eleanor asks me. "Close it. It's freezing."

"Sorry," I say, realizing as I struggle to roll the window back up that I am disgustingly self-absorbed. I decided I didn't deserve to be comfortable and made Eleanor uncomfortable as a by-product. I cannot figure out how to roll the window back up. I keep unlocking and relocking the doors.

Eleanor uses the parental controls afforded to the driver to roll my window up for me.

"Sorry about that," I repeat.

She snorts. "It's fine."

Jeff violently pitches his coffee cup into the sink. The mug shatters against the other dirty dishes, and coffee splatters out of the sink and onto the counter. He spins around, not knowing I was standing behind him. Our eyes connect, and I stand motionless, alarmed to have witnessed Jeff's display of anger.

Our staring contest is quickly won by me when Jeff breaks, covers his face with his hands, and starts crying.

I came into this room planning to cure my hangover with a fourth cup of coffee. I did not come equipped for this.

"Are you okay?" I splutter, unable to hide how alarmed I am by the intensity of Jeff's shifting emotions.

"Grace," he cries into his hands. "Officer Parks called me. The toxicology test showed her death was suspicious."

"Oh God," I respond quietly.

Fuck. I shouldn't have said God's name in vain.

"I'm sorry," I say quickly. "About Grace and for saying 'God'—"

"I can't believe it." He continues to cry into his hands. His shoulders shake.

Am I supposed to hug him?

"It's okay," I say, putting my hand on his quaking shoulders.

He hugs me tightly. The unexpected embrace rattles my spirit right out of my body. I watch from the ceiling as my hand pats Jeff's back while he sobs into my shirt.

Why would anyone murder an old woman?

I am gazing into the face of the murderous nurse. I have opened a news article on my computer. I am examining her picture. She has short brown hair and glasses. She has wrinkles between her eyebrows and tanned, weathered skin.

I could take one wrong step off a curb and be crushed by a bus. I could choke on a piece of bread. The arteries around my heart might be clogging right now. I probably already have cancer. Someone in my apartment building might burn a frozen pizza tonight and fry me to death in my sleep. A mosquito could give me malaria. I don't know how to tell if I'm inhaling carbon monoxide. I could be struck by lightning. I could have an aneurysm. I could starve to death. A tornado could tear me from my seat and pitch me into the sky. I could have a stroke. I could be crushed in a tsunami or an earthquake. I could get rabies. I could drown in an undertow. I could catch the plague. The earth could open up a sinkhole and swallow me. I could get typhoid . . . and a psychopath could kill me? The fact that a person could deliberately end another person's life is hard for me to wrap my mind around. Given all the ways to die that are already looming over me, I have to worry about psychopaths, too?

I am staring intensely at my own hands. I am sitting in a pew, zeroing in on the wrinkles on my knuckles and the veins beneath my skin. I am thinking about how these have always been my hands. I was born with them. I used these to hold bottles, blocks, crayons. Everything I have ever eaten. Every book I have ever read. Everything I have ever touched has been with these appendages.

I will never have any other hands but these.

"The peace of the Lord be with you always," Jeff's voice bellows through the church.

"And with your spirit," I repeat in unison with the crowd.

"Let us offer each other the sign of peace."

All the people around me turn to extend their wrinkly hands toward me.

"Peace be with you," they tell me, shaking my cold, clammy hand.

I stare intensely at their hands as they shake mine. Their skin is wrinkled, transparent, and spotty. I think about how their hands were once baby hands. I think about babies gripping adults' fingers. I think about how these people have probably had their own babies and held them with the same hands.

"I need to shake a few other people's hands, too, dear," an old man tells me, trying to pull away from me.

"Sorry," I say, letting go of him.

I think about corpse hands. I think about skeletons. I look down at the bones in my hands and try to count how many are in there. There are at least three on each finger. Are there bones in knuckles?

"The body and blood of Christ," Jeff shouts at the head of the church while holding up a chalice and a small gold pot full of what is, allegedly, the body of Jesus Christ himself.

I glance around the room to see if anyone else looks put off by the grisly, cannibal concept.

The crowd booms an affirming, "Amen," and I realize as they do, that I, alone, am disconcerted.

Jeff pops a piece of God into his mouth and chews.

I hope the perfume I'm wearing masks that I didn't shower today. To be honest, I don't remember when I last showered. To shower, I have to encase my cast in plastic grocery bags and hold my arm outside the shower curtain. It is difficult to muster the motivation to take on that sort of task.

To be even more honest, I barely showered before I broke my arm. The one benefit of breaking my arm is that I now have an excuse to justify why I am a disgusting slob.

Everyone is standing up to get in line for their own bites of the Lord.

I feel nauseous and thirsty. There's a fountain at the back of the church, churning holy water. I fantasize about taking a big swig. Baptizing my stomach lining. Washing away the sins of my gut.

"Are you going?" the man next to me asks.

"Sorry," I say as I shuffle out of my pew with everyone else. I cup my hands in front of me, mimicking the people around me.

"The body of Christ," the old woman at the front of the line says to me while holding up a small white circular piece of God's human body.

I nod, and she places the flesh in my hands.

I reluctantly chew on God's bland, Styrofoam-cracker body while Jesus's woeful eyes stare down from the crucifix above me.

"I'm sorry to hear about Grace," an elderly woman consoles Jeff.

We are in the basement of the church having tea and lemon cake.

"Thank you, Mabel." Jeff nods.

"Has the nurse been convicted?" she asks.

"Not yet," Barney pipes in. His mouth is full of lemon cake. "The system is broken. The woman's confessed and the toxicology test verifies it, but for some reason the cops refuse to say Grace was one of her victims."

"Excuse me," Jeff says to us, putting his tea down and leaving our corner of the basement. He walks across the room and sits next to a man in a wheelchair.

"Did you hear she also murdered Geraldine Axford?" Barney asks Mabel.

Mabel chokes on her tea. "Oh my goodness! I knew Geraldine."

"Well, my condolences." Barney chews. "They have her on security footage doing it."

"Oh, heavens." Mabel puts a hand to her chest.

"They think she killed Alfred Wilkins, too." Barney shovels more lemon cake into his mouth. "Did you know Alfred, Mabel? Married a protestant."

"No." Mabel shakes her head. "That's terrible."

Barney elbows her. "Yeah, it is terrible he married a protestant."

He and Mabel both cackle.

"Haha." I feign a laugh to fit in.

The dirty dish castle in my room has developed a sour smell. The old smoothie cup has grown a little ecosystem inside of it. It is full of green, fluffy mold. I have been drinking right from the tap when I'm thirsty, rather than rinse out one of these cups. The structural integrity of the pile is dependent on the cups. If I move even one, the whole thing could fall apart.

Eleanor texted me.

Is everything okay?

I read her text twice, confused. Why did she ask me that? Was there a shooting near my house, or something? Is there some sort of storm warning?

I open the news app on my phone to see if there's something going on. The top story is about a two-hundred-year-old tortoise named Joan.

I'm fine, I text her back. Why? Are you okay?

You've just been quiet lately, she writes.

I exhale, relieved to learn there isn't an asteroid about to hit earth, or an active shooter in the streets.

Rather than address her comment, I send her the article about the tortoise.

Isn't this cute? I write.

"I guess Sharon's become a hoarder since Cliff left her," my dad shares while severing off a piece of his red steak.

Sharon and Cliff were a couple who used to come over to play Trivial Pursuit with my parents.

"I heard you can't step two feet in her house without tripping over old newspapers, Tupperware, or broken appliances."

My mom opens a bottle of beer for my dad.

My dad says, "Thanks, honey," before continuing. "She's apparently developed a rage problem, too. Cliff said one of their grandkids asked her if they could use some of her newspapers for some papier-mâché craft and she flipped out! She can't part with her garbage." He tuts. "The woman is insane."

"Can I have one?" Eli asks my mom, nodding at my dad's beer.

I am on the third book of the Bible. This one is called Leviticus. I turn the page and read:

If anyone curses his father or mother, he must be put to death.

That strikes me as pretty extreme. Do they mean curse as in use obscenities toward, or curse as in hire a witch to perform a solemn utterance intended to invoke a supernatural power to inflict harm on them?

I can't help noting the use of the male pronouns. I wonder whether this directive applies to me. Am I subject to a womanly loophole? Whoever wrote this book prioritized men so much, he forgot about the other half of humanity. It seems like I can curse my parents with no repercussions at all.

If a man lies with a man as one lies with a woman, both of them have committed an abomination. They must be put to death.

Yikes. Thank God this one doesn't seem to apply to women either. I'm disappointed God is so homophobic that he forgot about lesbians, but I guess I would rather be forgotten than put to death.

Wait. Would I?

Do not cut your bodies for the dead or put tattoo marks on yourself. I am the LORD.

I pull the sleeve of my arm down over my wrist, where I have tattooed a small question mark. Finally, a sin I'm subject to.

Do not wear clothing woven of two kinds of material.

What? Why not?

Do not degrade your daughter by making her a prostitute.

That one seems well-intentioned, at least. The use of the word "degrade" is a little disparaging because I don't think sex work is necessarily degrading; however, I certainly agree that no one's parent should be making their child a prostitute.

Do not lie. Do not deceive one another.

"Whoops," I say out loud, thinking about my position here.

"Whoops what?" Jeff says.

I look up. I didn't realize he was in the room.

"Oh, nothing," I say.

"What are you reading?" he asks.

"Leviticus," I reply, holding up the Bible.

"Oh, Leviticus." He smiles. "Anything good in there?"

"Not yet," I accidentally admit.

Barney pops his head into the room.

"A young man is here for you," he says to me.

"What?"

A short, dark-haired man enters the room behind Barney.

"Gilda?" the man addresses me.

"Yes?" I reply.

"I'm Giuseppe." He reaches his hand out for me to shake.

Oh God. I forgot about Giuseppe. I shake his hand. He has gel in his hair, and he is wearing clothes that fit a little too snuggly. I can see his pained biceps through his tight, salmon-colored blouse. There are sweat stains under his arms.

"Are you all set to go for sushi?" he asks, grinning.

I am sitting in Giuseppe's car with my hands folded in my lap.

He has the radio on. He is playing electronic dance music. His cologne, scented shampoo, body wash, air freshener, deodorant, and aftershave have combined to create an overwhelming, nauseating scent. I am holding my breath. He is shouting over the music that he hasn't had anything to eat all day but a protein shake. He went to the gym earlier. He was swamped today, but he managed to "hit the gym." He tells me he had a lot of client calls earlier. I learn as he shouts that he is twenty-nine years old, a Gemini, and a life coach.

"You know, if you actually want something, and you go for it, without limiting yourself, the universe will make it happen," Giuseppe says after eating more than half of the spicy crispy salmon roll that we ordered. "I tell my clients all the time, the only thing holding you back from living the life you want is you."

I sip my water and glance around the room. I imagine Eleanor walking into the restaurant. I picture her spotting me on a date with this guy.

I slouch down in my chair.

"If you want to write a book, or make a million dollars, or accomplish anything, all you really have to do is visualize that you have already done that, and then it will come to be. That's how energy works."

I sip my water again.

On my first date with Eleanor, we went to the nature museum. It was free to go on Thursdays. There were dinosaur bones on display. I was really fascinated by them. I wouldn't shut up about them. I realized near the end of the date that I had monopolized the conversation, and that I had been a terrible date. My anxiety had manifested in me being unusually chatty. I was afraid of there being awkward silences. I was also worried she might bring up things that we had messaged about before we met in person. We had been messaging for days. Before meeting her, I'd told her things I don't normally say out loud, like stories about my family, and how strange I'd been feeling lately. At the end of the date I felt self-conscious, and got quiet.

We were standing in front of megalosaur bones. I was thinking deeply about how I had sabotaged myself, and about how she probably would never talk to me again.

"It's weird to meet someone in person who you've already gotten to know, isn't it?" she said.

"I'm sorry for talking so much," I replied. "I'm anxious."

She said it was okay, she could tell.

I asked her if this was the worst date she'd ever been on and she said no.

She then told me more than one story about terrible dates she'd been on. She was once robbed by a date, she'd said. Another time, her date took her to a garbage dump to watch bears.

I told her the second date sounded good to me, so she drove me to the dump. We watched bears pick through garbage. She held my hand.

"Take me, for example," Giuseppe goes on. "I run a very successful firm, and it's because I don't limit myself. You just need to act like the person you want to become, and then you'll become it. It's as simple as that."

"What if you act like someone you don't want to be?" I ask.

He pauses. "What?"

"What if you act like someone you don't want to be, would you become that, too?"

He frowns. "Why would anyone do that?"

*   *   *

"I had a lovely evening with you," Giuseppe tells me as he pulls up to my apartment.

"Me too," I lie.

"We should do it again sometime," he suggests.

I don't reply. I stare blankly forward out the window.

I wonder if Eleanor wants to come over.

I can sense that Giuseppe is gawking at me. I feel him start to lean in. I pretend to cough.

"Excuse me," I say, hacking as hard as I can.

"Are you all right?" he asks, patting my back.

I continue to pretend to choke as I recoil from his touch.

I gag. "I'm fine! Sorry. I just need a glass of water."

I start to exit the car, still pretending to choke.

"See you later!" I shout at him while covering my mouth and spitting until I have escaped his line of vision.

I google Giuseppe's name and browse the search results. I click, hoping to find a criminal record, a warrant out for his arrest, or some evidence that would give me a reason to justify not seeing him again.

I do not find anything legally incriminating; however, I do discover that he runs a YouTube Channel. I scan the titles of his vlogs, still hoping to discover some incontestable deal breaker that I could reference when asked why in the world I, an eligible Catholic bachelorette, would reject him.

"Becoming your best self."

"The secret to life."

"How to win the game."

I click through the videos, listening to snippets of Giuseppe preaching that: "The people who have achieved what you want to achieve don't have anything you don't. They just believe in themselves."

I pause. That's not true. What if a paraplegic person wants to become a gymnast?

"Be your authentic self and people will be drawn to you!"

I pause again. What if my authentic self is unpleasant, and makes people feel uncomfortable? What if I am a psychopath?

"We are all capable of becoming whatever we want to be! You already have everything you need to do whatever you want!"

What about poor people? Or people who are discriminated against? What about people who are not cognitively capable of doing what they want to do? What about women who want to be Catholic priests, or men who want to be nuns?

"Your life has a purpose!"

"You exist for a reason!"

"You matter!"

I scowl.

I balance a water bottle on the stack of dishes piled next to my bed and wonder, do straight women find men who are bad at logical reasoning unattractive? I deliberate for a moment, considering whether I could justify rejecting him based on the fact that he is disturbingly irrational.

In elementary school, I refused to be Paul Nguyen's girlfriend, citing the fact that he used his forks underhanded, like a shovel. It was brought to my attention that that was a trivial reason to not date someone as nice as Paul Nguyen. Rumors rapidly emerged that I must be gay.

Both Giuseppe and Eleanor just texted me.

I open Eleanor's text. It says, Do you want to go see a movie tonight?

I reply, Boy, do I.

Giuseppe texts me again. I reluctantly tap the notification.

His first text said, Hi Gilda.

His second says, How is your day?

I swipe his conversation and hover my thumb over the red Delete option. I hesitate before tapping Delete. If I ghost him, he'll tell his sister-in-law, and she might tell others. People will wonder why. They'll think it's suspicious.

I deliberate for a moment.

I think about how awful I would feel if Eleanor were secretly dating Giuseppe.

I grimace.

I'm not really dating him, though, I tell myself. *This is acting. I'm an actress.*

Maybe, rather than ignore him, I should just bore him. Maybe I can get him to lose interest in me.

I type just: Good.

Excellent! He replies with a smiley face. I just had lunch with my old friend Brandon. Now I'm working! Are you working today?

I reply: Yes.

He replies with another smiley face.

Eleanor and I are seeing a movie. It is a comedy about two women who run a vending machine business. I am trying to pay attention to the plot, but I am too distracted by Eleanor's laugh. This abrupt honk erupts from her whenever something delights her. She sounds like a duck.

I am enraptured by how entertained Eleanor is by this movie. She thinks I'm laughing at the movie, but I'm not—I'm laughing because I am endeared by her. I'm looking at her exposed gummy smile and listening to her quack with laughter. I find it so endearing, it becomes difficult for me to inhale. My vision is blurred in tears, and I am incapable of speech.

*   *   *

"You know, these are easy to replace," Eleanor comments, holding up my broken TV remote. "They're only like five dollars," she explains. "Why don't you get a new one?"

I shoved all my dirty dishes into my closet earlier, to spare Eleanor the sight of them. I didn't think to hide my broken things.

My phone is ringing.

"I should, yeah." I nod while fishing for my phone in my pocket. Giuseppe is calling me.

"Who is that?" Eleanor asks.

"Nobody." I click Decline.

Eleanor snores. The first time she slept over, she warned me before we went to bed. She said, "Are you sure I can sleep over? I'm a terrible snorer. You're going to wish I weren't here."

She told me that she never used to go on sleepovers when she was a teenager because of her snoring. She said she's always been insecure about it.

I thought it *would* bother me but lied and said it wouldn't, to spare her feelings. I said, "I can sleep through anything," even though the truth is that I find it hard to fall asleep at all.

Eleanor doesn't struggle to fall asleep. Her head had hardly hit the pillow before her engine started revving up.

Our faces are pointed toward each other. I had fallen asleep facing away from her before my hip started to hurt and I had to roll over.

She asked me for a glass of water before we went to bed. Knowing every glass I own is rotting in my closet, I froze. Ultimately, I rinsed out an old Gatorade bottle and filled it with tap water. She took the bottle and said, "Do you not have any cups?" I stumbled to explain that I preferred water in old Gatorade bottles, and thought maybe she might too. She was gracious enough not to press the issue, but I don't feel great about it.

The light from outside my window turns my bedroom blue. I am looking at Eleanor's sleeping blue face. I stare at her, noting she has a scar on her chin and faint laugh lines forming around her eyes. I stare until I start to think that maybe I shouldn't look at her while she sleeps. Maybe this is creepy.

Her snoring is very loud.

Snore.

My eyes are heavy.

Snore.

I close my eyes.

Snore.

I feel oddly calmed by Eleanor's presence. The heat from her body is warming up the bed. Her breathing and snoring is lulling me to sleep.

Snore.

I feel my own breath deepen. My limbs feel heavy.

Snore.

I fall asleep.

"What's your spirit animal?" Giuseppe asks me over the phone.

I am sitting in the kitchen at the church. I'm on my lunch hour. I'm eating leftover egg salad sandwiches from a funeral. They aren't good. I'm worried they've spoiled.

"My what?" I reply.

He keeps calling me. I ignored his call three times today, but he kept calling.

"Your spirit animal," he reiterates.

"I don't know what that means."

"It's a totem meant to represent the traits and skills that you align with, and are supposed to learn from," he explains. "It's a component of the neoshamanic belief that a spirit guides, helps, and protects us."

"Oh," I reply. "I have no idea. What's yours?"

"I'm a lion," he answers immediately.

"A lion?" I repeat.

"You can see it too, right? The lion spirit represents courage, leadership, and strength in overcoming difficulties."

"What difficulties have you overcome?"

"Well, starting my business," he explains. "It's very difficult to be an entrepreneur. What animal do you think guides your spirit?" he asks again.

I search my mind for the animal I imagine Giuseppe would find the least likable.

"Maybe a pig," I reply.

"Oh, interesting—the boar," he replies. "That represents abundance, and fertility."

I text Ingrid a picture of Giuseppe and write: **What do you think of this guy?**

Ingrid is very straight. I want her to authorize that Giuseppe is abhorrent.

I can see that she's typing.

He's cute, she writes.

Fuck.

"I have to tell you something," Eleanor says.

I look at her. My heartbeat speeds up. What?

She looks into my face and I try to anticipate what she's going to say.

Maybe she wants to break up.

Maybe she saw me with Giuseppe.

"I already watched this movie last week." She nods at the TV in front of us. "I thought you'd like it, so I wanted to watch it again with you."

"Oh," I exhale.

"I'm sorry I lied and said I hadn't seen it," she says, throwing a blanket over us.

"That's okay," I reply.

Every time the movie makes me laugh, I notice Eleanor grin at me. I try to subdue my laughing to avoid being looked at, but the movie is funny.

A scene in the movie depicts a woman puking. Her friend is cleaning up after her.

Eleanor gags. "I couldn't clean up someone else's puke. No way."

"Me either," I reply. "I have a weak stomach."

"I guess if I really, really loved them I could," she adds.

I nod. "Yeah."

I am cleaning up Eli's puke.

I came to my parents' house to help my mom bake cookies. I opened the door, took a big sniff of the air to smell whether my mom had begun baking, and perceived immediately that someone had vomited. After almost vomiting myself, I followed the smell until I discovered Eli cocooned in his bedsheets on the bathroom floor surrounded by a pool of his own barf.

My mom isn't home yet, and Eli is still retching.

"Why are you so hungover?" I ask him through the towel I have bandannaed around my mouth and nose.

"This is crazy, but I think it has something to do with how much I drank," he jokes.

I snort. "You're an idiot."

Eli is recovering in the living room, watching *A Christmas Carol* and clutching a mug of tea.

"I wonder if Eli ate something off," my mom mulls while stirring dough in a large bowl.

I purse my lips, allowing her comment to hang in the kitchen silently for a moment.

I glance at Eli, note that he's half-asleep, and whisper: "I think he might be having some mental health issues. I think he should see someone about it—"

My mom bats her hand in the air as if to swat my idea out of the room. "Did you know your father has been working a lot of overtime lately?" She changes the subject. "His next paycheck is going to be double what it usually is."

I watch her press a fork into the tops of small balls of brown dough.

"He's a workaholic, your dad," she hums. "He's worked late almost every night this week. You know, when I married your father, one of the qualities I hoped he'd pass down to you kids is his work ethic. I wanted you to have my hair, and his work ethic—"

I didn't inherit her hair.

"I've been working every day this month," I announce.

"What? You have?" She wipes her hands off on her apron. "I didn't even know you got a job! Where is it?"

I hesitate before I reply. I can't admit that I work in a church. She'll have too many questions.

"In an office," I tell half the truth.

"Wow!" She grins. "I'm so proud of you! What kind of office?"

I look around the kitchen.

Bob Cratchit's voice ebbs into the room.

"An accounting office," I lie.

I am lying on the floor of my kitchen, holding my phone up to my deadened ear.

Giuseppe is talking about himself.

He has a dog named Ernie.

His dad owns a restaurant.

He has three brothers.

"Are you introverted or extroverted?" he asks.

"Introverted," I reply mindlessly.

"I'm extroverted," he tells me, as if that weren't apparent.

"What is your biggest fear?" he asks me.

"Dying, I guess," I reply.

"I'm afraid of living an unfulfilled life," he counters, making my answer sound trite.

"Did you grow up rich or poor?"

"Middle-class, I guess," I say.

"Me too."

"Do you believe in fate?"

"No."

"I do," he says.

"Do you believe in luck?" he follows.

"I guess," I say.

"Me too."

Two very tall people are getting married today. The church is choked with their pink roses. All of their guests are wearing pastel; pastel heels, pastel ties. I did not get the memo and am consequently wearing gray. I feel like a storm cloud in a spring meadow.

It is unclear what my role is today, but I was asked to stand at the entrance to the church, and because of that, I suspect my role might be: gargoyle.

I am leaning on a stone pillar, staring through the open door at the bride and groom. They are about to recite their vows to each other. Microphones are placed at the front of the church so when the bride opens her enormous mouth to speak, her voice echoes through the building like the lurid narrator in a movie trailer.

Her booming voice tells us all that this balding man is her best friend. Everyone who is watching them starts tearing up. She bellows that she cannot imagine being in a happier place than sitting beside him on their ratty sofa. The crowd coos in approval. She howls that she wants to grow old and gray beside him while he grows old and gray beside her.

I eye her dress and then zero in on all the flowers in the room. I think about how much it cost these people to stand in this room to make noises with their mouths at each other.

"What's your favorite kind of food?" Giuseppe interviews me over the phone.

"Pizza," I reply, monotone. "What's yours?"

"Kale," he answers immediately.

"Kale?" I repeat in disbelief.

"Yup," he confirms. "Kale is a superfood. I can't get enough kale. Don't tell me you don't like kale?"

"I don't like kale."

He chuckles. "Your body is a temple, Gilda. Nutrition and regular detoxification is what helped me bring my body out of the red zone, and catalyzed a huge change in my health and well-being. You have to feed yourself right. What you eat affects everything. It affects your energy level, your mood, your horomes, your aura. It's really important."

"Good to know."

Half-digested pepperoni splatters in the bowl of my toilet while I shove my middle and pointer fingers deep into the back of my throat. I ate two large pizzas alone, and now I feel so violently ill that I have decided my only option is to make myself puke.

*   *   *

What's your favorite food? I text Eleanor.

Waffles, she replies. Why? What's yours?

"Finding your passion isn't just about money and your job. It's about finding yourself," Giuseppe explains on our next call. "People who truly know who they are, they are the successful ones. I am a self-actualized reality strategist, and I'd rather be me than be living as, let's say, a successful politician—for example. Do you know who you are, Gilda?"

A cat is gaping at me through a window. He is sitting on the back of a floral print couch. I saw him while walking to the church for work. I stopped to look at him up close.

He is a very good-looking cat. He has green eyes and the tips of his small teeth peak out from his upper lip. He is a little overweight, but it looks good.

It's strange to think of how small I am, and then to consider how much smaller cats are. In the grand scheme of things, I matter as much as this cat does. Worse than that, everyone around me matters as much as this cat does. Worse than that, I think this cat should matter. I think this cat should be considered incredibly important.

The cat tries to paw at me through the glass. I look at the pads of its feet. At the wisps of fur that surround his pink toes.

I look down at my hands. I stare at my palms.

"What did you want to be when you grew up?"

I am inside my empty bathtub. It doesn't have water in it.

"Do you mean when I was a kid?" I ask.

"Yes," Giuseppe replies. "Did you always want to work for the church?"

"No. I wanted to be a vet."

"What was your favorite subject in school when you were a kid?"

"Physics," I reply limply. I liked learning things like why the sky is blue, or how much I'd weigh on Mars.

"I liked drama," he tells me. "Do you prefer winter or summer?"

"They're the same to me," I reply.

"I love summer, personally," he tells me. "What excites you and makes you want to get up in the morning?"

"Uh," I reply. What kind of question is that? I stumble to come up with an answer. "I guess," I start. "Like, um. I—Well, I mean—"

He laughs. "I'm sorry, Gilda. I know it's late. We should probably get off the phone."

My family has a home video of Eli and I talking about what we want to be when we grow up. I am eight years old in the video and I am wearing all purple. Purple pants, purple shirt, and purple socks.

I answer confidently: "An animal doctor."

Eli's answer is: "Grandma."

My parents find Eli's answer hysterical. Their laughing overtakes the audio of the video.

My dad tells my mom: "We'll have to tell your mother he said that."

"He just loves his grandma." My mom chuckles.

The video flashes to a new clip of Eli and me. We're a little older, and we're in the backyard. The sprinkler is on. We don't know our parents are watching, or that we're being filmed. We're wearing bathing suits and plastic sunglasses. Eli has one hand on his hip, and one hand holding a juice box.

I am jumping through the sprinkler. There is a rainbow in the grass under the sprinkler. I do a cartwheel over it.

"Why is there a rainbow?" Eli points. He has a little-kid lisp.

I must have learned about rainbows in school, because I reply knowledgeably.

"When sunlight goes through something like water," I explain, "it slows it down. If it goes through it on a slant, it bends it, and that makes a rainbow."

Eli is no longer listening. He's picking up a rock.

"Sunlight," I continue my lesson despite having no student, "looks like it has no color, but it actually has all the colors. White is every color. That's why sunlight can make a rainbow. All colors are in sunlight. It refracts."

It is midnight and I am at mass. This is a peculiar behavior Catholics exhibit on Christmas Eve. Even the elderly forgo sleep to attend. The church is dimly lit, and everyone is holding a candle. It smells like incense, and the choir is singing "O Holy Night."

"Where are you sitting?" A man touches my shoulder. Giuseppe.

I turn and face him. He's standing, arms linked with a short, middle-aged woman.

"Hi," I say, disconcerted to see him.

"We'd love to sit with you," he tells me, smiling. "Come find us and sit with us, will you?"

The woman with him is grinning at me.

I nod. "Right. Sure. I'll try."

He turns to the woman. "Mom, this is Gilda, the girl I was telling you about."

The woman's grin widens. "Lovely to meet you, dear," she says, reaching out to squeeze my hand.

"Hi," I whisper.

"You're as cute as he described you." She beams.

The choir music stops.

"We better take our seats," Giuseppe says, shuffling his mom ahead of him. Before shuffling along with her, he leans in and kisses my cheek. His tepid, damp voice says, "Merry Christmas, Gilda," right into my ear canal, and my entire body recoils.

*   *   *

"For those who have been taken from us in death," Jeff bellows from the pulpit. "Particularly those who have died since last Christmas, including Jim Andrew, Gloria Faith, and Grace Moppet. May the peace and joy of heaven be theirs always."

"Lord hear our prayer."

It's Christmas. The house smells like dead bird and gravy.

"You need a haircut," my dad comments offhand to Eli.

Eli's hair is long.

"No he doesn't," I pipe in. "His hair looks good like that."

Eli is drunk. He keeps pouring spiced rum into a mug shaped like Santa's head.

My parents are oblivious. My mom is humming "Jingle Bells." My dad is sipping on his own glass of something.

"Don't drive." I pull at Eli's arm while he struggles to put his shoes on. He has his car keys in his teeth, dangling from his mouth.

"I'm fine to drive," he argues. "I'm going to my friend's house."

My parents are in the back room watching *It's a Wonderful Life*.

I purse my lips. His face looks different when he's drunk. It looks swollen and flushed.

"No, you're not." I tug at his arm.

He pulls away and lumbers out the front door toward his car. I follow him.

I yell, "Stop, Eli!" as he climbs into the driver's seat and begins to peel out of the driveway.

I run toward his car as he leaves, but he's gone.

I stand staring at the empty driveway for a few seconds. I am not wearing shoes, or a coat, and it is snowing. The tracks Eli's car made in the road are being filled in by fresh snow.

I cross my arms and continue to stare at the empty driveway. An intrusive thought about Eli driving off a bridge ebbs into my mind's eye. I see his car soaring off the edge of a bridge and sinking into dark water. I imagine him trying to roll his window down, getting caught in his seat belt, and drowning. I think about his motionless chest.

"Have you seen my purse?" my mom asks me.

I scan the room around me. "No, I haven't."

"I put it by the front door. I can't seem to find it now . . ."

"What do you need your purse for?" my dad asks. "It's Christmas. Everything's closed."

"I'd just like to know where it is," she explains, frazzled.

After rummaging around the house for ten minutes, she addresses me again. "You wouldn't take my purse, would you, Gilda?"

"What?" I reply, flabbergasted by the allegation.

"I'm not accusing you," she tries to assure me. "I'm just checking."

I pause, then say, "What the fuck?"

"Hey!" my dad shouts from the other room.

"You think I took your purse?" I shout.

"I didn't say that!"

"If I had to guess who took your purse, Mom, I'd say it was Eli. He's drunk right now. He just drove out of here and neither of you said a fucking word. I think he took money out of my wallet, too—by the way. I was stranded in a coffee shop the other day with no money, probably because he stole it. He's turning into a real dirtbag, your kid."

"Don't say that!" My mom shakes her head, dismayed to be faced with that reality.

"He's got a problem," I continue. "Can we all please admit that Eli has a drinking issue?"

"It's Christmas!" my dad yells irrelevantly.

"I can't find any of my painkillers, either," I announce. "I have a broken fucking arm and I have no painkillers. I think he took those too."

"Gilda, stop it! It's Christmas!" my dad shouts again.

"Yes, Merry Christmas, Dad; I think your son is an alcoholic. He should go to AA. He can't keep a job. He dropped out of school. He needs help. He needs to go to therapy. He needs some psychiatric help—"

"*Therapy?*" my dad repeats, as if I just used the most belligerent curse word he's ever heard. "He doesn't need therapy. My son is not fucking deranged!"

"He needs to go to therapy," I repeat with emphasis.

"Get out!" my mom shouts.

"Get out? You want me to leave because Eli's an alcoholic?"

"Shut up, Gilda!" My mom shakes her head. "You're being insensitive!"

"Insensitive?" I repeat. "You just accused me of stealing your purse! The person who stole your purse is probably driving the wrong way down a one-way right now, Mom, like a blind mole! I'm insensitive? What if he kills himself?"

"A blind mole?" my dad says. "Why would you use that to describe—"

"I don't know why my word choice is what you're focusing on! What you choose to focus on might be a part of the problem, though."

"What the hell does that mean?" my dad roars.

"This isn't the right time to discuss this," my mom announces.

"Okay, should we save this conversation for Eli's intervention, then, or wait for his funeral?" I ask.

"Get out!" my mom yells.

part three

Ordinary Time

"**I** fought with my parents," I admit to Jeff through the lattice wall that divides us in the shadowy confessional booth.

Jeff asked me to attend confessional. This is when Catholic people sit in a closet with a priest and fess up to everything they have ever done wrong. I had to go behind a red curtain to get in here. The booth itself is ornate. The outside is covered in little stars and cross carvings. It's too dark inside to see if there are carvings in here too. I'm touching the walls to feel for them.

I did not feel particularly obliged to share my depravities with my employer; however, I could tell that Jeff wanted me to, and refusing felt rude. Moreover, I have been feeling guilty about arguing with my parents about Eli, so I figure that I might as well experiment with confession as a solution to that guilt.

So far it is not helping.

I have decided, of course, to omit many of my transgressions. In order to uphold my status as a Catholic, and as an employee at this church, I have, for example, not exposed myself as a gay, atheist, gluttonous, lying sloth.

"I also fought with my brother," I confess.

We sit quietly while I search my mind for more sins that I feel comfortable divulging.

"I ate pork—is that a sin?"

"No." Jeff clarifies, "Not for us."

*   *   *

Jeff said my penance is to say five Hail Marys, three Our Fathers, and to call my parents. I do not know the words to either of those prayers, and I have not called my parents. Usually, when there's conflict in my family, we distance ourselves until whatever we fought about is a memory that we can pretend didn't happen. It's too soon to do that. I want to call to ask if Eli is okay, but I'm afraid to. I keep opening my phone to call them, then closing it.

I was four years old when Eli was born. We didn't know if he would be a boy or a girl. I wanted him to be a girl. I thought boys and girls were on opposite teams, and that if he was a boy it would mean that I would have to watch boy TV. I shuddered at the prospect every time Ninja Turtles or Mighty Machines came on TV.

I remember my dad picking me up from kindergarten and taking me to the hospital the day Eli was born. I remember seeing Eli's little wrinkly face squished in my mom's armpit, and I remember asking gravely, "Is that a boy or is it a girl?"

My mom told me, "He's a little boy, and his name is Elijah."

Eli never made me watch boy TV. He liked all the same shows I did.

Eli has not replied to my texts since Christmas.

Please reply, I text him again.

Please reply.

Please reply.

Please reply.

*   *   *

"Do you and your brother get along?" I ask Eleanor.

We are lying on her bed.

Eleanor has a brother, too. He's older than her. She told me he lives two hours away and that he is a librarian.

"Yeah. We're good friends," she says. "Do you and Eli get along?"

"Kind of," I say. "But he's got some issues."

"Well, that runs in your family, doesn't it?" she jabs lightheartedly, though I sense some sincerity.

"How dare you?" I reply, using the same tone.

She cackles.

"Hey, I almost forgot. I got you something." She stands up abruptly, leaving me alone in her room.

I wait for her to come back, paused on her bed. I look around the room in her absence. Her walls are all white. She has a lot of potted plants. There's a disorganized desk in front of her window. There are books piled on her nightstand. *The Color Purple. The Price of Salt—*

"Here it is!" She returns, carrying a box of Thin Mints. "You said you love these, right? A woman's daughter in my office was selling them, so I got you a box."

She hands the box to me.

I look at the box, then at her smiling mouth, and time stops.

I feel strangely derailed by this gesture. The image of Eleanor committing something I said offhand to her memory, spending her money, and gifting me this makes me feel, for some reason, heartbroken.

I begin to mouth the words "thank you" and to simulate a smile despite the strange, crushing sadness I'm experiencing.

I hold the box in my hands, my heart pounding.

"That's nice of you to remember something I said," I manage to spit out, heat pounding off my face while I try to veil the black bile I feel boiling inside me.

I find it so bizarre that I occupy space, and that I am seen by other people. I feel like I am falling through space and Eleanor just threw me a rose. It's such a sweet, pointless gesture. It would be less devastating to fall through space alone, without someone else falling next to me. Whenever someone does something nice for me, I feel intensely aware of how strange and sad it is to know someone.

She beams. "Of course I remember the things you say."

I push the box of cookies into my cupboard, behind a pack of communion wafers, where I can't see them. I slam the cupboard door shut so hard after hiding them that it breaks off one of its hinges. The remaining hinge is enough to keep the cupboard attached. It hangs from the wall like a loose tooth.

I gaze at the sky through my bedroom window. I see white clouds rolling across the blueness. I see a beam of light cut from the window to my closet. I see millions of specks of dust twisting in the light beam. I smell deodorant in my sweater. I hear wind whistling through the cracks in my window. I hear the fridge hum. I hear air entering my nostrils and leaving. I feel my heart beat.

I took the dishes out of my closet and carried them to my sink. It took five trips. One mug fell from the pile and cracked on the floor. I am now standing at the sink with pink rubber gloves on. Soap suds are growing in the water. I pick up a dish and the sponge. I try to scrub stuck-on red sauce from a bowl. There is old, rotten milk in the bottom of a glass cup. I am scrubbing frantically, sweating over the sink.

Eli still hasn't texted me back.

I open my phone. I run my thumbs over the flat, scratched screen. I tap Eli's name, and text, Are you alive?

Hello?

Are you alive?

I followed a man who looked like Eli into a pet store. I was walking to work when I spotted him. I stood behind him in the dog treat aisle until he turned around, and I realized he wasn't Eli. He was just a guy who kind of looked like Eli.

I'm now standing in front of a cage with three gray kittens in it. On my way out of the store, I heard their faint meows like a siren's call. I followed the meows to this cage. I have my fingers through the bars now. I'm watching two kittens roll over each other, play fighting. The other kitten is rubbing her face on my fingers. They are from the animal shelter. There's a leaflet beside their cage with their names, ages, and a bit about them. Their names are Jane, Garrett, and Lorraine. They are twelve weeks old. They have their shots. Jane is described as sociable and chatty. Garrett is a little more shy and reserved. Lorraine, who is rubbing her face on my finger, is described as affectionate and calm.

"Are you looking to adopt?" an employee asks me.

I look at Lorraine's green eyes and tiny pink nose.

Despite wanting to say yes, I say "No, thank you," and leave the store.

"The police are inept!" Barney shouts, slamming a folded newspaper on the table in front of Jeff and me.

"What's going on?" Jeff asks, picking up the paper.

"Read that!" Barney shouts. "It's an outrage!"

Before either of us are able to absorb any of the print, he shouts: "It says they're not including Grace in Laurie Damon's case!"

"What?" Jeff gasps, his eyes racing over the paper. "How could Grace's case not be addressed? That doesn't make sense—"

"It says there isn't sufficient evidence to build a case for Grace!" Barney roars, his face red.

"That's outrageous," Jeff says, covering his mouth in disbelief.

"I am calling on behalf of St. Rigobert's Church," Barney shouts into the phone.

He has the phone on speaker. Jeff and I are standing behind him.

"We want to know—no, we demand to know—why justice is not being served for Grace Moppet. This killer nurse obviously murdered her! You guys told us she had a quantity of drugs in her system that she couldn't possibly have access to! How do you explain that? How do you explain an old lady having that amount of drugs in her system? The nurse confessed! She said she killed her! What is wrong with you people? You can't even convict with a confession? You should be ashamed—"

"Sir, I need to ask you to calm down."

"We could all be murdered in cold blood tomorrow, and you lot wouldn't do a thing to address it!" he bellows. "We demand that justice be served!"

"I understand you're upset, sir, but Grace was not murdered by Laurie Damon," the officer explains.

"Like hell she wasn't!" Barney roars.

"Grace's death is suspicious, and we are continuing to investigate it. Laurie Damon is not a probable suspect. We suspect Laurie is trying to take credit for deaths she's not responsible for. Killers do this sometimes; they want to break serial killer stats for cred. She says she killed Grace, but it just doesn't add up. The toxicology report does show a large amount of secobarbital in Grace's system, but the time line just doesn't make sense. Grace died on a Saturday evening. She was seen that afternoon and was found dead the next morning. We've got Laurie on security footage at the Elgin Hospital during that time. She's accounted for every second. The security footage does not show her leave the hospital until well into the next morning. It's impossible that it was her. We want justice served too, sir," the officer explains. "That's why we can't attribute Grace's death to Laurie."

Barney's flared nostrils decrease in size as he processes the officer's statement.

"You're telling us there's another murderer out there?" he clarifies.

"We are conducting an investigation."

I open the church's email:

Dear Grace,

How were your holidays? I hope you were able to spend time with your family and enjoy the holiday season.

The kids came over to my house. Cindy helped me cook. I made your apricot tarts. They were a hit, as usual.

I would be lying if I said I was fully in the spirit, however. Jim's absence was really noticeable. He used to wear a hat like Santa's all day on Christmas. We put the hat on his chair at dinner.

I am trying to be more grateful for what I have remaining in my life. I have my health, for example.

How have you been, Grace? Have you been feeling well? We're old birds now, aren't we?

Happy New Year.

Love,
Rosemary

*   *   *

"I would like to pray now for my friend Grace Moppet," Jeff calls out from the pulpit. Red light is coming through the stained glass windows and creating shadows on the tile floor. "Grace recently left us for her heavenly home, and she has been on my mind. I'd like to ask everyone here to spend a moment praying for Grace with me."

Murmurs rustle in the crowd as everyone bows their heads.

Jeff recites: "Hail Mary, full of Grace, the Lord is with thee. Blessed are thou among women, and blessed is the fruit of thy womb, Jesus. Holy Mary, Mother of God, pray for us sinners, now, and at the hour of our death. Amen."

The church is silent. Pews creak.

I look up from my folded hands and scan the room. Everyone has kept their eyes closed. Their heads are bowed. I zero in on their moving, praying, wrinkled mouths.

Everyone in this room has managed to grow old despite how easy it is to die. They all escaped their childhoods alive despite tuberculosis, polio, and whatever other horrible illnesses afflicted humanity when they were kids. They drove without seat belts, in cars full of cigarette smoke. They survived literal wars. Terrible things have probably happened to every single person in this room, and yet here they are.

Here I am.

I close my eyes and focus on the darkness behind my eyelids.

Black.

It's grim to imagine an old woman making it all the way to the end of her life, just to be snuffed out illogically.

I tighten my eyes closed, harder.

It's bizarre that a body can be animated one second, and then turn lifeless permanently.

Black.

When we die, our bodies are garbage. We rot.

Black.

I can't believe that I'm alive.

Black.

I can't believe that I can believe anything.

There was a time when my dad threw a porcelain doll against my dresser. It shattered. Bits of the doll's face ricocheted onto my bed, and into the carpet. He had stormed into my room unexpectedly, collected the toys on the floor I'd amassed, gathered them in his arms, and then thrown them into the hall. When he noticed he missed the doll, he picked it up, and pitched it into the dresser.

He did this under the guise of being angry that I hadn't cleaned my room; however, I was an astute ten-year-old, and knew that wasn't the whole truth. He was having a breakdown.

His brother died the week prior. It was unexpected. My dad and my uncle had fallen out of touch. They hadn't spoken in years. I never met him.

Before my uncle died, there were instances when my dad yelled and got angry, but it was rare for him to break things, or behave violently. The instances before never felt as heavy as what was happening then. The day before, he screamed at Eli for not putting his shoes away. He grabbed Eli's arm really tightly while Eli cried and screamed, asking him to let go.

I remember sitting with Eli in my room, holding my headless porcelain doll, while my mom told us, "He's just out of sorts, kids."

I found out later, through a second cousin on Facebook, that my uncle had substance abuse issues. He'd been homeless. He'd overdosed.

* * *

I type out a message to Eleanor. It says: My brother isn't replying to me. He drove drunk on Christmas and I haven't heard from him since. I can't call my parents' house because I got in a fight with them, and I don't know what to do.

I read the message over twice before I erase it.

"Flop is dead," I announced to my parents after discovering the inert, lifeless remains of my pet rabbit. Her once bouncy life-form had malformed into a puff of motionless white fur.

"Jesus Christ," my dad griped as he struggled to rise from his reclined chair.

"Oh, sweetie, can I get you something to take your mind off it?" my mom fussed. "Would you like me to get you some chocolate milk? Do you want a cookie?"

My eyes were as wide open as Flop's were.

"What happens when you die?" Eli asked me.

We were lying in my bed, looking up at the glow-in-the-dark stickers stuck to my bedroom ceiling. They were solar system stickers, little moons and Saturns.

I was ten and Eli was six.

"I don't know," I admitted, feeling small beneath the planets on my roof.

"Just nothing?" he asked quietly.

"Maybe," I whispered.

Bright blue skies are shining down on a sandy white beach. I am standing with zinc on my nose, and a paperback tucked under my arm. *The Color Purple*. I put my hand above my eyes to shield them from the sunlight, and spot pterodactyls in the distance—picking at a corpse like vultures the size of giraffes.

"Shoo!" I shout at them, waving my arms above my head.

"Get away from him!" I run through them like they're a horde of seagulls surrounding a discarded hot dog. "Get away from him!"

My brother's body is lying crumpled in the sand.

I'm screaming, but there is no noise. I've reached an inaudible pitch beyond my own senses. There are veins protruding across my slick, red face. My fists are full of sand, and I am retching.

I wake up.

I check my phone to see if Eli has replied to me yet.

I type, **Do you remember when Flop died, Eli?**

You remember how I found her?

I think about it all the time.

Do you know what I mean?

Can you please reply to me?

I'm worried that you're dead.

The image of my body being shredded by a train driving over it flashes across my mind's eye.

I am on a bus driving over train tracks. I am going to the church. I look away from the tracks, into the glow of my cell phone screen. My heart rate increases when I see a text notification appear on my phone screen. I open it hoping it's from Eli, confirming that he is alive. It's been eight days since I heard from him.

I swipe to see that it's just a text from Eleanor.

What are you thinking about right now?

I direct my gaze away from my phone, toward the window on the other side of the bus. I stare up at a very tall escarpment and imagine myself doing backflips off the edge and twirling down deep into the dark water below.

Are you okay? she texts me again.

Hi, Grace,

I am just writing to share Jim's obituary with you. I have attached a picture of it.

Love,
Rosemary

I open the attached image. It's a scanned newspaper clipping of a smiling old man wearing a polo shirt and a flat cap. I read:

Jim was born in Newfoundland. He, his parents, and his older sister lived there until 1955. He loved animals, and he was a talented piano player . . .

My eyes tear up.

He will be dearly missed by his wife, Rosemary, his children, grandchildren, and his sister.

I can barely see through all of the tears in my eyes.

He was a beloved son, brother, husband, father, and grandfather.

I am in the church bathroom screaming "Is Eli there?" into my phone.

"Oh my God, what's wrong?" my mom responds, frantic.

"Is Eli there?" I demand again, louder this time.

I picture my brother's cold, waxy face decaying in dirt.

"No. Why? Is everything okay?"

I picture his photo in the newspaper.

"Have you heard from him?" I clutch my pounding chest while the image of Eli's motionless one scorches my mind's eyes.

"No! Why? Is he okay? You're scaring me—"

My mind starts writing him an obituary. Stop.

"Have you heard from him since Christmas?"

Beloved brother, and son. Stop.

"Yes, of course I have—I saw him this morning. Why? Is he okay?"

I exhale. The image of Eli's dead, motionless chest dissolves as the weight is lifted.

"He's ignoring my texts," I explain, panting. "I was worried he died."

"Oh my God, Gilda!" my mom shouts. "What a terrible thing to say. What is wrong with you?"

People are filing out of the church. Barney and I are standing by the back entrance, observing the slow crowd of people migrating gently out of the building.

"Have you heard anything about Grace?" I ask Barney.

"No." He crosses his arms, his eyes scanning the weathered faces of the feeble parishioners as they leave, as if he's trying to spot suspects.

"What do you think happened to her?" I ask.

"Well, someone killed her," he says curtly.

I nod. "Yeah, I guess the question is who."

"No." He shakes his head. "The question is why. If you understand the motive, you understand who did it."

"Oh." I nod. "Any idea what the motive might have been, then?"

"I suppose money is often the reason," he remarks.

"Do you know if she was rich?" I ask.

"I don't know," he says.

"It's usually someone who knows them," he goes on. "Rarely are people murdered arbitrarily."

"Do you know if she was married?" I ask.

"I don't think so," he says.

"I suppose it could've been random," he says. "I've been seeing some wild things on the news these past years about psychopaths. Wouldn't surprise me if some lunatic attacked an old woman."

Officer Parks is in Jeff's office.

They have been in there for over an hour.

I am tempted to put my ear to the door.

I google "Grace Moppet" and scan the results for her obituary. I click until I find her name. I pause after opening the link, to appreciate her picture. She has permed, ivory hair. She is wearing pink lipstick and large gold glasses. She looks very sweet, like someone who stocks a candy bowl and talks a lot to cashiers.

Her eyes connect with mine.

Hi, I mouth, watching to see if she somehow greets me back.

I feel relieved and disappointed when she doesn't.

I scroll down and read:

MOPPET, Grace of St. Thomas, passed away on Thursday, October 11, 2019, in her 86th year. Cherished wife of the late Richard "Dick" Moppet and beloved daughter of Matthew and Christina Smyth. Grace was born on October 1, 1933. She was a member of St. Rigobert's Catholic Church and worked there for ten years as the church's administrative assistant. She worked many years prior as a cashier at Elgin Corner Store. Grace's parents, Matthew and Christina, passed away when she was a teenager, and she will be missed as both a sister and a mother figure by her younger sisters Mary, Faith, and Elizabeth. The family will receive friends at Sunny's Funeral Home, 60 Elgin St., St. Thomas, on Sunday from 1:00–3:00 p.m.

I scan the obituary again for clues about how Grace might have died.

I reread the line about her husband. He's dead. He died before she did—so he couldn't have done it.

She worked here, and as a cashier at a corner store. She was an orphaned "mother figure" to her sisters. I don't think she could have been rich, given all of that. That means the odds of someone killing her for an inheritance are slim.

According to Barney, that leaves one remaining possibility: a psychopath killed her.

Did a psychopath kill her?

"Gilda?" Barney's voice interrupts my train of thought.

I look up.

"Can I ask you a favor?"

I hesitate. "Sure."

He leans in, his eyes glancing back and forth as if to check if anyone is eavesdropping on us. "Are you comfortable shopping online?"

I pause. "Yes. Well—for what?"

"I need a book," he explains, his voice quieting. "It's called *How to Catch a Murderer*."

I am lying in my bed with the lights off. I can hear sirens in the streets below my window. I wonder whether I locked the door.

I imagine a murderer skulking outside my apartment. I imagine the silhouette of his hand reaching toward my doorknob. I yank my blankets up to my chin, hopeful that my downy duvet might function as a shield against my prospective killer.

Rustling noises in the hall make all the hairs on my arms stand at attention like useless little soldiers. I close my eyes and imagine explosions. Gunfire. Bombs. I picture hands coiling around throats, and pillows being pushed down over faces. I picture poison being poured into glasses and cars veering off roads into crowded sidewalks. I think of ropes wrapping around throats and about gasoline, matches, and—

Stop.

Think about something else.

I think about Grace and her decomposing body.

Stop.

Think about something else.

"What's your mantra?" Giuseppe asks me.

"My what?"

"Your mantra," he says. "Mine is: I love myself, I believe in myself, and I support myself."

I don't respond.

"Let's think of one for you," he continues. "How about: I am capable and worthy."

I scowl. "What do you mean capable and worthy? Capable and worthy of what?"

He laughs. "Okay, maybe that one isn't for you. What about—"

"Do you know anyone who was murdered?" I interrupt him, hoping to direct this terrible conversation toward something I find more mentally stimulating.

"What? No," he says. "Why?"

"Isn't it crazy how people get murdered?" I probe. "I mean the whole concept of murder. Isn't it nuts?"

"I guess," he replies hesitantly. "That's sort of a dark topic, though, isn't it? You shouldn't allow that kind of bleak energy into your lifespace. Think about things like living and vivacity instead."

"All right," I reply, while thinking intensely about dying and listlessness.

* * *

"Do you know anyone who was murdered?" I ask my parents while pouring a can of soda into a glass filled with ice. The fizzing noise and clinking ice cubes muffle my mom's response.

Eli is in his room and has not come downstairs.

She replies, "What? No."

"Boy, do I," my dad says. "A man we hired to do some landscaping murdered three women from town. He was a nut. What was his name, honey? Arthur?"

"Oh, don't talk about Arthur!" My mom swats at the air.

The LOST CAT poster outside my apartment has half-disintegrated. I can no longer make out Mittens's name. I am paused in front of it, staring at the gray, peeling image.

The sun is setting, and the sky is pink.

I wonder if Mittens's family adopted a new cat.

"Ever since I was a little boy, I was obsessed with happiness. I wanted to know the secrets of happy people. I wanted to know what separated happy people from unhappy people."

Giuseppe calls me every night. I don't know what to do to make him stop.

"What separates them?" I drone, praying he picks up on my tone and realizes that I am uninterested.

I wonder what Eleanor is doing.

"Happy people cultivate gratitude; they're active members of their community, they feel deeply connected to the earth, and to the people around them. They're often spiritual."

The phone is silent for a minute before Giuseppe asks me: "Are you happy, Gilda?"

I'm lying on my bathroom floor staring at the mold growing around the ceiling fan.

"Not usually," I answer mindlessly.

"What?"

"Uh," I say, realizing I have slipped up in my acting.

"I mean, yes—I'm happy," I correct myself. "I'm super happy. I thank God every day for blessing me with all this happiness."

"Murderers hide in plain sight," Barney tells me.

He's leaning on my desk with his nose in the book he made me order for him.

"The worst criminals look like everyday people," he goes on.

I stare at my computer screen.

"You ever hear that saying, '*Criminals always return to the scene of the crime*'?"

I nod.

"I bet whoever killed Grace comes to this church all the time."

"This isn't where she died, is it?" I ask.

"I don't know," he replies dismissively. "Did you know a lot of murderers wet the bed when they were kids?" he continues. "They often had head injuries as children, too. Oh, and have you ever heard of a trophy? It's the little mementos that murderers collect from the people they kill."

Jeff hands me a stack of paperwork. The ring on his finger catches the light as I take the papers from him. My chest tightens.

"Could you please tab these?" he asks.

"That's Grace's ring, right?" I nod at his hand.

He looks down. "Yes, I wear it to remember her."

"Did she give it to you?" I question.

"Well, she left it on her desk," he explains. "But don't worry, it's just costume jewelry—I would have given it to her sisters if it were valuable. It's just a little memento."

I google the word "priest" and scan the startling search results.

SHEPHERDS WHO PREY ON THEIR FLOCKS

WHY DEPRAVED MEN ARE ATTRACTED TO THE CATHOLIC CHURCH

INSIDE THE MIND OF A PERVERTED PRIEST

Jesus Christ, I mouth while I read an article that explains that predatory men are attracted to being priests because it puts them in a position of power over vulnerable people. I glance up from the article at Jeff's office door. An ominous energy overtakes me.

"What made you want to become a priest?" I ask Jeff quietly, hoping I can interrogate him subtly.

"Oh, I just felt a calling to it," he hums. "I imagine it's sort of like people who feel born to be parents, or doctors, or artists. Does that make sense?"

He is standing next to the office kettle, holding a ceramic mug. I stare at the mug intently, ruminating about how everyday items can be repurposed as weapons. A ceramic mug, for example, could easily be used to bludgeon someone.

I think about how angry he was when he found out Grace's death was suspicious. I think about how he cried when he found out. I wonder whether a murderer would cry. I wonder if he's a good actor.

"You never wanted to get married, or have kids?" I interview him further, still mindful of how elusive my questions need to be.

The kettle whistles. Jeff turns to pour hot water into his cup. "Not

really, no, but even if I had—I feel like God's chosen me for the life I
have. Would you like some tea, dear?"

"No." I shake my head. "Thank you."

I am perusing an online forum that suggests priests are more likely
to be debauched because they don't want to be husbands or dads.
Hundreds of commenters have agreed with the sentiment; priests are
freaks because they do not succumb to the primal drive humans all
have inside of us to pair up and procreate.

Jeff not wanting to be a husband or a father doesn't befuddle me,
because I don't want to be a wife or mother. It is not difficult for me
to commiserate with a person who does not kowtow to the traditional
roles of his or her gender.

Because I have that insight, I decide to contribute to the forum:

> I, for one, am less confused by priests not feeling called to be
> husbands and fathers than I am confused by them feeling called
> to be anything at all.

Almost immediately, a commenter replies: What the hell?
I delete my comment.

A single beam of light breaks through a crack in the curtains and
shines, like a laser pointer, directly into my eye.

I sit up, blinded.

"Where am I?" I ask the darkness, worried.

No one answers me, but my vision begins to recover. The shadows
of couches and tables begin to form. I am now able to distinguish for
myself that I am on the couch in my parents' living room.

I can hear someone washing dishes in the kitchen.

"How did I get here?" I ask.

"What?" my mom shouts over the sound of running water.

"How did I get here?" I ask again.

"What do you mean? I don't know. You probably took the bus. What are you talking about?"

I am sitting on a bench in front of the grocery store. I am watching people bumble around the parking lot. I watch a woman's grocery bags give out; glass tomato sauce explodes on the concrete. I stare at her mouth. She's frowning.

I blink.

I watch a stray cart roll into a car door.

Crash.

I need to gather the momentum to walk into the grocery store.

Stand up.

Stand up.

Stand up.

People brush their arms against mine as they reach for their products. The store is crowded. A woman with a baby strapped to her chest hurdles past me, diving for the last box of reduced-price Kraft Dinner.

The fluorescent light is burning my eyes.

"Gilda?"

I turn and face a girl who I went to high school with, whose name I no longer remember.

"Oh hey," I say, still searching my memory for her name.

Katelyn?

Kirsten?

"How have you been!" She grins.

"Great!" I try to match her enthusiasm, while her name remains forgotten. "And yourself?"

Tara?

Sarah?

Michelle?

"Oh, I've been fantastic." She beams while flashing the engagement ring she has on her finger. "You remember Devon Cunnings, don't you?"

I nod even though I don't remember.

I don't even remember you, I want to say.

"We started dating in college." She smiles down at her hand. "We never really noticed each other in high school. I was dating Paul, remember? We bought a house uptown, on Cherry Street. It's got a lot of bedrooms, which is great because we are thinking of kids already." She laughs.

"What happened?" she asks, nodding at my arm.

"Oh, some kid asked to sign my cast and drew a penis, so my brother painted over it with this—"

She laughs. "No, I mean, how did you break it?"

"Oh, I was in a small car accident."

"Oh gosh!" she says.

"I'm fine, though," I tell her.

I don't think she really cares if I'm fine. She just wants to tell me about her husband, and her house, and her plans. She wants to be validated, to feel good about herself. She wants to prove to me that her existence matters. I wonder how I can signal to her that she's succeeded.

It's strange that I am able to give her any kind of validation. Who am I to her? Why does she care what I think of her? I don't even remember her. I can't think of anything she could say to me that would validate me. She could tell me I'm the most interesting, important, beautiful, successful person that she has ever laid her sorry eyes on and it would mean as much to me as if it came from someone trying to get me to join their pyramid scheme.

Jane?

Clara?

"It sounds like you're doing really well," I tell her. Her eyes light up. I add, "I'm so happy for you. You look great, by the way."

She grins.

The milk is all marked to expire in two days, and none of the cartons look clean. I reach for one at the back of the shelf, even though it looks just as bad, hoping to get one that fewer people have touched.

"This milk expires in two days!" my mom says, exasperated, after I hand her the milk.

I had gone to the store to get it for her.

"Sorry," I apologize.

"Why didn't you look for one with a better date?"

"I didn't think of it," I lie.

A perfume of sweat and alcohol overtakes the room. I pinch my nose and scowl at the source of the smell.

Eli just walked in.

"What are you doing here?" he asks me from the doorframe.

"Visiting," I reply, while I watch him stumble to take his shoes off. Our parents are in the back room, watching TV.

Eli accidentally takes off one of his socks with his sneaker.

"You know, you haven't replied to any of my texts since Christmas," I confront him.

He rolls his eyes, now tripping to take off his other shoe.

"I thought you were dead," I tell him.

He snorts. "I wish I were dead."

I feel intense anger boil in my stomach. I stand up.

"Take that back," I tell him. I feel like there's an electric current running through me.

He scoffs. "I wish I were dead," he repeats.

I punch him in the shoulder. He falls backward.

He laughs and repeats, "I wish I were dead. I wish I were dead."

I shove him in the corner. He keeps repeating, "I wish I were dead."

I punch him. "Stop saying that!"

"Stop saying it!"

"What the hell is going on?" my dad's voice roars.

I keep punching Eli. He doesn't hit back.

"Break it up!" my dad shouts.

I kick my dad as he tries to pull me off Eli. I break his glasses. My mom is shouting. The coffee table is overturned. I've broken the decorative plates.

"What is wrong with you, Gilda?" my mom cries.

A frozen brussels sprout falls out of the bag I have pressed up to my bruised eye. I let it roll under my childhood bed. I imagine it staying there forever. I think of it molding and putrefying.

There is a vent in my bedroom that carries sound from the rooms below it. I can hear my parents murmuring.

"I don't know what's wrong with that girl," my mom is saying.

"She's a grown adult."

"Why is she picking fights with her little brother?"

"She needs to take a long, hard look at herself."

This room is the site of almost every breakdown I ever had before I turned eighteen. I remember hyperventilating in here.

It's difficult for me to process my thoughts. I can hardly begin to examine anything before stopping myself and asking: *Why?* Why do I care that I feel this way? Why does it matter, for example, that my little brother is an alcoholic? Why does it matter that he says he wishes he were dead? Why do I care so much about this?

I can't make myself feel better about anything because almost every thought process I have is thwarted by my consciousness leaving my body and watching myself.

There I am.

Look at me thinking about how I don't want Eli to be an alcoholic.

Look at me now, I'm crying.

That's ridiculous.

Hey! Stop crying.

It doesn't matter.

Consider the vastness of space!

I remember Eli shouting, "I can post whatever I want! It's art, you idiot!"

My dad grounded him for paintings he posted on the internet. He was fifteen and he had painted a series of up-close, odd angles of human genitalia.

My parents' artistic interpretation of the work was that it was attention-seeking, and painted solely to embarrass the family. I thought it was good. I'd have hung it up in my house.

"Not under this roof!" my dad roared.

"I wasn't under this roof when I posted them. I posted them at school," Eli quipped back.

"What is wrong with you?" my dad said. The kettle in the kitchen was whistling.

My mom said, "Stop, don't escalate this. He can just take down the pictures."

Eli said, "I'm not taking them down. Fuck you."

My dad gripped Eli's arm. He said, "Watch your mouth."

Eli pulled away. "Are you going to fight me like you fought with Uncle Teddy?"

One night Eli and I overheard my parents through the vent in my room. My dad was confiding in my mom that he and his brother fought a lot as teenagers. He was crying when he told her. He said he was worried it was part of why Teddy became the way he did. I'm sure it wasn't, and I'm sure Eli didn't really think it was either. My dad slapped him.

Every time my family argued, my initial response was to fantasize about moving far away and never speaking to any of them again. I thought about starting a new life on a new continent. By the time I was in my bed, waiting to fall asleep, I started to feel bad for everyone.

In the morning, when everyone woke up, we would avoid each other. Eventually, after a few days, we would just pretend it didn't happen. Someone would tell an unrelated joke, my mom would make everyone tea, and my dad would talk about the weather, or the neighbors.

The trees outside my parents' house are bigger than I thought they were. I am sitting on the curb outside the house, staring at my surroundings.

Some of my childhood memories are more vivid to me than my memory of yesterday is. One night, for example, I played hide-and-go-seek on this street with a group of neighborhood kids. I remember each kid that was there. It was dusk and the black concrete road reflected the orange glow from the streetlights. Our shadows were stretched across the road and were moving and running along beside us. We climbed over our neighbors' fences and ran through the back-yards of strangers, jumping into their pools and petting their dogs. One dog was a Pomeranian, and the other was a Golden Retriever. We sat on this curb drinking Slurpees. My Slurpee was red and blue flavors mixed. I remember exactly how my mouth tasted and how I felt.

Am I the same person now?

Younger than that, I pretended that the road in front of my house was an ocean. I drew chalk drawings of starfish, whales, and a raft on it. I had Band-Aids wrapped around my fingers and the sticky part of the Band-Aid collected a pastel residue from the chalk. I lay down with my eyes closed on the chalk-drawn raft in the middle of the street. I thought about sharks, and about what it might feel like to see a shark fin circling you in the water.

I was laying in the street, thinking about how I could be run over, and I wasn't standing up. Both of my parents saw me, ran into the street, and were furious at me for lying there. They made me go to my room. My dad yelled, "You could have died! And then what?"

And then what?

I spent the rest of the day looking out my window at the ocean-road, wondering what would have happened if I had died. And then what? And then what? And then what? There was a spider trapped with me behind the glass. I looked at her up close; at the bows in her thin legs, and at her small monster face.

Another night I stole my parents' car and backed into the light post across the street. I was sixteen. I remember touching the post and it feeling smooth and cold, and I remember touching the car where it hit and that feeling chipped and uneven. I drove to the beach and thought about killing myself there—not just because of the car, but because I had been depressed for years—but instead I decided to go to McDonald's and order a bag of fries. The McDonald's employee asked me to clarify my order, and I repeated, "One bag of fries, please."

When I got home, I gave the fries to Eli with no explanation.

"Oh . . . thank you," he said cautiously, evidently confused by the gesture.

I bought them with the intention of eating them myself. I asked myself, "Is there anything I want right now?" and then answered "fries." I therefore decided to buy the fries instead of killing myself because that seemed logical. You shouldn't kill yourself when you still want to eat.

I then allowed myself to think too deeply about stealing the car, backing into a light post, and considering killing myself, *and then what? and then what? and then what?*—and then I thought: *Eli might like to have a bag of fries.*

* * *

I can hear Eli crying in his room through the wall that separates our bedrooms.

I am distracting myself from that noise with my phone. I am scrolling through Instagram. My profile contains two photos. One is of a garbage can captioned "me," and the other is of a cat I saw once. I haven't posted anything in four years.

I don't often look at what other people post, but today I am. Today I am looking at the aging faces of my acquaintances and people who bullied me in elementary school. I look at their babies posed next to chalkboard signs that indicate the baby's age in months. The baby boys are dressed in suspenders and the girls are wearing large bow headbands. Their bald baby heads and confused wide eyes stare up into the camera as if to say: *What the fuck? Why am I next to this sign? Why aren't you holding me?*

Men my age are beginning to lose their hair and grow beer guts. Almost every photo I scroll past is of a row of women dressed in floral summer dresses attending a baby or bridal shower. Occasionally there's a bachelorette photo picturing phallic-shaped décor and food. These attempt to sprinkle a little za za zoo in the bleak, unending, contrived photo ops of people seeking some sad validation.

For a moment, this exercise makes me feel superior to them. Somehow my picture of a garbage can makes me feel like these people should all envy me. I am above all of this; I have a higher awareness. They are all losing a game I won't even bother playing. Once another moment passes, and I hear Eli sobbing through the walls, I realize that I wish every single one of these people felt sincerely significant and validated. I wish these horrible pictures reflected some authentically meaningful sign of their existence.

My hair is purple, my skin is gray, and I am floating in a pond.

"You are a grown adult," my mom's voice swims into my consciousness.

Frozen brussels sprouts rain from the sky.

"Why are you picking fights with your little brother?"

I kick my legs in the water.

"You need to take a long, hard look at yourself!"

I am looking at myself in a magnifying mirror. At my pores, and at the little blond hairs that grow all over my cheeks. I am staring at the creases in my eyelids. At the weird pattern of wrinkles under my eyes. My eyelashes change color as they grow; the roots are black, and the tips are blond. There are thin red veins in my eyes, and there's yellow around my pupils.

I blink.

I am lying in an icy bathtub with my clothes on. I am maneuvering the tap with my feet. I turn the tap on and allow spurts of cold water to enter the tub, then I turn it off, and then on again.

On.

Off.

I was standing in my bathroom when I felt the onset of an attack budding in my stomach. Unwilling to accept an attack lying down, so to speak, I decided I would try to prevent it. I couldn't think of what to do and thought that it might help to submerge myself in cold water—and so here I am. Lying, fully clothed, in my icy bathtub.

I place a dirty plate and an empty mug on my nightstand.

A teenager is sitting beside me on the bus. She is hushing into her cell phone. She looks like she is about thirteen years old. She has severe acne, and her fingernails are covered in chipped blue nail polish.

She keeps giggling awkwardly and saying, "Totally," into her phone.

I stare at her mouth.

She seems so nervous.

"Totally."

"Haha, totally."

"Oh, totally!"

She hangs up.

I hear her exhale.

She fidgets, then dials a new number.

"Mom? Guess what? Lara called me," she hushes, excited.

"Yeah, I think that she wants to be my friend," she whispers.

My heart sinks.

"I know, I hope that she isn't tricking me, or something," she continues.

I feel my heart fall so deep into my stomach that I start picturing it flopping out of my body onto the floor of the bus.

The girl is tugging at the bottom of her T-shirt. It is too small for her and rides up, exposing her fleshy midriff.

I close my eyes and try to tune out her conversation.

"I know, I won't get my hopes up," her small voice swims into my thoughts.

"Are you okay?" a stranger asks me as I rush off the bus.

"Oh yes, thank you—I'm fine," I say, crying. "I'm just having an allergic reaction."

"I feel weird," I disclose to the emergency room doctor.

"What's the matter?" she asks.

"This is going to sound strange," I admit. "But I just can't believe that there is a skeleton inside me."

"What do you mean you can't believe there's a skeleton inside you?"

"I just can't believe it," I repeat, hushed.

I am clutching my arm beneath my coat. I intentionally cut the skin on my forearm very deeply. I have not admitted that to the doctor. I came here for stitches but realized as I waited that they might admit me or lock me up for this.

Maybe I should say it was an accident.

"It was an accident," I say.

"What was?" she asks me, confused.

"Sorry, nothing," I grumble. "I'm just not really feeling well."

"Are you depressed?" she asks.

"Yes," I reply. I feel blood drip from my arm onto my hand.

"When did you first start feeling depressed?"

I pause to think. "I think I was eleven."

"Eleven? That's a long time to be feeling this way. Did something happen when you were eleven?"

"No, not really," I answer, discretely rubbing the blood off on my dark jeans.

I have a clear memory of myself when I was eleven. It was summer, and I was lying in a field of yellow long grass. There were ladybugs everywhere, and fast-moving, white rolling clouds in the sky. I remember telling myself to remember that moment as a sort of experiment. There was nothing particularly unforgettable about the moment. I was just alone with my thoughts and decided to actively choose to remember something.

Memories of being younger than eleven were starting to fade. I didn't feel eleven; I often accidentally answered that I was ten when people asked. I felt like time was moving quickly. I felt nostalgic for being younger, and it bothered me that I'd forgotten things. Who was my teacher in first grade? What color was my living room before my parents painted it? Who was my best friend in kindergarten? I felt like I was never in the moment I was in. I was always looking back, or worried about the future. I remember it was windy and the grass was swaying; ladybugs were clinging to the swinging blades or flying away. I felt incredibly sad and aware of how strange it was to feel so sad in such a bright, pleasant setting.

I came to the realization that every moment exists in perpetuity regardless of whether it's remembered. What has happened has happened; it occupies that moment in time forever. I was an eleven-year-old girl lying in the grass one summer. I knew in that moment that was true and recognized that I would blaze through moments for the rest of my life, forgetting things, and becoming ages older, until I forgot everything—so I consoled myself by committing to remember that one moment.

I was finally awarded selective serotonin reuptake inhibitors for all my hard work as a depressed person. I am waiting for the pharmacist to fill my prescription, and to present me with my medal. Thank you to Dr. Chan for nominating me for this honor, and my brain for burdening me.

The pharmacist waves me over to a private area in the drugstore. Customers eye me as I walk to the secluded area.

The pharmacist explains, while I nod, that this medication might cause nausea, upset stomach, sexual problems, fatigue, dizziness, insomnia, weight change, and headaches. I'm to call the doctor if I have suicidal thoughts.

"Hello, doctor?"

"We're not doctors, this is Telehealth. We will advise you to see a doctor, depending on your issue. What's the problem today?"

"Never mind."

*   *   *

I haven't gone to work in two days. The dishes in my room have piled up again.

Eleanor texted me a picture of a bird.

I'm reading a book about birds, she writes. This one is called a lilac-breasted roller.

It's pretty, I reply.

I thought you'd like it, she writes.

I zoom in on the picture. I look at the bird's purple and blue feathers, and its little black beak.

You're being quiet again, she writes. You'd tell me if you weren't doing okay, right?

Yes, I lie.

I add, Send me more pictures of birds.

The cars that are driving under this overpass are speeding. No one is driving the speed limit. They are zooming by on their way to wherever they are going. I am dangling my feet over the edge. I wonder how long it would take me to fall from where I am to the ground below. I am thinking about how enormous my thighs look pressed down on the concrete, while simultaneously thinking about how small I am in the grand scheme of things.

I am thinking about Grace being killed by Jeff, Flop dying alone in her cage, Mittens being burned to death, Eli drinking, sad teenaged girls, homeless people in the winter, and nuclear bombs.

Sometimes when I'm driving, I think about veering into traffic.

If I stand near the edge of anything, I think about stepping off.

I can't take a pill, clean with bleach, or use a knife without it occurring to me that I could end it.

The night sky is dotted in bright little specks; the night sky is dotted in monstrous fireballs. I am the size of ten million ants, and I don't make up even one percentage of the weight of the rock that I'm floating on. Everything matters so much and so little; it is disgusting.

One of my shoes is untied. It would be awful if my shoe fell off and hurt someone driving beneath me.

I tuck my legs in.

I have positioned myself in front of the receptionist's view in the ER. I am pretending to read a pamphlet in order to appear occupied. The pamphlet is titled BEDWETTING. I hadn't looked at its title before pretending to read it.

"How can I help you today, Gilda?" The receptionist looks up at me from her paperwork.

"Me again." I wave. She looks at the pamphlet in my hand. I try to return it to the display table I found it on, but I accidentally mess up all the other pamphlets in the process.

"You can't get rid of me, eh?" I laugh while knocking some of the pamphlets off the table.

She smiles at me disingenuously. "What's troubling you today?"

"It's probably just anxiety again," I concede, "but I don't want to die in my apartment because I have a cat, and I read that he'll eat my face, and I wouldn't care about that, but I have a family and they're open-casket people so—"

"Please have a seat." She nods toward the waiting area.

"Thank you." I nod.

I don't really have a cat. I said that I did because I felt compelled to provide a concrete reason why I don't want to die alone in my apartment. The real reason is much more difficult for me to pinpoint.

"I went through a dark period before I started my business," Giuseppe tells me.

We are going through a drive-through. I ordered two hamburgers and a milkshake.

I wish I were with Eleanor.

"I felt directionless," he continues. "Hopeless. I see it all the time in my clients."

"How did you fix that?" I ask.

"Oh, that's the secret." He laughs. "It's actually so simple. You just have to choose happiness," he explains.

"Choose happiness?" I clarify.

"Easy as that!"

He exchanges our money for the food, and hands me my items. He then parks, turns to me, and asks: "So, have you ever kissed a guy?"

I choke. I had just unhinged my jaw like a python and taken the largest bite of a hamburger that I could stretch to make.

He starts patting my back as my life flashes before my eyes.

Does Giuseppe know I'm gay? I thought I had been so convincing. How did he find out?

He laughs. "I guess I didn't segue into my question that well. I only asked because I know you're a devoted Catholic," he explains. "I wondered if you have certain purity standards because of your faith. We've seen each other a few times now, and you haven't seemed to want to—"

"Oh," I say. "Yes. Yes, that's exactly it."

I have chosen happiness. Out of all the emotions set out on the table, I have selected it. It is by far the superior option. It's insane to think I would have ever picked one of those shittier emotions before—when all the while, I could have chosen shiny, shimmering, iridescent happiness.

I am ready to feel happy, universe. Lay it on me.

* * *

I am still waiting for the happiness I chose to kick in.

I am at work for the first time in three days. Before going to work, I put two dishes in the sink. I've told myself I'll do two dishes at a time, and then eventually all the dishes will be done.

"Where have you been?" Barney asks me. "We were worried."

"I called," I lie. "I left a message. Did you not get it? I've been sick."

Jeff enters the room from behind me. "I'm sorry to hear that, dear," he says. "Are you feeling better?"

"Yes," I reply brusquely.

Barney has reprinted his flyers warning parents about homosexuality. I pick up one of the fresh posters from the printer. Despite mentally telling myself not to say anything, something possesses me to ask, "So what's this all about?"

Barney takes the poster from me and explains, "We're doing some awareness sessions for parents of teenagers."

Almost everyone who attends this church is older than sixty-five. I don't think many people here have teenaged children.

"The world is falling apart, Gilda," Barney continues, sighing. "Not all young people are as close to God as you are. The fact is, homosexuality is a sin, and as much as these modern-day liberal kids want to argue it, it's an abomination. We have to protect our children."

I purse my lips.

He hushes his voice. "Now, personally, I don't care what anyone does in their bedroom as long as I don't have to hear about it, but these days it's all we hear about."

I look into Barney's face. I look at his wrinkled white skin, and at his gray eyebrows.

In what universe is being gay all we hear about? Who is Barney hanging out with?

"Some things are better kept to yourself," he says. "Other people's bedrooms are none of my business."

I squint. When a straight person mentions their partner to me, I don't feel like they're telling me about their bedroom. I think about how they live with them, pay the same bills, and maybe have kids together. I think about how they probably vote the same way. I think about how, when they die, they will be buried in the same plot. I don't think about how they have sex.

"I just don't want to hear about that kind of thing," Barney says.

The first girl I dated was named Cammie Anthony. She was a year older than me. She had failed eleventh-grade calculus and had to take it again with my class.

The specific chemicals that are released when we have a crush are called norepinephrine, dopamine, and endogenous opioids.

I remember Cammie reaching to hold my hand in a movie theater. We went to see a horror movie, and it was unclear if we were going as friends or on a date.

Norepinephrine is what causes our bodies to have sweaty palms and increased heart rates.

I remember lying awake in my bed texting Cammie until three in the morning.

Dopamine is energizing; it makes us feel motivated and attentive.

I remember every time my phone pinged with a text from Cammie, I felt happy.

Endogenous opioids are part of our reward system. It's what makes having a crush feel enjoyable rather than just crushing.

Oxytocin and vasopressin are the chemicals that make us feel calm, secure, comfortable, and emotionally attached to long-term partners.

It's always been hard for me to feel happy. I think the triggers that prompt my brain to transmit happy chemicals are broken. The only time I have felt happy at all recently was when I was watching a movie with Eleanor and she was laughing.

When I think about the Catholic church, and about most religions in general, my theory is that they came to be as a solution to our existential dread. It's comforting to imagine that everyone who is dead is just waiting for us in the next room. It's calming to imagine that we have an all-powerful father who is watching over us, and who loves us. All of it makes us feel like our lives have some divine meaning; it helps us feel happy. It's ironic that a belief system theoretically created to help me feel safe and meaningful takes away one of the few things that makes me feel like my life is worth living at all.

I google Eleanor's name and scroll through the search results.

I learn she writes reviews for every hotel, restaurant, and business she visits. I read each review and note not a single one is negative. She gave one café five stars despite her review mentioning that they messed up her order. She wrote: "Absolutely love their matcha latte. I ordered a macchiato, but I'm glad my order got a little mixed up because this is my new favorite drink!"

I find the relics of her high school experience preserved in some archaic photo-sharing platform. I look at the photos of thirteen-year-old her, wearing a bucket hat, drinking a bottle of Smirnoff Ice. I find one photo of her smiling weakly at the camera; she has braces and blotchy skin. I keep clicking through the photos until I reach the last one in the album. It's of her and her friends laughing. I zero in on her squinted eyes and breathe air out of my nose while thinking about how ridiculous her laugh sounds.

I find an article from her college and learn she won an award for a short story she wrote. There's a picture of her holding a plaque and shaking hands with a smiling woman. I read the article and learn the story was about the last living bee. There are quotes from the story peppered throughout the article.

"What are you going to do?" a slug asks the bee. "You've got a weapon, you know. You could get retribution. You could sting someone for this."

"No," replies the bee. "I think instead I will just make the last bit of honey."

"Eliza is pregnant!" Barney announces. "Come look, Gilda! Can you believe it? Come look at these pictures she took!"

I stare at him, unmoved.

"Come on!" he shouts.

"I don't even know who Eliza is," I tell him.

"My daughter! Come on," he says again, gesturing at me to come look. "You're talking to a grandpa now. Can you believe it?"

I stand up and peer over his shoulder. He has his phone open and is flipping through photos of a young woman standing in a cornfield with a balding man. The woman is wearing a pink cardigan paired with cowboy boots. In one photo, she and her husband have both their hands on her gut.

Barney grins as he clicks through the photos. I notice the girl's outfit changes a few times, but her husband is wearing the same plaid shirt in every single shot. I think about how she had to change in that field somewhere while this guy stood there waiting. The image of a naked pregnant woman standing in a field while her husband holds her clothes distracts me as Barney continues clicking through all ninety-five photos.

"Doesn't this make you want to get married and have a baby?" Barney beams, nudging me.

I smile.

No.

*   *   *

My mother had a baby, and her mother had a baby, and her mother had a baby. Every woman in my family before me lived to have a baby—just so that baby could grow up to have another baby. If I don't have a baby, then all of those women reproduced just so that I could exist. I am the final product. I am the final baby.

I tried to take two more dishes out of the pile of dishes in my room, but they were load bearing, and the pile fell. I watched the dishes tip over like a Jenga tower. Every single dish shattered. Shards splintered across the floor like shrapnel. I stood, stunned, holding the two cups I'd pulled from the pile, taking in the unsalvageable ruins.

I don't feel like my antidepressants are working. I think they are giving me tremors. I feel shaky. My mouth is dry. I'm sweating more than usual and, perhaps most inconvenient, I keep thinking about killing myself.

Streetlights blur past the car window. Giuseppe is taking me for a drive. I told him that I didn't feel like going, but he insisted.

I am a hostage in his car, forced to sit and listen to him ramble about regret.

"Can we turn on the radio?" I ask.

"I don't believe in having regrets," he says, ignoring me. "Everything in my life has brought me to become who I am now. If I regretted anything, I wouldn't be who I am. That's why I don't think anyone should ever regret anything."

Giuseppe is too ignorant and arrogant to grasp that some people don't like where they are in life, or who they are.

"Do you have regrets, Gilda?"

"Yes," I answer, breaking character.

"What?" he asks, staggered. He expects me to nod along to everything he says. "No you don't. Don't say that."

"Of course I have regrets," I reiterate. "I regret a lot of things."

Giuseppe hardly knows me. For all he knows, I'm a cannibal.

"Do you believe cannibals shouldn't regret cannibalizing people?" I ask.

"What?" he asks.

"I regret getting in this car," I groan. "Sometimes I regret being born at all. I regret more things than I don't."

"What are you talking about?" He turns to look at me, confused.

"You're an idiot," I hear myself saying. Stop. "And you're the worst kind of idiot because you have no idea that you're an idiot."

He opens his mouth, stunned.

I continue: "I'm over here crippled by how insignificant and stupid I know I am, and yet you're out here just vomiting daft, illogical thoughts as if you know anything."

Stop.

"Despite being absolutely certain that I am oblivious, I am equally as sure that I am less oblivious than you are. Here's a news flash for you, Giuseppe: You don't know anything. You're a fraud. You don't demonstrate even a shred of awareness regarding the reality of things. You've deluded yourself into thinking you've figured something out that other people haven't, but you haven't either. If anyone figures life out, it's not going to be you. It's easy to feel like you understand everything in life when you're big-headed, self-important, and stupid."

Stop.

"You have never said anything that I thought was astute. You have no authority to talk about life in any capacity. The only reason you are successful at all is because you have exploited other people's naivety and desperation."

Stop.

"Ignorance is bliss, Giuseppe, have you ever heard that? If you ever find yourself feeling particularly blissful, take a moment to appreciate it's probably because you are incredibly stupid."

"Well you're a fucking dyke!" Giuseppe shouts, startling me.

I hesitate. "How did you know—"

"You're a stupid bitch!" he yells. "Fuck you!"

I realize as he continues to shout defamatory names that he was just insulting me using the random slurs that came to his mind and is not actually aware that I am gay.

"Get out of my car!"

I am walking on a dusky road with no sidewalk. I watch the dark silhouettes of pine trees sway around me. It's quiet except for the sounds of branches creaking. I feel afraid for a moment before recognizing that I don't think I really care what happens to me. I could accidentally be hit by a car, abducted by a serial killer, or get lost out here—but all of those possible outcomes cause me just as much grief as the prospect of returning to my house and going to sleep.

I start walking in the middle of the road.

"Are you all right?" Jeff asks me.

I look up from my hands.

"I'm fine."

"You seem like you have something on your mind," he comments.

"I'm fine," I repeat, glancing at the suspicious ring on his finger.

"Would it help you to attend confessional?" he suggests.

"No, thank you," I answer.

"All right, dear." He nods, turning to leave the room.

"Wait!" I shout after contemplating something. "Who do *you* confess your sins to?"

"Pardon?" He turns around.

"Who do you confess your sins to?" I repeat, louder. "When you have something on your mind, who do you confess it to?"

"Oh, usually other priests," he answers. "I visit other churches. Why?"

A grief-stricken, stone woman is ogling me. She is the statue guarding Our Lady of Sorrows, which is the Catholic church on the other side of town. I hesitate before entering the church; its name is not exactly inviting, and the miserable stone woman at the entrance is also a bit of a repellent. If I were to avoid buildings built for sad women, however, I would be homeless—so, despite my physical inclination not to, I enter the off-putting church.

The building is dim and somber. I can hear each step I take vibrate through it. There is maroon carpet casing the floor, and red stained glass windows letting bloodshot light spill all over the pews. I feel like I am a crumb moving through a human body.

I roam the outskirts of the pews until I find the confessional booth. I move the black curtain and sit down on the confessor's side of the booth.

"Hi," I greet the priest expecting me.

"Hi," the old man's brusque voice responds. "You're who called?"

"I am," I reply. I made an appointment before coming.

"Have you attended confessional before?"

"Yes."

"Go ahead, then."

I clear my throat. "I was wondering, if someone confessed something terrible to you—"

"That's not how you begin," he corrects me.

"Right. Sorry." I clear my throat again. "In the name of the Father, and of the Son, and of the Holy Spirit. I was wondering, do you report confessions to the police?"

"No," he replies. "I have a duty not to disclose anything. It's called the seal of confessional."

"Even something terrible?" I stress.

"I have an absolute duty not to."

"Has anyone ever confessed something you thought the police should know?"

"Yes, but I do not report confessions to the police."

"Interesting," I remark, mulling that over in my mind.

"Do you have something to confess?" he asks me after a moment of quiet.

"Oh," I blurt. "No."

"There's nothing you regret doing?" he presses.

"Well, I regret doing a lot of things," I admit.

"Like what?" he probes.

I don't really feel like talking about the things I regret, but this man came to this booth expecting to absolve me of my trespasses, and I don't want to disappoint him.

"I regret lying," I admit.

He hums to acknowledge he has heard me.

"I have been kind of pretending to be someone I'm not," I explain. "I wish I didn't do that, but I'm sort of trapped in it now."

"Hm. I pray that you escape," he replies.

"Thank you."

"God will forgive it," he adds. "What else can I absolve you from?" he asks.

I pause to think. I mentally turn the pages in my hefty catalog of regrets I keep archived in my mind.

"I used to sneak into my brother's room," I hear myself disclose. "He would steal my things sometimes, so I'd look through his room to find my missing belongings."

This is something I try not to think about. This is one of those memories that I've tucked into the back corner of my consciousness.

"I should never have gone into his room. I should have respected his privacy, even if he stole my things. I shouldn't have gone in there."

The priest hums again to acknowledge that he hears me.

"This is something I want to be forgiven for," I explain. "I feel bad for doing it."

Eli had a shoebox full of Polaroids under his bed. I found the box when I was looking for my missing cell phone charger. The box was overflowing with photos of Eli wearing women's clothing. Some of the clothing was mine.

I sat on the edge of his bed, looking into the box. When I first saw the photos, I laughed. I thought, how ridiculous. I then realized that most of the clothing he was wearing was mine, and I felt fleetingly angry that he had stolen it from me. My anger simmered when I noticed the contented expression on his face, and the way he had accessorized my blouse. The longer I looked the more I realized that it wasn't funny, and I wasn't angry.

"Can I be forgiven for doing that?" I ask.

"Of course you can," he tells me.

"Murderers sure are something," Barney tells me, holding the book he had me buy him. "I think all mentally ill people should be removed from society," he tuts. "I can't believe we're living in a world where these sickos can just roam the streets. Some of them are teachers! Childcare workers!"

"How will we know who is mentally ill?" I ask.

"Well," he says, opening his book. "This book outlines the common characteristics in psychopaths. I think anyone who meets these criteria should be watched."

"What's the criteria?" I ask.

"They were usually bullied as kids," he tells me.

"They get involved in petty crimes, like theft."

"They have a hard time staying employed."

*   *   *

Today is my birthday. I have existed for twenty-eight years. That is 336 months, or 10,220 days. That is one year longer than Kurt Cobain and Janis Joplin lived, and five years older than my mom was when she had me.

If I lived on Mercury, I'd be 116. I'd have orbited the sun that many times. On Venus, I'd be forty-five. I'd be fourteen on Mars. On Saturn, Uranus, Neptune and Pluto, I wouldn't even be one yet.

I was born late. I existed inside my mother's gut as a fully formed baby for a good two weeks longer than most humans do. That means I'm probably 10,234 days old.

If I live as long as Grace did, I'll live 31,390 some-odd days. That doesn't seem much longer, in the grand scheme of things. Even in the minor scheme of things, it seems short.

I read once that women are born with all the eggs that they will ever produce in their life. That means the egg that formed me is as old as my mother. From that perspective, part of me is fifty-one.

My parents and Eli are singing happy birthday to me. My mom baked me a chocolate cake. She drew a large letter *G* on top of the cake in yellow icing and covered the cake in thin pink candles.

"Make a wish!" she says, gesturing toward the candles.

I stare into the glowing flecks of fire and wish:

I wish that I find something distracting enough to occupy my mind with thoughts unrelated to the futility of my existence, or that I die in the least disruptive way possible for my family.

I blow out the candles.

"Now don't tell us!" my mom says. "Or it won't come true!"

"Thank you for making me a cake," I say, looking into her beaming face.

I look at her mouth; at her smiling.

"I can't believe it was twenty-eight years ago when we had you."
She grins.

"It's stupid," Eli warns me.

Despite being in a fight, he still got me a birthday present.

I tear glossy paper into pieces and unveil a painting on a canvas.

"Wow," my mom says from behind me.

"What a beautiful painting!" my dad remarks.

He painted me a picture of Flop.

"This isn't stupid," I say, grinning at the painting.

My mom sent me home with a Tupperware container jam-packed
with leftover cake. She said, "You could pack it in your lunch for
work!"

I smiled and nodded. "Good idea."

The second I get into my apartment I undress and crawl into my
bed like a naked rat in a den.

My phone is ringing.

"Hello?"

"Gilda! What are we doing tonight?" Ingrid asks me.

I look down at my container of cake.

"Meet me at the Fox!" she says. "Let's get a drink."

"Oh, I don't really feel like—"

"Too bad!"

Ingrid bought me a stuffed animal for my birthday.

She grins as she hands it to me.

"You remembered," I say, taking the stuffed animal from her.

It's a pig.

"Of course I remembered! It's our tradition!"

I smile despite feeling brokenhearted by the gesture.

"That's so sweet," I say, tears filling my eyes.

"You must be drunk!" she teases, grabbing my shoulders.

"I'm wasted," I lie.

A band is playing. The lights are moving in sync with the music. Whenever the drum beats, all the blue lights flash on and then off. The red lights flicker in sync with the bass. When the singer hits a high note, all the lights point to her.

"How is everyone doing tonight!" the singer shrieks into the crowd.

Amid the screaming replies, I allow myself to say out loud, "I actually haven't been feeling well lately."

I look behind me and see that the room has been swarmed with people. I think about how strange it would be to see other animals do some of the things humans do. What if birds had concerts? I start to imagine a flock of hundreds of birds surrounding one little bird while it sings to them. That is what this is, when I think about it. We're a herd of animals watching another animal make noises.

"Eleanor," I hear myself slurring into my phone, "what if birds were like people?"

"What if birds had concerts, wouldn't that be weird?"

"What if they had weddings?"

"What if they got each other gifts?"

Eleanor redirects my hand whenever it goes anywhere near her stomach. She's never told me explicitly not to touch her stomach, but I recognize that she doesn't want me to by how she grips my hand and moves it to her hip or her rib cage. She's thinner than I am, but that doesn't seem to matter. She thinks something is wrong with her stomach.

"I like your stomach," I tell her, thinking I'm subtle.

"Fuck off," she replies, laughing.

It's strange people don't like how their bodies look. It's strange we waste any of our time concerning ourselves with how our skin drapes over our bones or how fat cultivates.

"You're really pretty," I tell her.

She laughs really loudly. "Fuck off."

Jeff has gone to give last rites to dying patients at the hospital. I am sitting at my desk, staring straight ahead—through Jeff's open office door. There is another door inside of Jeff's office which leads into the rectory, where he lives.

I stand up and walk quickly through both doors. I do not think about what I'm doing before I do it. I shut the doors behind me and pause.

I am inside Jeff's house. It smells like cinnamon and laundry. I look around the room. I eye his brown sofa, and the knickknacks he's collected on his side tables. He has a lot of porcelain figurines of birds. There's an oil painting of a garden hanging over his primitive TV, and books stacked on the floor.

I walk through the living room into the kitchen. I find papers piled on his counter. I flip through them. They are mostly bills. There is one postcard from a family. It says they are having a lovely time in India. They saw elephants and ate tandoori chicken.

I open drawers and pull out piles of photos. I pause to look at Jeff in the photos. He is much younger in them. He has brown hair. I sit down at the table and continue to flip through the photos until I spot Grace's face.

I study the picture. She and Jeff are standing together outside. They are at a picnic. Both of them are holding white paper plates. They are eating corn on the cob and hamburgers. Jeff is grinning and Grace is laughing. It looks like he told her a joke—

I hear keys jingle in the front door.

Fuck.

I drop the pictures back in the drawers and shut them. I rush toward the back door I came in through and try to open it—but find that it has locked itself behind me.

Fuck.

Why did I do this?

I rush away from the door, looking for someplace to hide. I run into the bedroom, throw myself to the ground, and roll under Jeff's bed. There is not much room for me to fit, and springs from the mattress dig into my back. I close my eyes tightly and try to imagine that I am not where I am.

I am not where I am.

I hear the door shut.

I hear steps move closer to me.

I am not where I am.

The steps stop.

I open my eyes and see Jeff's brown loafers standing right next to me.

Fuck.

I put my hand over my mouth and say a prayer to every God I have ever heard of that he doesn't find me here. Please Jesus, Jupiter, Elohim, Zeus, and Ra. Have mercy. I can't explain this. There is no acceptable reason I could give to justify why I am hiding under his bed. If he's a murderer—I'm dead. If he's not, I wish I were.

Jeff kneels next to me and I feel tears start to roll down my cheeks as the horrible reality that he has found me dawns on me. I wish I could will myself to die before he sees me.

Die, body, please.

I close my eyes and wait to either die or to be spotted, but neither outcome transpires.

Instead I hear Jeff's voice say, "In the name of the Father, and of the Son and of the Holy Spirit . . ."

My heart calms slightly. He is praying. He hasn't found me. He is just kneeling next to his bed to pray.

"Lord, please help me to understand those things that lead others into despair. Please help me bring justice to my friend Grace, who has found her home with you, and please help me to forgive whoever has done this. Please also help me to be less sad, and to find comfort in the peace you give to those who die. Amen."

After four hours of listening to Jeff watch a *Waltons* marathon, while my body becomes number than a corpse under his bed, I finally hear the angels sing. Jeff is snoring. I move as slowly and silently as I can out from under the bed, like a worm emerging from underneath a rock. I tiptoe right past Jeff's slumbering body, out his door, into the outside space.

I stand outside. I exhale like a pardoned criminal just freed from years in prison.

I feel so intensely relieved to have escaped that hideous predicament that I am on the brink of tears. I feel intensely relieved to have learned that Jeff is not a cold-blooded old-lady killer. He is just a sad old man.

I spend a full millisecond savoring the reprieve I feel learning my employer is not a killer, and that I was not found hiding in his house, before anxiety nudges itself back into the forefront of my mind's eye.

"*Hey, wait a minute.*" My anxiety raises its hand.

"Yes?" I acknowledge it.

"*If Jeff didn't kill Grace, then who did?*"

part four
─────────

Lent

"The Hebrew People of the Old Testament understood that human life was short, and that everyone would eventually get sick, grow old, and die. When the Hebrews disobeyed God, they were called to repent, and to turn away from their sins. The people would put on clothes made from rough cloth, cover their heads with ashes; they would fast and pray for God's mercy."

Jeff pauses.

"Dear friends," he continues after a moment of silence. "Let us ask our Father to bless these ashes, which we will use as the mark of our repentance."

The crowd replies, "Amen."

Jeff sprinkles holy water on the ashes.

People start to stand up. I shuffle forward with the crowd.

When I reach the front of the room, Jeff smiles at me, rubs ashes on my forehead, and says, "Remember: you are dust and to dust you will return."

Barney is still engrossed in his book about murderers. I am starting to wonder if I should suspect him. Is he putting on a show, reading that book everywhere he goes? Is he trying to throw everyone off?

"What do you think of Barney?" I ask Jeff, wondering if he is suspicious of him too.

Jeff is sitting beside my desk sipping coffee.

"Barney? Oh, he has a good heart, doesn't he?" Jeff smiles.

Barney walks to and from work every day. He lives a few blocks over from the church. I know that because I just followed him home.

I trailed far enough behind him that he didn't notice me. I crept along the sidewalk close to the bushes so I could hide behind them if he turned around. He didn't.

I am now standing at the side of his house, peering into his kitchen window. His kitchen has yellow wallpaper. There is a calendar on his wall that has not been flipped in two months. He has junk scattered all over his counters. Piles of dirty plates, pots, and pans. There is also a dirty bucket, a flat of water bottles, an open box of cereal, overripe bananas, and a dead houseplant.

He is making himself pasta. He's standing over the pot, waiting for it to boil. He keeps sighing.

After witnessing Barney spend his sinister evening alone, eating macaroni from the pot in silence, I decide to leave. I skulk along the side of his house to the driveway.

Just as I emerge, a car pulls in. Its headlights put a spotlight on me. My heart stops.

"Hello?" the driver addresses me. It's a woman.

I ignore her as she climbs out of her seat. I notice that she is pregnant. She must be Barney's daughter. I walk quickly forward, toward the sidewalk.

"Hello?" she calls after me again. "What were you doing beside the house?"

I start to run.

She yells after me, "Hey! What the hell? What were you doing?"

I bolt. I run down the street. Cold wind blasts against my ears.

I rocket through a park and down a fenced-in pedestrian path. I cut through a backyard. I jog down a sidewalk. I keep running until my chest hurts. I turn into a corner store. I decide to hide in there. I enter the store panting.

The second I enter the bright light of the corner store the cashier addresses me.

"Hey! You there!" she shouts.

My heart stops again. Did Barney's daughter call the police, and did they warn this corner store cashier to look out for me?

I turn to look at her. "What?" I say.

"You have something on your face," she tells me.

"What?"

"There's a smudge on your face," she tells me. "It's on your forehead. I just thought I'd tell you. I'd want someone to tell me if I had something on my face." She smiles.

"Oh." I exhale, rubbing off the ashes Jeff smudged on my face today. "Thank you."

I notice the store is selling dishes. I buy two bowls, two plates, and two glasses to replace my broken dishes.

I am riding the bus home, reading articles about murderers on my phone.

Juana Barraza was a professional wrestler who killed over forty old women. She strangled and bludgeoned them to death. She said she did it because of lingering resentment she had toward her mother. Her mother used to trade her for beer to men.

Thierry Paulin killed about twenty old women. He killed one woman by forcing her to drink drain cleaner. Others had their heads stuck in plastic bags. Some reports said that he singled out women who seemed unfriendly. He said he did it to steal from them.

Ed Gein dug up his mother's dead body, killed two women, and used the bones and skin of corpses to create hideous trophies.

I look up from a photo of Ed Gein and realize that I missed my stop. I pull the bell and walk toward the back door of the bus.

I gaze at the passengers breathing around me while I wait for the bus to stop. I think about how strange it is that it's possible to end someone's life. It's like an ominous magical power, turning someone inanimate.

I remember watching rhinos chew branches at the Toronto Zoo. My fifth-grade class went on a field trip. I remember looking at the rhinos, listening to their teeth crunch twigs and wood, and thinking: those things are just like dinosaurs, and dinosaurs are just like dragons. I decided rhinos were like magical creatures. The only reason they aren't considered magical is because they're real.

I swallow an antidepressant with tap water. My mouth is still dry, and I am still sweating more than I used to; however, I am using a knife right now, and it's only slightly occurring to me that I could kill myself with it. I am mostly thinking about the apple I'm slicing, and about how fruit is sort of magical.

There are a lot of things on earth that I think would be considered magic if they weren't real. Dreaming, for example. The fact that babies are created inside of women's bodies; the whole concept of conception. Castles. Trees. Whales. Lions. Birds. Rainbows. Water. The northern lights. Volcanos. Lightning. Fire.

Murder is like a dark magic. If we didn't know it existed, finding out it did would be like discovering vampires exist, or that hell is real, or that there are real monsters under our beds. Murderers have discovered this and realized it's a real power they can use. Despite being an inconsequential animal on a pebble in space, they've found the closest thing they can to making sparks fly from their fingertips and they want to hone it at the expense of anyone. They want to feel powerful.

"Someone tried to break into my house last night!" Barney proclaims as he storms through the church's front doors.

I pause. I had been watering the ferns by the entrance. I stand still, afraid he knows it was me.

"This community is in shambles!" he bellows. "We're living among criminals! We aren't safe in our homes!" He looks at me. "Do you have mace, Gilda?"

"What?" I reply.

"Pepper spray," he reiterates. "Bear spray? A weapon? Do you carry anything to protect yourself?"

Before I say no, I hesitate. I wonder if he's asking me that to see if I'm vulnerable. I wonder if he's pretending to ask me out of concern but is actually feeling me out to see if he can attack me.

"Yes," I decide to lie. "I do."

"Good." He nods.

I am typing gibberish into a Word document while I observe Barney pace around the church. I watch him interact with Sister Jude. She pats him on his shoulder while he tells her about the attempted break-in.

"That's terrible," I hear her comfort him. "I'm so sorry you're going through this, Barney."

I watch him talk to a group of parishioners. They all exchange expressions of concern and unease as he tells them he was almost robbed. He mentions that his daughter saw the perpetrator. He tells them it was "a young woman."

"A young woman?" one of the elderly men repeats him, aghast. "My God. It's becoming more and more difficult to profile criminals in this day and age, isn't it? How are we supposed to know who we're safe around?"

I stare at Barney's face. I squint at him as he nods reverently at his audience.

I know this church doesn't do background checks, because they didn't do one on me. Jeff didn't ask me for so much as a résumé before hiring me. Barney could be an escaped convict, for all we know. He could be a serial killer.

A couple is getting married today. The bride is blond, and she is wearing white despite something I overheard her soon-to-be mother-in-law say in the hall.

I am standing at the back of the church, watching the couple at the front. They are looking into each other's faces, holding each other's hands.

I look around the church—at the crowd of people watching. They are all smiling up at the couple. Some of them are teary-eyed.

I wonder, why do we do this? We give each other rocks and wear expensive clothing to sign papers saying we will be someone's partner until one of us dies. We involve the government.

I look around the room again, at the happy faces of the people sitting in the pews. They love this. They love watching these two get married.

The bride and the groom are grinning at each other.

Something in my mind clicks. This makes them happy. They buy expensive clothing and involve the government because it makes them happy.

I run a sharp knife through a cold, uncooked chicken breast. I look at the pink, fleshy insides. I notice specks of deep red veins in the cutlets.

"Is that normal?" I ask Eleanor.

She nods.

We are cooking dinner together at her house. I brought wine I stole from the church.

I don't cook and I'm not contributing much.

Eleanor has been stirring a saucepan with hot sauce, brown sugar, and red pepper flakes in it. She splashed some of the wine I brought into the pan.

She seasons the chicken and pours the red sauce on it. I stare at the bloody, bright red chicken and wonder: What does human meat look like?

"Aren't you hungry?" Eleanor asks me as she moves a fork of the meat to her lips.

I don't want to offend her by not eating what she cooked.

I cut a piece of the chicken off, put it to my mouth, and chew.

"Do you like it?" she asks.

I nod.

I am looking into Eleanor's face on her pillow.

Her eyes are brown.

"Your eyes are brown," I tell her.

"I know," she replies, smiling.

"Do you think you'll want to get married one day?" I ask her.

She snorts. "Wow, I can't figure you out!"

"What do you mean?" I ask.

She laughs. "Half the time you don't text me back, and now you're talking to me about marriage? Don't you think it's a little early to ask me that kind of question, Gilda?"

"I just wondered," I explain, "in general, do you think you'll ever want to get married to anyone?"

"Well," she answers, rolling on her back, "I'm not really sure."

She has freckles.

"You have freckles," I tell her.

"I know," she replies, smiling.

I dream that Barney is tightening a belt around my throat.

I dream that he's put my head inside a plastic bag.

I dream that he's forcing me to drink Drano.

He's put a pillow over my face and a knife up to my throat.

He's tied a rope around my neck and put a gun to my temple.

He's put a bomb in this room.

I'm screaming, "Please stop! Stop!"

I lash out and kick. "Just kill me!"

My stomach turns and I open my eyes.

I am in Eleanor's bed and I feel nauseous.

Maybe it'll go away if I fall back asleep, I tell myself.

I close my eyes.

My stomach turns again. I look up at the dark ceiling. I feel cold sweat roll off my forehead.

I sit up and quietly walk toward the bathroom.

I turn the light on and look at the toilet. The second my eyes register the toilet they send a cue to my stomach that it's a safe time to puke, and I fall to my knees.

I try to be quiet, but I keep making loud, involuntary gagging noises.

Stop, I tell my body.

Gag.

Stop.

I can't control the noises I'm making, or that my body keeps twisting my back and neck as I puke. I have no control over myself; I am trapped in this malfunctioning physical vessel.

Gag.

I hear stirring in the bedroom.

"Gilda?" Eleanor's voice carries through the hall. "Are you sick?"

I try to reply that I'm okay, and that she should go back to sleep, but opening my mouth inspires the vomit in my stomach to erupt. I puke on the floor. Fuck.

I glance around the bathroom. All of her towels are white. I don't know how to clean this up.

Gag.

I hear her feet slap against the floorboards toward me.

Stop puking, I tell my body as it pukes.

She opens the door.

"Oh no, you're sick," she says.

"I'm okay, it's all right, don't worry," I say. "Go back to bed. I'm fine."

She turns the tap on and fills a glass by the sink with cold water. She hands it to me.

I try to say thank you, but I can't do anything besides throw up.

She takes her elastic out of her own hair and uses it to pull my hair back.

I keep trying to say that I'm okay, it's all right, don't worry, but every time I open my mouth I puke.

I wrap my arms around the bowl of the toilet and vomit red, half-digested chicken into the water.

As I feel pressure build up in my eyes, my stomach continues to turn, and my throat burns from my own stomach acids. I watch as Eleanor takes one of her clean, folded white towels from its basket and uses it to clean up my puke.

"Do you think it was a man or a woman?" Barney asks me. He's sitting on my desk.

"What are you talking about?" I reply.

I wish he weren't sitting so close to me. I still feel sick.

"Whoever murdered Grace. Do you think it was a man or a woman?"

"A man," I reply, eyeing him.

"You think so? Why?" he asks.

"Just a hunch," I say quietly.

"I don't know," he mulls. "I think it might've been who tried to rob me."

I google "homicide and gender." I learn that about 90 percent of all murderers are men.

"Father Jeff?" I knock on Jeff's office door.

"Yes, dear?" He looks up from his notebook.

"Do you have a minute?"

"Of course, come in." He puts his pen down.

I sit down on the chair across from his desk.

"I've been thinking about Grace a lot," I tell him. "Do you mind if I ask you about her?"

"Oh," he replies. "Of course. What would you like to know?"

"She's been on my mind a lot," I tell him. "I feel terrible about what happened to her."

"Me too." Jeff nods. "Grace is happy in heaven now, though, dear. Is that a comfort to you?"

I nod, but it isn't.

"What did Grace do before working here?" I ask.

"Oh." He thinks for a minute. "Well, she worked for a time as a cashier at a corner store."

"What else did she do?" I ask.

"Well . . ." He thinks. "She volunteered with the Friends of the Library. She loved to read. She used to monitor recess at St. Gabriel's. She loved children. She used to do a lot of crossword puzzles. She was very social. She was quite involved in the church. She used to run our canned food drives. She was very charitable."

"So, she was a nice lady?" I ask. "People liked her?"

"Oh yes." He nods. "Yes, everyone loved her. She was very kind."

"Do you think someone killed her to steal from her?"

"I'm not sure," Jeff replies. "She was from humble means, so it would surprise me."

"Did she have anyone around her who seemed crazy?" I ask. "Did she know anyone who had drug problems, or anything like that?"

Jeff shakes his head. "None that she ever mentioned to me."

"Barney's been talking to me about it a lot," I say quietly. "He's reading that book about catching murderers."

Jeff nods. "Yes, it's obviously weighing on him, too."

I nod.

"Who do you think killed her?" I blurt.

"Oh, I'm really not sure," he says. "She was a very sweet, quiet woman. I can't imagine why anyone would do anything to harm her. I've chosen not to occupy my mind with those apprehensions though, dear, and to leave it to the police and to God. It doesn't help to dwell on those types of wonderings."

I google Barney's name. I scroll until I find a link to his Facebook profile.

His profile picture is a selfie taken from a very low angle. He posts a lot of links to Fox News. His relationship status is set to married. He has not mastered Facebook's privacy settings; every photo album he has is open. He took a trip to Florida three years ago. Prior to that he attended some sort of car show. This summer he went to the beach and took a lot of blurry photos of a beach towel. There is one picture at the very end of the album of him smiling with his arm around his daughter. I click on her profile.

She posts a lot of statuses regarding how far along into her pregnancy she is.

"The baby is the size of a walnut!"

"The baby is the size of an apple!"

"The baby is the size of a cantaloupe!"

Barney has liked every single status.

I am creating a fake Facebook profile.

I choose the name: Homer S. Gerster.

After selecting a photo of an old man from Google images, I open Barney's daughter's profile and click "Add Friend."

I am sitting at my desk listening to the hum of the light above me. I am watching the clock in the corner of my computer screen tick through time. It's 2:41. It's 2:42. It's 2:43. My eyes wander across the screen. They zero in on the sent email folder.

I click, scroll, and unearth hundreds of emails written and sent by Grace.

I click rapidly through each email, speed-reading every word, while simultaneously disparaging myself for not thinking to look here earlier.

She sent condolence emails to bereaved families.

Dear Williams family,

Our parish family has you in our thoughts and we are praying for you and John's spirit every day.

Please see the enclosed passage about losing a loved one.

With love and God's blessings,
St. Rigobert's Church

She forwarded the emails forwarded to her. "Look at these funny pictures of hamsters!" she wrote. She sent one titled "Funny church signs." It has pictures of church signs that say things like: HOW DO WE MAKE HOLY WATER? WE BOIL THE HELL OUT OF IT.

She sent Rosemary recipes. I read one for chocolate fudge. She wrote instructions regarding how to make kombucha and Turkish delight.

She wrote:

Rose,

Tell Jim I saw a man who looked just like him at the drugstore last night. I screamed "Jim!" over and over. When the man finally turned around and I realized it was not Jim, I recognized what a miracle it is they haven't committed me to a seniors' home yet. I have been laughing about it all day.

Love, your friend,
Grace

Her most recently sent email to Rosemary was for her birthday. It said:

Dear Rosemary,

Happy belated birthday! My memory is going, Rosie. I'm sorry I didn't email you last week. If I ever miss it again, please consider this email my forever happy birthday. I hope every birthday, and every day you have left on this earth, is so happy you can barely stand it!!!

I comb through the emails for any mention of Barney.
I search his name and find one. It says:

Dear Barney,

We miss you at the church and are praying for you.

Love,
Grace

He replied:

God bless you and thank you, Grace. I'm doing ok.
Barney

I read both emails about ten times.

Why wasn't Barney at the church, and why were they praying for him?

Local schoolchildren are putting on a play for mass today. The play is called *Stations*. It has attracted a larger than usual congregation.

The lead actor is a blond ten-year-old boy. He has a wreath made of twigs on top of his small golden head, and he is wearing a large white bathrobe. He keeps tightening the bathrobe belt around his little waist. I look at his hands as he tightens the belt. He has a purple Band-Aid on his finger. I look up at his mouth and notice the residue of whatever he ate for lunch has created an orangish mustache above his upper lip.

Just as I begin to grow attached to this kid, a ten-year-old girl with a beard drawn on her face condemns him to death. The lights in the church go out.

When they come back on again, the ten-year-old boy is given a wooden cross to carry. The cross is impressively realistic; it looks sturdy enough to withstand an actual crucifixion. It's not man-sized, however, because this kid wouldn't be able to carry it. It's a child-sized crucifix.

The little boy falls down while lugging the cross. Is that part of the play? I glance around. No one else in the audience looks surprised by the tumble. It's either a part of the play, or this audience has low expectations.

One of Jesus's classmates, dressed in a pale-blue bedsheet, kneels beside him. I think she's playing his mother. She's touching his face with her small hands. The lights go out.

In the fifth scene, one of Jesus's male classmates helps him carry the cross. Isn't that nice? This is my favorite scene so far.

A female classmate wipes his face off with a washcloth. She holds the cloth out toward the audience. We see that Jesus's face has been drawn on the cloth. The drawing of a grown man's face, with a large beard and long brown hair, contrasts starkly against this blond child's pale, freckled face.

He falls again in the seventh scene. I think that his robe is too long, and he's tripped over it. I think he's wearing his dad's bathrobe.

A bunch of girls wearing bedsheets surround him and pretend to cry.

He falls again. I think this time it was intentional.

A crowd of his classmates rip his robe off him. Thankfully, the child is wearing a T-shirt and shorts beneath the bathrobe. The scene still feels inappropriate.

Now one of his classmates is pretending to nail him to the cross. He is swinging an actual hammer an inch away from his hand. I wince every time he swings, afraid he'll misjudge the distance and hammer the palm of this kid's little hand.

I think he is pretending to die now; he is looking up into the ceiling of the church.

He looks down at his feet. I think this is the end.

Wait, they're taking him off the cross.

Now they're lying him down on the carpet of the church.

The lights go out.

Everyone is clapping.

I am clapping as well, to blend in.

We all stand up. We are cheering.

"Good job, kids!" someone shouts.

A man whistles.

"Encore!"

"Beautiful stations this year, weren't they?" Barney remarks to the old man standing across from us.

The man has his thumbs beneath his suspenders. He nods. "The girl playing Mary suited the part especially, I thought."

"I thought she did as well," Barney agrees.

"What did you think of it?" The man turns to me.

I sputter, "It seemed like the cross was pretty heavy."

They both nod. Barney mumbles, "It did seem heavy, yeah."

"What's going on with all this Grace Moppet hullabaloo?" the old man changes the subject. "Any updates? Do we know who did it yet?"

Barney shakes his head. "We've received very little news, I'm afraid. The police are taking their sweet time getting to the bottom of it. I've been looking into it myself. I've got a couple of leads. I don't know if I trust the police to sort it out, to be honest. Did I tell you my house was almost robbed?"

"It was?" the man asks, aghast. "When?"

"A couple of nights ago. The police haven't done anything. They told me there's no evidence. I've called them at least eight times about it, and they've asked me to stop. Can you imagine? They can't solve a simple attempted robbery, let alone a murder case. I don't have much hope."

The old man tuts, "What's the world coming to?"

"Do you think anyone who goes to this church was involved?" I ask Jeff.

I have returned to his office to ask him more about Grace.

"No, I don't think so," he answers. "I can't think of anyone."

I stare at my hands. I start to think about skeletons, and the bones in my fingers.

"Would you like to say a prayer for Grace with me, Gilda?" Jeff offers.

"Sure," I reply, folding my skeleton hands in my lap.

Jeff looks down and recites, "Saints of God, come to Grace's aid! Come to meet her, angels of the Lord! Receive her soul and present her to God the Most High. May Christ, Who called you, take you to Himself; may Angels lead you to Abraham's side. Give her eternal rest, O Lord, and may Your light shine on her forever."

Who is this? Barney's daughter messages me.

She accepted my friend request.

Hi, I reply, this is Homer.

Do we know each other? she writes back.

I'm an old friend of your dad's, I reply. I knew you when you were little. How is old Barney doing these days?

Oh, I'm sorry, I don't remember you. He's been doing okay. Did you hear my mom passed away last year? We've all been struggling with that. I'm expecting a baby soon though, and he's looking forward to being a grandpa.

His wife is dead?

I'm sorry to hear about your mom, I write.

I start to imagine that Barney is a serial killer. I imagine that he murdered his wife.

Was it unexpected? I ask.

She had cancer for quite a while prior, Eliza writes. Did you know her?

No, I reply. How has Barney been dealing with all of that?

He's okay, she shares. My mom was always a homemaker, so he's been struggling a bit with cooking and cleaning. I had to teach him how to do laundry. He's doing his best. I'm sure he'd like to hear from an old friend. I'll tell him you said hello.

Barney is eating a Tupperware container full of macaroni. I have watched him move his fork to his mouth over and over. He has poured himself a glass of tap water.

I stare at his hands; at the gray hairs growing on his knuckles, and his worn, fat fingers.

I zero in on his gold wedding ring.

He coughs a little as he swallows a spoon of his depressing lunch.

I look at his thinning hair, the wrinkles around his eyes, and at his unruly old-man eyebrows. I look at his eyes and think about how those have always been his eyes. Even when he was a little boy, that's what his eyes looked like.

"What's the worst thing you've ever done?" I ask him quietly.

"Pardon?" he replies, choking a little on his macaroni.

"What's the worst thing you've ever done?" I repeat.

"Oh." He looks at his food. "That's a big question. Why?"

"I was just wondering if you have any big regrets."

He hums. He snaps his fingers. "Yes. Yes, I wish I took better care of my teeth. I've spent some serious money on my teeth. Do you take good care of your teeth?"

I nod, even though I don't.

"Good," he says, spooning more food into his mouth.

A small black ant races across the table in front of Barney.

"An ant!" he shouts. He attempts to kill it with a clenched fist. He bangs on the table over the ant three times, but each time the ant remains unharmed and continues racing across the table.

I look at the macaroni that he has spilled on his shirt. I look at his unironed shirt, half tucked into his pants, and at how nothing he's wearing matches.

I watch him continue to attempt, and fail at, killing the ant.

This man doesn't know how to make himself lunch. He doesn't know how to clean his house. He doesn't know how to iron his clothing, and he literally cannot kill an ant.

If Barney didn't kill Grace, then who did?

I can see the top of my own head. This sensation is unsettling; however, maybe I should be grateful for it. It's sort of like a superpower, to float outside of your body. It's kind of like flying. People pay to see the world from an aerial perspective. That's why lookouts have coin-operated telescopes mounted on them. People climb mountains for the view. Window seats in airplanes sell out first. Maybe it's pessimistic of me to categorize this feeling as unsettling. Maybe my physical perspective has warped itself to encourage me to change my inner perspective.

Maybe I'm supposed to stop caring about who killed Grace.

Maybe I'm supposed to stop worrying about Eli having a drinking problem, and maybe I'm not supposed to care that my parents don't acknowledge it.

Maybe I need to stop thinking about all these negative things.

Maybe I need to look on the bright side.

"Hey, look on the bright side," I tell my body.

Hi Grace,

I haven't heard from you in a while. I hope all is well with you.

Things have been quiet around here. I've been spending most of my time knitting and tending to Lou.

Last Sunday, I paid my sister June a visit. She was just moved to a nursing home. Her son wanted her to move in with his family, but she requires too much care now. She seems comfortable in the facility, but she is a bit confused. She doesn't know what she's doing there. She keeps insisting that she's twenty-eight years old. It's not worth telling her otherwise. She is insistent that she just turned twenty-eight.

She mentioned places and names I haven't heard in years. Remember how we used to go to that drive-in? Remember that old department store on Elm Street? She keeps asking for things that I don't think exist anymore. She wants a glass of Tab. She wants to visit that cottage we owned in the eighties. She also mentioned Freddie Wilkens. Do you remember Freddie Wilkens? I wonder how he turned out.

It's funny what's stored in our minds that we don't realize. I don't think June would have remembered who Freddie was if I had asked her a decade ago, but somehow now it's as if he's fresh in her mind.

She also mentioned Rebecca Purst. Remember her? My heart fell when she said her name. June doesn't remember how her life turned out. Remember that terrible abusive man she ended up with? They lost all their kids because he was such a predator. She died of cancer quite young, remember? Such a sad story. She was a really sweet girl when we were all young. It's so strange to think of how our lives can be rerouted.

Remember that boy I was seeing before Jim? He ended up living in Costa Rica. Can you imagine how different my life would have been if I had stayed with him? I remember you used to talk about becoming a nun! Can you imagine?

It's fun to reminisce, isn't it? I wouldn't go back in time myself, though. As much as I miss the people, I wouldn't want to be in my twenties again. Is that strange of me? I suppose I'm content with how everything turned out and would hate to risk messing it up.

June actually didn't recognize me on Sunday. I said, "Hi, June, it's Rosemary" and she looked at me with bewilderment. When she finally recognized me, she shouted, "You look so old!" The nurse in the room was mortified before I laughed and said, "I am old!"

I hope you've been well, Grace.

Love,
Rosemary

For no apparent reason, my heartbeat is racing, and I am struggling to breathe.

Exercise mindfulness, I tell myself.

Look around and tell yourself what you see.

I see dust on my dresser.

I see socks on the floor.

I see clothes hanging in my closet.

I own six identical green hoodies. I don't know what possessed me to buy six green hoodies. I don't particularly love hoodies, let alone the color green. And why are all my jeans gray? I own a T-shirt with a drawing of an eye on it. I have another T-shirt with a tree stump drawn on it. Why? Is this my style? Why does the concept of style exist at all? Do I drape fabric over my body for the same reasons turtles have shells? Is it because I'm like a bird, and these are my feathers? Is it for some other reason? Why did I pick these colors? How much money did I spend on these things? What will happen to this stuff when I die? Will everything be donated and worn by people who I've never met? What if someone I have met wears them? What if they unknowingly walk around in their dead acquaintance's green hoodie? Which of these things did I buy from a thrift store? Did anyone already die in these things?

I see a dirty plate on my bedside table.

I see light coming in through my window.

I see my phone lighting up.

I look down. Eleanor texted me.

I was out of my mind when I dressed myself this morning. I over-thought my outfit to the point of absurdity. I somehow landed on pairing men's gray sweatpants with an XL gray T-shirt. I reasoned, through some mental acrobats, that these were my only acceptable pieces of clothing. Some hateful spirit possessed me into thinking I'd look ridiculous in anything else. It didn't occur to me that going to the movies with Eleanor meant that I was dressing for a date, and that poor Eleanor might find me—dressed like a large, gray blob—repugnant.

I am washing my hands in the theater's bathroom. The soap has already been rinsed from my skin, but I keep activating the automatic tap water and rewashing because it has just dawned on me that I should be ashamed of myself.

I exit the bathroom and wave a pruned hand at Eleanor, who has been patiently waiting outside for me. I am humbled by how starkly I contrast against her fashionable, put-together outfit. She's wearing jeans and a clean, tailored T-shirt. I squint at her face. Is she wearing mascara?

"Why are you looking at me like that?" she asks.

"Sorry," I reply, looking away.

The people around us probably think I am her strange charity-case cousin who she has benevolently taken out to the movies despite being discernibly strange and unattractive.

The movie theater employee rips our ticket stubs. He smiles warmly at fashionable Eleanor, but the heat in his expression cools when his eyes land on me.

We arrive at our aisle. I hand Eleanor my bag of popcorn and ask, "Can you please hold this for a second?" before I genuflect and make the sign of the cross.

She snorts. "What the hell are you doing?"

What the hell am I doing?

I don't like the movie we're watching, but I am still grinning up at the expansive screen. Eleanor finds the movie funny; she keeps snorting and slapping her knee. A thrill of happiness washes over me as I listen to her ridiculous chortle.

"Did you like it?" she asks as we exit the theater.

I throw my empty popcorn bag in the trash.

"Yes." I smile at her.

"Everything in your apartment is broken," Eleanor comments. "You have a cracked mirror, a broken cupboard, a broken TV remote. Your closet door doesn't shut. Your can opener doesn't work. I can't lock your window. Why don't you ever get anything fixed?" she asks. "Do you want me to help you get these things fixed?"

"Oh, no thank you, I'm on it," I lie.

"You're being quiet again," she adds. "Are you doing okay?"

I look into her face.

"I'm fine."

An unanticipated knock on my front door shocks me awake. I sit up, panicked, and then fumble to look at the time on my phone.

"Who is that?" Eleanor asks.

"I don't know," I reply, rubbing my eyes.

The person at my door knocks again.

I stumble to answer. I squint quickly at my reflection in the cracked bathroom mirror as I pass by it. My hair is matted at the back of my head, and there are lines indented on my cheeks from my pillowcases.

I open the door and find a police officer leaning on my doorframe.

I notice my neighbor has her door open. She is peering out to see what's going on.

"Hi there," the police officer greets me, his eyes scanning my face.

"Hi," I reply.

I am sitting in a sparse, gray room at the police station. Two police officers are sitting across the table from me. I was given a can of orange soda.

I am not sure why I was brought here. They asked me to come, and I said okay. I am trying to ignore my internal dialogue while it attempts to speculate why.

I feel my heart rate increase as I explore the various possibilities in my mind. I look around the room for something to distract myself with. The room is bare; there's very little to look at. There is a clock in the room. I can hear it tick.

Focusing on the *tick, tick, tick* is making me feel antsier.

I inhale and stare down at my hands. *Tick. Tick. Tick.* I focus on the lines in my knuckles. *Tick. Tick. Tick.* On the shape of my fingernails.

The officer who came to my door is filling out some paperwork. Without looking up at me, he asks: "I saw a pretty beat-up-looking car outside your apartment. Is that yours?"

"Yes," I answer, nodding.

I have not repaired my car since I was rear-ended at that stoplight.

"How'd it get so beat-up?" he asks, still looking down.

"I got in a car accident," I explain. "A woman hit me at a stoplight."

"Did you file a report?"

I shake my head.

"Why not?"

I stammer, "I'm n-not sure."

I didn't file a report because I didn't have the motivation to. I suspect that this rationale might be difficult for people with the drive to complete basic tasks to understand, so I am choosing not to share it. I would rather ignore the problem than go to a police station, fill out paperwork, and talk to an insurance company. The task of filing a report is more daunting to me than accepting the loss of my car.

The policeman tilts his head. "So, according to you, you were stopped at a red light, following all the rules, someone rammed into the back of your car—totaled your car—and you didn't so much as file a claim with your insurance company?"

"Yeah, I mean, I guess—I just haven't gotten to it yet," I lie.

"Do you drink, Gilda?"

"Alcohol?" I clarify for some reason. My existence as a living human person implies that I drink water and other liquids.

I correct myself quickly, "No, I d-don't drink."

"You don't drink at all?"

"I drink a little, but I wouldn't call myself a drinker, no."

"Did you have much to drink before that accident?"

"No."

"Nothing at all to drink that day?"

"No, I-I don't think so. It was like eight a.m."

"So, you don't remember?"

"Am I a suspect for something?" I ask. "Do you think that I did something—"

The men hesitate before replying.

"Did you know Grace Moppett well?"

"Did I know Grace well?" I repeat, registering the question. "No, I d-didn't know her at all."

"You never met?"

"No. I started working at the church after her—"

"This is your opportunity to be honest, Gilda."

"What? I am being honest."

"May I ask," the officer softens his voice, "why are you so nervous, then?" He leans forward. "You've been stuttering and fidgeting since you came in here. You look pale, and you are breathing irregularly—"

"I'm always like this," I assert, slamming a pointed finger on the table in front of me.

The policemen have left me alone in the sparse room to stew.

I am listening again to the *tick, tick, tick* of the clock.

I feel like I am outside my body; I feel like I am watching myself from the ceiling. I am staring down at the top of my head.

I look awful. My clothing is wrinkled and I'm slouching.

Why am I slouching so much?

Sit up.

You look like a criminal.

Sit up!

One of the officers returns to the room.

I sit up.

He is not looking at me. I try to make eye contact with him, but he is avoiding it. His face looks pink. Is he blushing? Is it normal to feel like the cop questioning you is shy?

"Are you gay, Gilda?" he asks.

"What?" I didn't expect that question.

He waits for my response.

"Yes."

He looks in my eyes. "That's kind of curious, isn't it? What is a gay girl doing working for a Catholic church?"

"What is anyone doing, doing anything?" I reply.

He contorts his eyebrows. "What?"

I don't say anything.

I once again feel myself begin to float out of my body, up to the ceiling.

He continues, "It's strange for a gay girl to be working for a Catholic church, don't you think? It's also strange that you haven't filed a report for your car. You seem off, okay? I'm concerned. You're coming across very strange."

I am watching his mouth open and close. Open and close. Open and close.

I hover above myself while he continues to tell me that I seem strange.

I do seem strange.

I watch myself struggle to form a facial expression that will not exaggerate how strange I seem. It is difficult in response to this subject to produce any expression that isn't weird. I can't smile, for example, that would be weirder. Maybe I should nod.

"Do you understand why I'm concerned?" he asks, contorting his eyebrows again.

Nod.

Nod.

Nod! I shout down at myself.

I nod.

I exit the police station in a stupor. I feel detached from reality. Every step I take forward is deliberate. I feel like I am operating my body like it's a vehicle. I am conscious of when I blink, and of when I inhale.

I look for my signal switch as I turn, before I remember that my body is not a car and does not have a blinker. I look around myself, hyperaware of the detail in the outdoors surrounding me. I see the sharp needles in the pine trees. Small specks of rust in the cars that drive by.

"Who is Giuseppe?" Eleanor asks me as I enter my apartment.

"You're still here?" I toss my keys on the table beside my door. I expected her to have left by now.

She's sitting on my bed with my phone in her lap.

I pause. "Did you look through my phone—"

"Do you have a boyfriend?" she asks.

"No."

Her bottom lip protrudes, and she covers her face with her hands.

"I'm sorry—" I start.

"I don't think you care about me at all!" she cries through her fingers. "I knew something was off, but I didn't expect this! You've been hiding that you have a boyfriend this whole time? Has it been the whole time?"

"No, Eleanor, I don't have a boyfriend," I explain. "This is just a misunderstanding. I really—"

"I read your text messages," she says. "He calls you pet names, and you obviously hang out all the time. I can see in your call history that he calls you a lot. You're obviously dating this guy."

"I'm really not," I try to explain. "This is kind of a funny story. I—"

"At least be honest with me now, Gilda." She uncovers her face.

"I am being honest—"

"Half the time you don't reply to me when I text you!" she cries. "I feel like you're not even half-interested in me. You give me these bleak little moments to string me along, making me think you like me. I have never felt more pathetic in my life. You put in no effort. I don't know why I keep trying to talk to you—"

"I'm really sorry—"

"Why do you talk to me at all?" she asks. "You obviously don't even like me."

"I do like you," I tell her.

"Why do you act like this, then?"

"Something's wrong with me."

"Tell me one thing you like about me. I bet you can't name one thi—"

"I like how loudly you laugh," I announce immediately.

She glares. "What kind of stupid reason—"

"It's not stupid."

She shakes her head and starts to stand up.

"I'm really sorry," I say again.

She leaves.

I text Eleanor Hi, but she doesn't reply.

    Hi.

    Hi.

    Hi.

    I scroll up in our text messages. I reread our past conversations. I notice how often she texts me, and how often I don't reply. I rarely ever write more than two words to her. I almost never initiate the conversation.

    Hi, I write again.

Cold wind touches my face. It's below freezing, and the air is burning my skin. I can barely smell or hear; all my senses are muted because I feel frozen. I touch my numb left arm with my numb right hand. I sink deeply into a blip of awareness that one day I will never feel anything again.

I arrive four hours late to work. I enter the church cautiously, hoping to evade the condemnatory glares of any prying parishioners.

    I slept in. My alarm went off, but it didn't wake me up. I slept through three hours of beeping. As an aftereffect, I now have a headache with a pulse, and inexorable anxiety regarding what else I am liable to sleep through.

    The church phone is blinking, meaning I have missed calls. There are also two emails in the church email inbox.

    I open the emails first. They're both from Rosemary.

The first email contains a recipe for hazelnut fudge.

"You'll love this one, Grace!" she writes.

The second email contains photos of her family reunion. She included a note in her email saying, "I just wanted to share a glimpse of my family with you, old friend."

I look through the photos. I verify that Rosemary is, as I suspected, a weathered old woman. She is wearing an apron in most of her photos, and she is laughing in every single shot.

That's nice that she's so happy, I think. It's nice that anyone is capable of happiness, really. It's amazing that the human body can produce the neurochemicals required to feel joy. I am disappointed to have been served so little of those chemicals—but I am glad nonetheless that this old woman has enough dopamine, and oxytocin, and whatever else she needs to sustain that smile—despite the fact that her husband is dead, her teeth are probably fake, and all human life is fundamentally inconsequential.

"Did the cops meet with you?" Barney asks me after materializing behind me like Jacob Marley.

"Yes," I answer, quickly closing the window on my computer—which was open to an incriminating web page titled: "How to Get Your Girlfriend to Forgive You."

"Why?" I ask. "Did they meet with you too?"

"Yes." He nods.

I feel the blood rush out of my face. I look up at him. Did they tell him I'm gay?

"I'm afraid they might be incompetent," he says.

"Why?" I ask, my palms sweating.

Does he think they're incompetent because they told him I'm gay?

"All they did was ask me about you!" He shakes his head. "They seem to think they need to look into you! You didn't even know her. They're inept."

"What did they say about me?"

"I don't remember," he says. "They had a bunch of questions. They asked things about your temperament and your behavior. They asked me if I noticed anything odd about you. They're incompetent—"

"So they didn't tell you why they find me suspicious?" I ask.

"No." He shakes his head. "I have no idea why they find you suspicious. Do you?"

I shake my head, wide-eyed. "No, I have no idea. That's why I wondered if they gave you any reason. So, they didn't? They didn't give you any reason why they find me suspicious? They didn't say there's something queer about me, or—"

I stop. Why did I use the word "queer"?

He shakes his head. "No, I think they're just grasping at straws. You shouldn't worry."

My arms are shaking.

"I'm not worried," I say.

When I discovered the corpse of my pet rabbit, I wondered if she'd died because of me. I wondered if I'd fed her weeds that were poison, or if I'd scared her. I knew rabbits could be frightened to death. I thought maybe I'd done something. Maybe I'd killed her.

I haven't eaten anything today. I do not have the motivation to leave my house to buy groceries, and I can't face interacting with a delivery person.

I also don't want to spend money. I am afraid I am about to be outed at the church and fired.

I open my fridge. I contemplate eating baking soda.

I open my cupboards. I grab a bag of communion wafers. Grabbing these unveils the box of Thin Mints Eleanor bought me. A surge of sadness overwhelms me at the sight of them. I feel tears in my eyes.

I slam the cupboard shut to conceal the cookies from my view. I slam it so hard that it breaks off its other hinge and crashes to the floor. A bowl on my counter crashes to the ground with it. The cupboard lands partly on my foot.

I scream, "Fuck!" and grip my injured foot.

I scream, "Fuck! Fuck! Fuck!" over and over at increasingly lower volumes as I adjust to life with my new injury.

Someone knocks on my door.

I hobble to answer it.

My neighbor is standing in my doorframe, clutching her robe tight to her body.

"I heard a noise," she says, peering into my apartment.

"Yeah, my cupboard broke off its hinge," I tell her.

She sees the broken cupboard, and eyes the broken mirror in my bathroom.

"You can call the landlord to fix those things, you know," she tells me, furrowing her brow.

"Yes, I know, thank you," I reply as I shut the door.

I keep applying and reapplying moisturizer to my hands. Every time I look at them, I am shocked by how old they look. My skin must be dry, I tell myself. I don't think these are really my hands.

Does dying feel more like falling asleep, or like suffocating? Does it feel like something else?

I wonder if it might be better to die through some violence to avoid really experiencing the sensation of death.

I think about Flop dying in her hutch. I think about the innocent thoughts of a flower-eating rabbit being consumed by the bleak and ominous reality of her death as she becomes incapable of breathing and her blood stops moving.

I think about Grace, wide-eyed and waiting for her heart to stop beating. I think about her inhaling and exhaling and stopping. Stop.

I think about myself.

"Why are the cops calling us, Gilda?" my dad asks me sternly via a voice mail.

"Why am I getting calls about my adult daughter from the police?"

"They asked to meet with me and your mother to discuss you."

"Do you know why the police want to discuss you?"

"Your mother and I are concerned, Gilda."

"Call me back."

I've got it all figured out. Humans are cancer. If we were to look at earth from a distance, we would look like white blood cells, and watching our evolution would be like watching cancer spread.

"Your mother and me are meeting with the police this afternoon, Gilda."

"I would love to talk to you before going, to get some insight from you regarding what's going on here."

"Are you okay?"

"Are you involved in something?"

"Call me back, okay?"

"We're worried."

I've got it all figured out. We're a parasite. Other animals on this planet coexist with nature. We don't; we're like scabies. Tiny mites covering the outer layer of earth, burrowing into it, infecting it. We are like tapeworm.

* * *

"We met with the police, Gilda. Pick up."

"Are you going to call us back?"

"Your mother is beside herself. Are you a criminal?"

"We told them you've never been crazy. We said you're a normal, healthy person."

"Why aren't you picking up? This is serious."

"They asked us about your relationship with an old woman."

"Did you know an old lady named Grace?"

"Call us back."

I've got it all figured out. We're bacteria. The universe is probably just a thread in some larger thing's eyelash, and we exist on it the way microorganisms exist in our eyes. We're like skin flora.

"Pick up, Gilda. I'm serious. We're worried."

"Are you getting these?"

"Did you lose your phone?"

"Call me back."

"Are you really working for a Catholic church?"

"Why would you do that?"

"Are you doing drugs, or something?"

"Have you really been going to the hospital every week? Why do the police think you're crazy?"

"Call me back, okay? Call me back."

I am eating an unsliced loaf of bread like an unsupervised goat in a bakery. I am biting off hunks and swigging back wine to help the carby mouthfuls travel through my throat into the crypts of my body like I am Christ at his Last Supper. This is, based on my understanding, how to treat your body like a temple.

My dad keeps calling me. I can't look at anything on my phone because his calls interrupt and take over the screen.

I bought this loaf of bread thinking I would turn it into sandwiches, or something. It occurred to me, however, that I don't own any meat, cheese, or lettuce. It also occurred to me that the sandwiches would be for me, and me alone. Why should I exert myself assembling sandwiches for just me?

It is disgusting that I eat. I consume sustenance while other living things starve. I fill landfills with wrappers and trash. It's unforgivable.

I stole the wine from the church. I don't know whether wine comes pre-consecrated or not. If this wine is the blood of God, I hope it poisons me. I hope God and Jesus are real and that my consumption of this blood wine is so unholy that I get smited right here and now.

"Hi," I text Eleanor.

She doesn't reply.

"Hi," I text again.

I am looking at myself in the mirror. Sometimes, when I look in a mirror long enough, I become very aware that I am an animal. I think about how if aliens came to earth and saw humans, we would probably look like apes to them. Sometimes I think we'd look uglier than apes because we have no fur. We are sort of like pig-apes with manes. Other times, I think maybe we look better than apes. Girls with nice hair and big eyes might be good-looking, like horses. If humans didn't wear clothes, we'd be worse-looking in most cases, I think. I believe that all bodies are beautiful philosophically—it's beautiful that our bodies work, and let us taste, and move, and do all that—but visually, I think you'd have to be nuts not to think that a lot of naked bodies are unsightly. I don't know whether I am unsightly or not. Sometimes I look in the mirror and try really hard to see whether I am ugly, or pretty, or somewhere in between, but I always end up thinking about how I am an animal, and how I just look like a pig-ape.

My hands look like they did when I was a kid, I swear. My fingers are short, and my fingernails are all chewed up. My skin is fresher and smoother-looking. I have a pink Band-Aid on my thumb. There is sand under my fingernails. I flex my knuckles. I make a fist.

I blink again and see my hands as they look today. Longer fingers. Rougher skin. There is a scar on my wrist.

I flip my palms around, examining my knuckles. I think about what my hands will look like when I am old. I think about age spots and wrinkles. I think about how, despite aging, my hands will still always be these exact hands. Barring some grisly disfigurement, I will be entombed with these things.

I am excessively aware of the way my hands are sitting in my lap. I keep repositioning how I have linked my fingers. The woman beside me isn't aware of her hands at all. She keeps accidentally touching me with hers. Maybe she is aware of her hands, and has no personal boundaries, but I don't think so. I think everyone else on this bus is completely out of tune with their hands.

"Look at your hands!" I hear myself demand of a stranger loudly.

"What?" The stranger looks at me, alarmed. I realize as her eyes connect with mine that I have just behaved oddly.

She distances herself from me while I struggle to make up a sane explanation for my request. I can't think of one. I end up saying nothing.

* * *

The police want to talk to me about you, Eli texts me.
Should I go? Did you do something? Are you okay?
Mom and dad are freaking out. Can you call them?
I can see you're getting these.
Text me back.
Are you okay?
We think you're a murder suspect.
Did you know an old lady named Grace?

How could anyone think I could kill someone? I can't even kill myself.

I close my eyes and focus on the darkness behind my eyelids.

Black.

I feel outside of my body.

"What motive could you possibly have to kill a woman?" I ask myself out loud.

I am standing on a bridge above a road and some water. I am watching cars beneath me run over the concrete.

What motive could I have to do anything?

I could jump; I could ruin everyone's day down there. I could absolutely traumatize some motorist on their way to wherever they're going.

I tighten my eyes closed harder.

Black.

Look at your hands.

Do you remember everything you've ever done with your hands?

Every moment exists in perpetuity regardless of whether it's remembered. What has happened has happened; it occupies that moment in time forever. You blaze through moments all your life, forgetting things, and becoming ages older, until you forget everything.

I am staring intensely at my own hands. I am zeroing in on the wrinkles in my knuckles and the veins beneath my skin.

I will never have any other hands but these.

It's bizarre that a body can be animated one second, and then turn lifeless permanently.

Black.

When we die our bodies are garbage. We rot.

Black.

I can't believe that I'm alive.

Black.

I can't believe that I can believe anything.

"What are you doing?" someone shouts at me from their car.

I hear ringing. I look over the bridge into the black water.

"Is she fishing?"

"She doesn't have any fishing gear."

"Are you okay?"

"Hey! Are you okay?"

"I'm thinking about fishing," I announce.

I am thinking about how it must feel for a hook to snag your cheek and for your body to be dragged into a space where you can't breathe.

What if someone outside earth thinks of humans as fish?

What if aliens drag us out where our heads will pop?

"Are you okay?" he asks me again.

I look into the car. There are two teenaged boys in it.

"Come over here," one of them says. "You're making us nervous. Are you feeling sad?"

I look into their faces. They are both very young. They were little boys a couple years ago, I can tell.

"I'm okay," I tell them. "I just went out for a walk. Thank you for asking me. That's very nice of you. You must be nice."

"Can we call someone for you?" he asks.

"Yes." I nod. "Please call 911."

*   *   *

"You're just a little depressed and anxious," the doctor tells me. "Do you think you're a danger to yourself?"

Yes.

"No." I shake my head. "I'm just feeling a little bit off."

"We all have those days," he replies. "You're probably just adjusting to your new SSRIs. I can send a referral to a psychiatrist for you, though."

"Thank you."

"Now, you've had this cast on you for two weeks longer than you were supposed to." He knocks on my cast.

"I forgot to come get it off," I explain as he prepares to saw it off.

I watch as Eli's drawing is cut in two, and my arm emerges from the cast like a fat, overdue chick from its shell.

I might be a robot. My hands are cold, and moving my fingers requires that I really put thought into it. I am aware of when I blink.

I blink repeatedly.

Black. Black. Black.

Someone is knocking on my door.

I roll over and listen to the knock, knock, knock.

"Gilda, it's me—it's Eli."

"Answer the door. Are you in there? Hello?"

"Did you do something, Gilda? Are you okay?"

"Can I help you?"

"Can you hear me?"

"Hello?"

"Do you need me to lie for you?" he whispers through the crack by the doorframe.

"Tell me what to say and I'll say it, okay?"

"If you're in trouble, I'll help you, don't worry."

"Are you in there?"
"Hello?"
"Hello?"

After sitting catatonically on my bedroom floor for hours, I stand up, gather every dish in my house, and throw them against my wall. I had to throw a cup twice for it to break.

When I was a kid, I was obsessed with animals. I exclusively took out books about animals from the library. I subscribed to magazines about dogs and horses. All I talked about were the fascinating facts that I unearthed about various pets.

Basenjis are the only dogs that do not bark.

Siamese cats have fur that turns darker in the parts of their bodies where they feel cold.

All puppies are born blind and toothless.

My family and I were sitting at the kitchen table, where I had just blown out all eight of the candles on my birthday cake, when my mom asked me, "So, what did you wish for?"

I almost admitted my wish before I caught myself and said, "I can't say, or it won't come true."

At that point, my dad reached under the kitchen table and emerged with a white metal cage. He placed the cage in front of me, and I was stunned.

After a moment of gaping into the cage, at Flop's twitchy nose and cotton-ball tail, I gasped, "Am I dreaming?"

I can't tell if I am dreaming or not. Am I in a store? I feel like I am on a movie set. Everything is familiar to me, but it's different. It feels like a plastic backdrop. It is all off and sort of otherworldly.

"Are you lost?" a blurry-looking woman asks me.

I stare at her.

She hesitates. "Are you okay, miss? Do you need any help?"

"I'm fine," I lie.

St. Rigobert's is a large building. It has a steeple with a small cross on top of it. It is covered in decorative carvings; little grotesques and gargoyles. The buildings surrounding it are all modern. It stands out in the skyline like a tall goth kid in a class photo.

I haven't gone to work for days.

I am standing on the lawn of the church, staring up into its large rose windows. I think about what's behind that glass. I think of the statues of Jesus and angels. I think about Jeff praying, and making coffee. I think about the old people bumbling around the pews, praying their rosaries, planning funerals. I think of the incense smell and the organ playing.

There is a statue of Jesus outside. It's perched above the front door like an owl. Jesus is wearing a crown and holding up one of his hands. I look into his stone face, and I swear his lips move.

"Why aren't you inside?" the statue asks. "You're supposed to be working, aren't you?"

"Is that what I'm supposed to be doing?" I ask.

"You said you're not much of a drinker, didn't you?"

The police asked me to come back to the station for more questioning.

I am hungover. I can smell God's blood in my sweat.

I nod.

"You smell like you've been drinking," one of the officers remarks.

"I have been," I reply.

They eye each other.

I am sitting across the room from myself, watching myself, like I am watching a weird ape in a zoo.

"Are you okay?" one of the officers asks me.

"I'm fine," my body replies as a reflex.

"Are you sure?" she asks, frowning at me.

"I have a headache, I think," I say.

"You think?" she repeats me. "You don't know whether you have a headache?"

"I feel very detached from myself physically right now," I admit. "My mind feels foggy. I can't really tell if my head hurts or not. I think it does."

She stares at me.

"Why do you think you feel that way?" she asks quietly.

"I'm not sure," I reply.

"Can you tell me what you did yesterday?" a police officer asks me.

I try to recall what I did.

I think I went to the store. I think I ate a loaf of bread.

No, wait—that was a few days ago.

"I don't remember," I answer.

"You don't remember?"

"I didn't do anything eventful," I explain. "Nothing worth remembering."

"Nothing worth remembering?" the police officer repeats me. "That's interesting. Tell me, what makes something worth remembering?"

I think.

I answer, "I guess nothing."

"There's nothing that makes a day worth remembering?" the police officer clarifies.

"If you really think about it, no," I say.

He tilts his head. "Would you say that you've got a clear memory of the recent events that have happened to you, Gilda?" he asks. "Do you ever forget things you did?"

I blaze through moments all my life, forgetting things, and becoming ages older, until I forget everything.

"Did you really not know Grace? Are you sure?"

He puts a picture of Grace down on the table between us.

"You're a good liar, aren't you, Gilda?"

"None of your family knew you were working at St. Rigobert's."

"No one at St. Rigobert's knew you weren't Catholic."

"Do you lie to yourself, too, Gilda?"

"Are you sure you're not repressing what happened?"

I look down at the photograph on the table. I look at Grace's white hair, and at her wrinkly, smiling mouth.

I think about rhinos, and about all the things on earth that would be considered fantasy if we didn't know they were real. I think about how reality and make-believe are blended together because nothing matters, and it's all illogical. Maybe all of this is a dream. Maybe I don't exist at all.

I put my hands inside the murky puddles in my mind, and in the dark grottoes in my stomach, and feel around. I pull out the terrible truth, which is: How would I know if I killed someone? Maybe I did.

I think I'm crazy.

"What are you thinking about?" the officer asks me.

"Rhinos," I tell him through tears.

I watched my dad dig a hole in the backyard from my window. He was burying Flop.

My mom saw me peeking over the windowsill and said, "Honey, don't watch that. Go watch cartoons with your brother, or something."

I ignored her and continued to watch until my dad lowered the shoebox casket into the hole and shoveled dirt over it.

After everyone went to bed that night, I snuck downstairs. I kneeled beside the dirt patch that Flop's body was under, and cried alone beneath the moon.

"Do you know who that is?"

I am standing behind two-way glass. An old woman wearing a pale pink T-shirt with cartoon cats tossing yarn is sitting on the other side of the glass.

I start to say no, before I recognize her.

It's Rosemary.

"That's Rosemary Reeves," the police officer says. "She's traveled all the way here from out of town to talk to us. Do you have any idea why we asked her to come here?"

I don't reply. I stare at Rosemary's face. She's brushed pink blush across her weathered cheeks. She has mauve lipstick on.

"She doesn't drive anymore, so her daughter had to drive her here," the police officer continues. "She took a day off work to get her mom here. Isn't that nice?"

I don't reply. I look at her folded hands. She's wearing her wedding ring.

"We invited her because we looked at the church computer and found that you've been emailing her, pretending to be Grace. Can you talk to me about that, Gilda? Can you explain why you would do that?"

I look down at my hands. They're sweating. I feel very inside of my body.

"Gilda?"

"We noticed a lot of strange things," the other officer continues. "We noticed the church Twitter page likes a lot of inappropriate tweets, and that the browsing history of the computer includes searches such as Grace's name, and searches related to murder."

I stop listening to the officer as the grotesque image of Rosemary learning that her friend is dead flashes before my eyes. I imagine her happy, pleasant expression deteriorating.

I feel my chest tighten. I feel very inside of my body.

"You've been lying to an old woman, pretending to be Grace. Why?"

I can't stand imagining Rosemary finding out about Grace.

"Are you going to tell her Grace is dead?" I turn and ask the police officers.

"Yes. Of course we're going to tell her."

"Don't do it," I request. "Don't tell her."

"Why have you been lying to this poor old woman?"

"Please don't tell her," I repeat, tears now building up in my eyes.

"Are you trying to finesse her? What is your endgame?"

"No. I just don't want her to know—"

"What is your motive, Gilda? What are you trying to do?"

"I just don't want her to be sad." I start crying.

Something pitch-black inside me overtakes my body. I am overcome with a sense of absolute hopelessness. The lights in the room go black. Did someone shoot me? I feel blind. I am on the ground.

Jeff is crying in his office. Stop.

Mittens is burning in a house fire. Stop.

Eli's skin is turning yellow. Stop.

Eleanor keeps giving me Thin Mints. Stop.

Ingrid bought me a stuffed pig. Stop.

Eli painted me a picture of Flop. Stop.

He offered to lie to the police for me. Stop.

I feel so profoundly inside of myself, I can't stand it. I can feel my life force rattling inside my bones like a rabid dog in a pen trying to escape where it's been trapped.

Am I screaming?

"What's wrong with her?"

People are touching me.

"Why are you so upset?"

"Something is wrong with her."

* * *

I have been put in a jail cell. I am sitting in a concrete room with a toilet. There is nothing for me to do in here but look at the gray wall in front of me, at the imperfections in the concrete. There's a crack running down the wall.

I don't know if I am just being confined in here, or if I am actually in jail.

There is a single ant in this cell with me. She's searching the ground with her feelers for food. I watch her zigzag across the ground, sniffing out something to eat.

I put my cheek against the dirty floor and look at her up close. I look at the bows in her thin legs, and at her small monster face. I wonder why an ant would live inside a police station, when she could live anywhere. She could go outside. She could live in a restaurant, or a forest.

Maybe she doesn't know that. Maybe it would be too hard for her to get there.

I think about putting her in my pocket and feeding her bits of my food.

I wonder how long ants live.

"I can't keep you as a pet," I whisper to her out loud.

I can't have a pet for the same reason I don't want to make friends, or get close to people. It's not just because they'll die someday. It's also because I am a bad pet owner. I can't muster the energy required to be a positive part of anyone's life. I can't even muster the energy to apologize for that.

I look down at my hands. The ant is crawling near my fingers.

"I don't have anything to offer you. I don't have any food," I tell her. "They patted me down before bringing me in here. There's nothing in my pockets."

I demonstrate that to the ant. I turn my pockets inside out.

I am surprised when crumbs fall out.

*   *   *

"What did you learn in therapy?" I asked Eleanor.

We hadn't met yet. We were still messaging on the dating app. It was after midnight. The glow of my cell phone was illuminating my face on my pillow. I hadn't felt engaged in any conversation I'd had in months, but I felt engaged talking to her. I was interested in what she had to say. Every time I got a notification that she had messaged me, I felt alert.

She said, "I learned that there is a circular connection between thoughts, behaviors, and feelings."

She said, "It works like a feedback loop. What we think affects how we feel and act. If I feel bad because I think I'm not a good friend, for example, I might avoid people, which will then make me feel worse. If, instead of avoiding people, I visit a friend, that behavior will affect my thoughts about how good a friend I am, which will in turn affect my feelings and my behavior in the future."

I got the impression Eleanor was more upbeat and optimistic than I was. When she talked about therapy, I thought it might work for someone like her, but it probably wouldn't for me.

"Did it work?" I asked her.

She said, "Yeah."

"Drink that glass of water," a guard instructs me.

"Do I get a phone call?" I ask, ignoring the glass of water.

"Sure," she replies. "You can have as many as you like."

"I thought I only got one."

"That's just in the movies."

"Eleanor, I don't want to bother you. I understand why you're ghosting me. I just have to tell you how badly I feel about upsetting you. I really feel terrible. I must be self-centered, or something. This might sound weird, but I can't face that I disappointed someone who bought me Thin Mints. I know that sounds stupid. Something is wrong with me. I feel like I am a robot, or something. Does that make sense? I can't concentrate. I can't say this properly. Sometimes I feel like the only escape I have is becoming completely apathetic to everything, or dying. I just don't want to upset people. I realize that's ironic because I upset you. And I'm probably blowing this way out of proportion. You probably don't care about this that much. I'm someone you half dated, who you had a subpar experience with—I'm probably freaking you out. I feel like I have to explain it. You should have stopped talking to me way before you found out about Giuseppe—who I really am not dating, by the way—but it doesn't matter. I realize looking back that I never got you Thin Mints. I don't even know if you like them. It's my fault. I wish I were nicer to you. I'm sorry."

"Jeff, I've been lying to you. The day you hired me, I wasn't coming for a job. I came in response to an advertisement for therapy. I've been pretending to be Catholic to avoid admitting that to you, and because I needed a job. I shouldn't have done that, and I regret it. I want you to know that I'm really sorry. I know that you forgive everything because of who you are, but you don't have to forgive me for this."

"Giuseppe, I should have never strung you along, or lashed out at you. I am not who you think I am. It was hard for me to be around you because I resent how happy and well-adjusted you seem, and I'm too critical. I don't know if you'll understand this—but I keep finding myself staring at my hands. I keep thinking about how I'll never have any other hands but the ones I do. Do you know what I mean? I can't really explain it. I guess I'd rather you didn't get it. I wish I'd never thought of it. I know I don't make sense. I'm just calling to say that I'm sorry for lying to you and for making you feel bad. I was trying to do the opposite originally, but I'm not good at it."

*   *   *

"Barney, I'm who your daughter saw outside your house. I wasn't try-ing to rob you. I was spying on you because I thought maybe you were the one who killed Grace. I know you didn't. I'm sorry for thinking you might have, and for skulking around your house. Listen, I have no right to ask you to do anything—I've been lying to you, I'm an atheist, and I'm gay—but I really want you to turn your calendar to the current month. Do you know what I mean? I heard your wife died, and I imagine that maybe she used to change the calendar. You've got to change it now, okay? It's sad and dark, Barney, but you just have to change that calendar yourself."

"Mom and Dad, I don't know if you'll remember this, but once I pretended that the road in front of our house was an ocean. I drew chalk drawings of starfish, whales, and a raft on it. I lay down with my eyes closed on the chalk-drawn raft in the middle of the street, waiting to be run over. You came out screaming and sent me to my room. I think about that all the time. Do you know what I mean? I understand wanting to pretend everything is okay when it is not. I get why you do that with Eli. I think it would be better for us to address it, though. I'm afraid I might be insane. If I could pick—I'd rather you never worry about anything. Do you know what I mean?"

"Eli, listen to me. Stop drinking. Please. Be whatever you want to be—if that's what you're so sad about. I want you to do whatever you want to. Wear whatever you want to. Grow your hair out. Listen—because this is really important. We are all just floating in space, okay? Think about it, we're just ghosts inside skeletons, inside skin bags, floating on a rock in space. If there is anything that would make you feel happy to do, please do it."

* * *

"You're free to go." A police officer opens the door to my human cage.

Moments ago, after ten hours of holding it in, I finally peed in front of the guard.

"I'm free to go?" I clarify, confused.

"We know you didn't do it," she explains.

"What? How?"

"We searched the church," she answers. "We found something that proves you didn't."

"What did you find?"

"A note. It was folded in a romance novel inside Grace's old desk."

Dear whoever might find this,

My mother took her life when I was sixteen. She didn't say goodbye to me before, and she didn't leave a note. I wanted to find a note from her so badly, I kept my hopes up that someday I would. I would open books in used bookstores, hoping, somehow, they were her old books, that she had secretly hidden a note inside of.

I am hiding this for anyone who might wish to find a note from me.

I am not going the same way my mother did, though I am taking my life. I am eighty-six years old, and it is my turn to go. I am ready for my trip to what is after this.

If I didn't say goodbye to you, goodbye. I have had a wonderful life. I don't know that I could have been happier. I am so grateful to have been alive.

Grace

part five

Easter

I am one of 7.53 billion people on a planet orbiting one of 100 billion stars in one galaxy among billions of galaxies in an ever-expanding universe.

"I'm Gilda," I say.

It's easy for me to accept that I am bacteria, or a parasite, or cancer. It's easy for me to accept that my life is trivial, and that I am a speck of dust. It is hard for me to accept that for the people around me, however. It's hard for me to accept that my brother's life doesn't matter, or that old women who die don't matter, or even that rabbits or cats don't matter. I feel simultaneously intensely insignificant and hyperaware of how important everyone is.

"I don't know what to say," I tell Rosemary. "I'm sorry. This was so bizarre of me. I had no right to keep it from you that your friend died, or to send you any emails pretending to be her. I don't know what's wrong with me—"

Rosemary touches the top of my hand from across the table.

I look at her mouth. She's smiling.

"Grace would have thought this whole thing was hilarious," she tells me.

She laughs. "I forgive you, Gilda. It's okay."

A strange, sad relief overwhelms me.

"She would have?" I ask, my throat tightening.

Rosemary nods.

"Are you just saying that?" I ask.

She shakes her head, still laughing. "She'd have thought this was hysterical."

I hesitate. "Are you just being nice to me because I'm crazy?"

"You're not really crazy, are you?" she asks, touching the top of my hand again.

"I don't know. I might be. I haven't been feeling well lately," I explain. "I've been struggling with feeling like nothing matters."

One day I will die, and one day everyone I know will die. One day everyone I don't know will die. One day every animal and plant on this planet will die. One day earth itself will die, and one day all of humanity, and all relics of human life.

"Do you ever think about how small we are? Do you ever think about space?" I ask her. "I keep fixating on dying, and thinking about why we exist, and how sad everything is. I've been starting to think that the only thing that matters is that people feel happy, and I was trying to spare you some sadness. I keep noticing so many people aren't happy, and it's been making me feel sick. I keep looking at everyone and thinking, *Oh my God, I just want them to smile.* I keep staring at people's mouths. Do you know what I mean? I keep thinking, *Oh my God, I just wish you were smiling—*"

Rosemary nods. "Yes, I have thought about that too." She looks at my mouth. "Now, do you ever think about how people might wish that for you?"

The police station buzzes as I am escorted toward the exit. I hear an officer's voice say: "She was performing under-the-table assisted suicides."

There is a TV on in the room, broadcasting the news.

A blond reporter is holding a microphone. "Laurie claims she is not alone in doing this. She alleges that in most hospitals, nurses and physicians offer hints and euphemisms for patients to interpret about ending their lives. She claims she chose to be blunt and honest with her patients. She allegedly offered to help them end their lives with their consent."

"She confessed to giving some of her patients the medication they needed to do it independently in their homes. Grace Moppet and Rita Davis supposedly injected themselves. We've been informed that Grace may have left a suicide note that seems to corroborate this. The note allegedly states that Grace was ready for the so-called curtains to be drawn."

The TV shows a clip of Laurie reading a statement to a crowd.

"I don't think anyone's goal should be to live as long as they can," she states into a small throng of microphones. "I am not ashamed of my involvement in the lives or the deaths of Rita, Alfred, Li, Grace, or Geraldine. I hope my admittance of this sheds light on the fact that none of this has to be so bad."

I exit the police station. It's midafternoon. My eyes had adjusted to the dimness indoors. It's sunny, and hard for me to see outside. I have one eye closed and one eye squinting. I put a hand over my eyebrows to create a shadow. I squint through my watering eye at the last heaps of snow in the shadowy corners beneath trees, and at the yellow dandelions in the grass.

When I was a kid, I picked every dandelion I crossed paths with. I collected carrot peels and apple cores. I would pocket berries, cucumbers, and lettuce from my own plate. I would combine all of what I collected into a large bowl to feed as a salad to my rabbit Flop.

When it was sunny out, I would put her cage on the lawn. She would bite blades of grass and clover and lie on her side. I remember her furry white stomach moving up and down in the sunshine. I remember her falling asleep.

I built obstacle courses for her out of cardboard boxes and newspaper. I taught her how to come when I called her, and to stand when I had a treat.

I remember she would hop around in circles in her hutch when she saw me. I remember she made clucking, purring noises.

I wake up.
    I make my bed.
    I take a shower.
    I comb my hair.
    I brush my teeth.
    I floss.
    I get dressed.
    I put my socks on.
    I put ice in a clean glass with water.
    I put bread in my toaster.
    I set out a plate.
    I cut an apple into slices.
    I take the toast out of the toaster and butter it.
    I cut it into four pieces.
    I sit down at my table and eat.
    I rinse the dishes I used and put them away.
    I run a dishcloth over the counter.
    I put my shoes on.
    I look in the mirror.
    I leave my house.
    I walk outside.

A thrill of happiness washes over me as I listen to Eleanor's ridiculous chortle.

We are sitting on the steps outside my apartment, waiting for my landlord. He is coming with a repairman to fix my cupboards and my bathroom mirror.

"Think about it," I tell her. "If we discovered a dandelion on a planet besides earth, that would be astounding. The fact that dandelions exist on our planet is therefore astounding."

Eleanor is inspecting a dandelion, nodding. "You're right."

"If we discovered pigs on another planet," I continue, "we would think of those pigs as incredible beings. Imagine if we found apes. If we found apes on another planet, we would think of them as the most remarkable, precious aliens—"

"Did you hear that?" She touches my arm.

I stop talking.

There is a whining noise coming from beneath us.

"What is it?" Eleanor asks me as I kneel down and peer under the steps.

"It's a cat," I answer, spotting the light reflecting off its eyes.

"Get it out," Eleanor urges. "Is it okay?"

I reach down and pull the cat out. It emerges from the darkness covered in dirt and burrs.

"Oh my God," I say, astounded.

It's Mittens.

I scream, "What the fuck? You're alive!"

Acknowledgments

Thank you, Corrina, Brock, Mallory, Mitch, Ainsley, Chad, Aaron, and Tod. Thank you also Gloria, Jim, Joel, and the rest of my family. Thank you, preemptively, to Bridget, for writing my future favorite book, and to my friend Liz. Thank you, Heather Carr, for your guidance, support, help, and kindness. I am so appreciative of the work you and the Friedrich Agency have done to help me prepare and share this book. Thank you also, Daniella Wexler. This story is a lot better because of your editorial talents and expertise, and I am so grateful to you for everything you have done to improve and share it. I am also sincerely appreciative of Jade Hui, Gena Lanzi, Isabel Dasilva, Liz Byer, Min Choi, Loan Le, and everyone at Atria Books for all the work you have done to develop and promote this story. Thank you also to Bobby Mostyn-Owen and Atlantic Books for sharing this story with the UK, and Simon & Schuster Canada for sharing it with Canada. Thank you to my English and writing teachers, especially Ms. Nedic, Dorothy Nielsen, and Vidya Natarajan. Thanks also to the band Muna for the song "It's Gonna Be Okay, Baby" and Phoebe Bridgers for "Funeral." I listened to these a lot while writing this. Thank you to Robert Peett and Holland House, Lucy Carson, Kristina Moore, the Canada Council for the Arts, and everyone I've forgotten or who helped me without me knowing.

Reading Group Guide

This reading group guide for *Everyone in This Room Will Someday Be Dead* includes an introduction, discussion questions, ideas for enhancing your book club, and a Q&A with author **Emily Austin**. The suggested questions are intended to help your reading group find new and interesting angles and topics for your discussion. We hope that these ideas will enrich your conversation and increase your enjoyment of the book.

Introduction

In this darkly funny and utterly profound debut, Gilda, a twenty-something atheist lesbian, cannot stop ruminating about death. She accidentally stumbles into a job as a receptionist for a Catholic church, and in between trying to memorize the lines to mass, hiding the fact that she has a girlfriend, and watching the dirty-dish tower in her apartment grow ever higher, Gilda becomes obsessed with her work predecessor's mysterious death. Full of delightfully awkward predicaments and pitch-perfect observations about the human condition, this novel is for anyone who searches for meaning in a chaotic world where they feel like an outsider, watching the daily rituals of life unfold as if through binoculars.

Topics & Questions for Discussion

1. Gilda takes a job at a Catholic church despite being a lesbian atheist, which seems distinctly antithetical, and part of the fun is watching this situation unfold. Do you think Gilda's attempts to hide who she is at work have a detrimental effect on her? Or is Gilda used to hiding things about herself?

2. Gilda's parents both seem to be unable to face difficult realities. How do you think her parent's—and, in particular, her dad's—reactions to her behavior as a child affected her as she grew up? How do you think they affect both Gilda and Eli now that they're adults?

3. Do you think it surprises Gilda when she hears Jeff crying after the death of a teenager from the congregation? How does witnessing someone else's grief affect Gilda, who is constantly anxious about people's deaths?

4. In what ways does working in the church subvert Gilda's (and perhaps our own) expectations of what the experience will be like for her?

5. What do Gilda's experiences with the health care system reveal to us about how acute anxiety is managed (or mismanaged) by health care professionals? How could her visits have been handled differently?

6. Gilda believes that Eleanor is trying to steal her identity when they first start messaging on a dating app. Does this allow Gilda to act differently—and more candidly—with Eleanor than with her previous matches? Why do you think this is the case?

7. Gilda's anxieties throughout the novel can often be debilitating. They leave her unable to do dishes or shower, they cause her to obsess over things she can't control (like the missing cat), and they often cause her to break into tears or have panic attacks at inconvenient times. What is it like for the reader to experience life through Gilda's eyes? How did that affect you? Was it eye-opening or deeply familiar for you? Do you share her fears and, if so, to what extent?

8. As we see, Gilda often says yes to offers—the job at the church, the date with Giuseppe, etc.—when they are presented to her. Why do you think she does this?

9. How does Gilda's worldview contrast with Giuseppe's opinion that you can do anything you'd like in life as long as you believe that you can?

10. Gilda often hides what she's thinking, like just how much she's preoccupied with death, etc. How do these small omissions snowball into bigger ones? At what point does personal information about your own anxieties become necessary to share so that you can live as authentically as possible?

11. Gilda's focus on death and the chaotic realities of existence can make societal conventions (such as what's considered a sin) seem small in comparison. How does this contrast of existential dread shine a light on the rules and conventions that so many of us abide by? In your opinion, does it make them seem more trivial and nonsensical? Or does the acknowledgement of death help give meaning to existence?

12. In some ways, Gilda is very preoccupied with existence and the meaninglessness of our temporary lives, and in other ways, she cares deeply about the details that shape the lives of humans and animals. How do these seemingly opposite notions seem to coexist or push against each other in her mind?

13. Barney tells Gilda that the characteristics of psychopaths are having been bullied as a child, committing petty crimes, and being chronically unemployed, which we know are all criteria that fit Gilda. What do you think it means to her to hear that she fits the profile? Do you think we paint with too broad a brush when we talk about people with mental illnesses?

14. Why do you think Gilda is fixated on hands—her own and other people's? Why does she think so much about how they are the same hands throughout people's whole lives?

Enhance Your Book Club

1. This book has been compared to the show *Fleabag*. Watch both seasons of *Fleabag* (or choose select episodes) and discuss how the portrayals of the two young women—Gilda and Fleabag—are both similar to and different from one another.

2. In the latter half of the novel, both Barney and Gilda try to solve Grace's apparent murder. Do the members of your book club have a fascination with true crime? If so, discuss what documentaries/docuseries, books, or podcasts you've seen/read/listened to. Have you ever played an amateur sleuth, whether in your own life or in trying to solve more famous crimes?

3. If this book were made into a film, TV series, or play, who would your dream cast for the characters in the book be?

A Conversation with Emily Austin

Q: This book is so beautifully written that we feel like we're experiencing Gilda's reality while we read it. If you don't mind sharing, how much of this perspective (anxieties, existential dread, thinking about death, and caring deeply about others' happiness) do you share with our main character versus how much of it did you draw from your imagination or research?

A: Thank you! I do have an anxiety disorder and struggles with depression, and there are some thoughts represented in this book that belong to both Gilda and me. There are also areas where we differ, though. I have close friends and family who I also drew from. One of my sisters used to wake my mom up to cry about how she would die one day, for example.

Q: In that same vein, what other portrayals of anxiety and depression did you pull from—in books, movies, tv shows, etc.—in order to create Gilda's character?

A: I went to therapy while writing this book and was given some material from my psychologist about anxiety and how it manifests. Gilda not feeling the pain in her broken arm was a symptom I remember reading in that material. I also listened to a lot of music by Phoebe Bridgers and Muna while writing this. I think I drew from that sometimes too.

Q: Pets like the cat and rabbit come up multiple times throughout the book. Why did you choose to weave the story of the rabbit throughout Gilda's present story line?

A: A pet dying is often the first experience a person has with death, and it made sense to me that Gilda would struggle to ever get over that first experience.

Q: A large part of the book takes place at Gilda's job at a Catholic church. Why did you choose that as the setting for much of the story? How do you think the backdrop of organized religion and a church community informs us about Gilda's journey?

A: I grew up Catholic, and I think thematically Catholicism is aligned with a person who is morbidly anxious; a lot of Catholic language and imagery is about death, bodies, and blood. I also think, for some people, religion can help soothe morbid anxieties. If you are fixated on death or on the purpose of your life, there is some relief offered to you by the Catholic Church and by most religions. When you are queer though, what is offered is usually less comforting. Queer people can be Catholic, but regardless of your faith or beliefs, I think it is fair to say that if you are driven to Catholicism to soothe your morbid anxieties, a straight person is more likely to feel comforted than a queer person is.

Q: Gilda's fascination with death—both her preoccupation with how everyone will someday be dead (hence the title) and her fear that it could come for anyone at any moment—is so prominent throughout the book. Why did you choose to have her focus on this?

A: I think most anxiety and depression boils down to recognizing our own mortality, and the fact that everyone we know will someday die.

Q: Gilda is unsure of so many things, but she is so sure of her sexuality, even from a young age. What did it mean to you to portray her sexuality and her relationship throughout the novel?

A: Gilda being a lesbian is as much a fact to her as the fact that one day she will die is. I wrote her as unquestionably queer because her character serves in part to show what the experience of being depressed and queer is like. Queer people are more likely to suffer from depression, and to die by suicide. Being queer is not inherently depressing; however, it is tied to homophobia, which is why queer people suffer from depression and anxiety at higher rates. Because of that, I meant to portray Gilda's relationship with Eleanor as one area of her life that makes her happy. It served to illustrate why it is so damaging to queer people to suggest their relationships are bad. This is why Gilda mentions that it's ironic that Catholicism was theoretically created to help people feel safe and meaningful when it takes away one of the few things that makes her feel like her life is worth living at all.

Q: We have a very close point of view to Gilda throughout the story— we feel like we're within her mind, listening to her thoughts. Did you ever consider telling the story from other perspectives? Why did you choose to remain within Gilda's head for the whole novel? Why was it important for the story you told?

A: One reason I like reading is because it helps me develop empathy for others and learn from other people's experiences. Another reason is because it helps me relate and feel seen. I think it would be difficult to understand what it feels like to be Gilda without being subjected to her thought patterns, and it would be hard to relate to her without knowing intimately what she is thinking. I do not think that I considered writing her from another perspective, and I think this story is best suited to this perspective, but it is interesting to consider how a different approach might have impacted the story.

Q: Why did you choose to have Gilda's parents be particularly unresponsive to the pain of their children? What did you want to portray with this type of parent-child relationship?

A: This relationship served in part to represent mental health stigma, particularly in terms of how members of older generations sometimes approach mental health, and to illustrate the negative impacts of that.

Q: The passage that reads: "I find it so bizarre that I occupy space, and that I am seen by other people. I feel like I am falling through space and Eleanor just threw me a rose. It's such a sweet, pointless gesture. It would be less devastating to fall through space alone, without someone else falling next to me. Whenever someone does something nice for me, I feel intensely aware of how strange and sad it is to know someone" (p. 135–6) is particularly beautiful and heartbreaking. How did you come upon this metaphor?

A: Thank you! I think when you are depressed, it is hard not to recognize the absurdity of life. It is difficult to understand the point of doing anything, and because of that, kind gestures can feel heartbreaking. This passage was meant to describe that sort of thinking: we are specks of dust in space being nice to each other, and it is very sweet and devastating.

Q: There are so many instances in the book where health care professionals, employers, the police, and even Gilda's friends and family could have done so much more to help her instead of leaving her isolated. Near the end of the novel, she even considers suicide. What did you want to say about how mental illnesses are treated through this portrayal?

A: People who need mental health care often lack access to it. There is stigma, human resource shortages, fragmented service delivery models, and a lack of research capacity for implementation and policy change worldwide. There are also issues in the quality of the service provided. I have personally faced the impacts of this and have witnessed close friends also be negatively affected.

Q: Do you have a next project in mind? If so, can you share anything about it?

A: I am thinking of writing a book about someone who writes the beginnings of books, because I have a lot of half written stories, and that might a clever way of salvaging them.